DEDICATION

To Anuhea and La'anui:

Cal is the parent I wished to be for you. A parent to empower and embolden so that you were able to find your own voice and thrive. I love you.

Dear Reader,

Thank you for making the choice to read this book. I am so happy to
share Max's story with you. I do think it is important to explain that
Max's story is a companion story to Griffin's, *In the Echo of this Ghost
Town*, so some of the narrative will be repetitive, and perhaps more
enjoyable having read *In the Echo of this Ghost Town* first.

Most of the time, the writing process surprises me. At one time, I had
thought *In the Echo of this Ghost Town* would be a dual perspective of
both Griffin and Max, but it became clear during drafting that Griffin's
version of events was the primary story. Max, however, wouldn't be
quiet, so I allowed her the space to tell me her version. *When the Echo
Answers* is the collection of her perspective.

Early readers expressed a love for Max's story. Many of them shared,
however, they felt reading Griffin's story first illuminated Max's more.
The readers wondered if they read the stories in reverse that they might
have missed out on the depth that *In the Echo of this Ghost Town* provides.
Ultimately, it is your decision which order to read them, but I thought
you might want this bit of information to decide.

Happy Reading!
CLW

1

"Dad." I breath the word like a prayer when the house comes into view through the pickup's window. I should be used to the condition of the houses on move-in day—I've lived in so many of them—but this one might be one of the worst I've ever seen. Besides the anemic-looking siding, the wrap around porch resembles broken bones held up with weak crutches while the ghost of its foundation sits in the middle of a field in dire need of surgery. I think, perhaps my dad has lost his mind.

"I know it looks a fright," Dad says as he turns our rusty pickup into the drive.

A fright is an understatement. The house looks like a strong wind will blow it over after the ghosts finish their century-old party in it.

"Dad," I repeat. I'm not sure why I'm surprised. Not really. Over the last eighteen years of my life, we've moved ten times, and with each move, the house has always looked like a dump, maybe with the exception of house three. "There's no way you're flipping this before I leave for school."

We bounce along a driveway that needs repaving—or our truck needs new shocks. It's hard to decide which. Maybe both.

The sun wanes in the afternoon sky, lighting everything in beautiful hues of gold, but it doesn't seem to help the dilapidated building I'm about to call a temporary home look any better. I can't look anymore and turn away from the house, thinking about the plan he shared with me on the drive: fix this one up in a hurry—before I leave for college—flip it to help pay for school expenses not covered by my scholarship, and move onto the next one closer to school. It isn't going to happen. Eight weeks isn't enough time.

"I know it looks bad. I know." He puts the truck in park. We sit next to one another in Rust Bucket, facing a front door that's cracked up the center. Silence stretches a few extra beats, then my father adds, "But, I'm going to hire someone to help with this one."

"Dad." I shake my head this time as the air leaves my lungs. He's never hired anyone before, aside from tradesmen who help with stuff he doesn't do. Taking on a hire sounds like a lot of extra cash. "For real?" I ask.

"Sure," he says and taps the steering wheel, as if offering himself reinforcement to make it so. He looks at me and smiles. "When we sell this baby—for sure."

"Dad–" I can't seem to find another word.

"No. No." He shakes his head and looks at the house. "It's got amazing bones," he says—just like he always does—and so far, in my eighteen years on this planet, he hasn't been wrong. We've always had a roof over our head, even if sometimes there are holes in it until he fixes them. And we've always had food to eat, even if we don't always have a place for a table. He's always made sure I had clothes and shoes, even if we've had to shop at thrift stores. Truthfully, I haven't ever wanted for much, even if I'm not one of those kinds of people who wants much.

"Come on," he says. "Let me show you." He climbs out of the truck, the door squealing as he pushes it open.

I follow him but leave my bag inside the cab.

He high steps through the grass and looks over his shoulder at me. "Wait. I'll make a path for you."

I watch my dad push down the grass with his feet. That's my dad, my knight in shining armor, willing to brave the grasses with his boots so that I'll be comfortable. I'm wearing shorts, and I shouldn't have. I know better. First night in a flip is always about jeans, long sleeves, and hard-soled shoes. Sometimes I think Hazmat suits have probably been in order like house number five when we had to go get a hotel room for a couple weeks.

I hadn't thought my clothing choices through this morning, annoyed that we were doing this yet again. It might be early July, but summer months don't matter to a house that's falling apart. The rodents don't care either. Or squatters. Or whatever kinds of other items we might find inside I don't want to consider.

When it's clear the stubborn reeds aren't going to lie flat, he walks back to me and offers his wide back.

"Hop on, Max-in-a-million."

"Dad. I'm a little old for this."

"Aw. Humor your old man."

I jump up and let him piggyback me to the porch, which I can see needs to be completely redone. I'm factoring cost. The crack in the front door looks like the crack in Amy's wall in the first episode of the eleventh iteration of Doctor Who. Shit. Replacement. Cha-ching. Rodents guaranteed.

"Don't worry. We'll patch it up until we get the replacement."

As if the front door is the only thing needs replacing, I think but don't say it.

When Dad sets me down, he climbs the steps that buckle under his weight with creaks and groans but thankfully don't snap. He looks over his shoulder at me with one of those excited twinkles in his stormy-sea-colored eyes which are striking in contrast to the rich, sun-kissed hue of his face. "You ready to see this masterpiece?"

"As ready as I'll ever be."

The front door opens.

And it's a dump, just like I thought.

He has to push the door open through a pile of dirt, and, upon closer inspection, leaves, which makes me think there must be a broken window. The stairwell is intact, but a few of the stairs are cracked like chipped teeth. There's a musty odor of decomposing wood. The condition of the house is terrible, and I look at my dad with wide eyes.

"Remember, Max–" Dad turns to me, hands on his jean clad hips—he obviously knew how to dress, though in my whole life, I can't remember my dad ever wearing anything different– "you have to look at the place as it can be, not how it is. See through the damage to all the ways we'll fix it to–"

"–make it new," I finish for him. "Yes. I know, Dad. But–"

"No 'buts,'" he says, holding up a hand. "Just look."

I sigh and nod.

It's an old farmhouse, but under the grime, age, and harsh reality of time, I can see little treasures. The hardwood floor is mostly intact for some spots, though I'm wondering about that subfloor that creaks as our steps echo through the empty rooms. There are gorgeous, stained-glass windows still intact, set in the framed doorways between rooms. The kitchen needs a complete gut, and it makes me hear alarm bells of all the cash about to bleed out into the remodel. The shiplap looks shot, but the fireplace in the living room is beautiful with what looks like original river rock.

"Well?" Dad's voice is hopeful.

I follow him up the stairs. "I can see why you like it."

He flashes me a grin, which is infectious. It always is.

I share a smile with him. My reciprocation seems to relieve some of his tension when his shoulders droop to normal position.

At the top of the stairs, the walkway splits and the spindles of the banister forms a U around the stairwell. Closed doors outline the space. I follow my dad to the left. "I think this could be your room, but you can choose."

He pushes open a door.

I have to give my father credit. Even though the house is a dump—and looks like it might be haunted—the bones of this room are magical. The steeply pitched ceiling, dormered windows with places to sit though they look like they might have nests of something. The walls are bleeding old wallpaper, but I can imagine a new pattern, a beautiful room. "It's got potential," I tell him with a grin.

His eyes twinkle again. "Let me show you the rest."

After the tour, I can see the promise of the house, but I don't see how he's going to get it done in eight weeks—even with help. This will take months, which makes me look sideways at him again. My dad is a smart man. He's been doing this a long time, and while his timing isn't always perfect, he must know this is going to take the better part of a year to finish even with help. Looking around, I know he knows it, and I wonder why he's adamant about the timeline.

"I'll order us some pizza for dinner?" he asks. A tradition on the first night of each of our moves.

"Perfect," I say and wipe my hands over the back of my shorts, then realize I've probably wiped grime on my ass. I glance over my shoulder and twist to check, though I'm not sure why I'd care.

"It could be our last one." I look up at him and notice his gaze flick away. He swallows, then with a dip of his head says, "I'll start moving stuff in."

"I'll sweep up the sleeping spaces for the mattresses and lay the tarps. Don't move mattresses without me."

He nods. "Wouldn't dream of it."

I move out the front door, down the porch, and through the tall grass to the pickup to get my change of clothes. As I open the truck door, I look back at the house as Dad emerges from the doorway to grab the first boxes we'll need to settle for the night. My heart expands in my chest, already missing him, though I haven't left yet. With my leaving-for-college deadline impending—eight weeks away—Dad's strange timeline coincides. I wonder if it has more to do with me leaving rather than the actual completion of the house. Maybe it's his way of trying to make me feel better, or himself.

The thing is it doesn't make me feel better.

I change my clothes and get started on my assigned move-in day tasks. By the time the pizza arrives, I've swept the bedrooms and laid the tarps for the mattresses; Dad and I have moved our mattresses and important boxes from the trailer hitched to the back of the truck. We'll have the rest to unload in the morning. The sun has gone down, and without electricity, we're living by lantern light.

"Dad, you have definitely underestimated how long this house is going to take," I say, drawing a piece of pepperoni from the box. "I mean, Holmes Street was about this size but didn't have as much work. We were there for two years."

"True," Dad says and takes a sip of his cola he just opened. "But it also had a basement that I finished, and I had that full-time job." He takes a bite and finishes it. "Remember Misten Avenue? That one was terrible, and we were there for less than a year."

I'd forgotten about that. "Give me that." I take his soda and hand him his water bottle. "You can't drink that."

He gives me one of his looks, his mouth tensing with impatience. He shakes his head. "I didn't hire anyone to help at Holmes or Misten. And I like soda."

"Soda is diabetes juice, and you're predisposed."

He chuckles. "Look at this temple." He flexes, which makes me laugh because he always uses the same lines. "It wasn't too long ago I was a linebacker–"

"–averaging two and a half sacks, a game. Yeah. Yeah. Drink the water, Dad."

We eat in silence a moment.

"What's the rush, Dad?" I ask, plucking at a piece of pepperoni.

"You're leaving for school," he says as if he's announced the date of my birth, just matter of fact.

"What does that have to do with it?"

He looks up at me, and I see a look I don't recognize on his face, but it burns out just as quickly when he covers it with a smile. "Just seems like a natural point to shoot for. Look for a new place closer to the college so you don't have to travel so far to visit."

"It's only three or so hours from here. An easy bus ride," I point out.

He maintains the smile, but I see it's not in his eyes. Maybe that's the lack of light cast by the lantern. He nods and takes another bite of his pizza. "What am I going to do without you to keep me on track? I might go off budget."

I swallow and take a bite of my pizza, feeling guilty. It's always been us. Dad and Max-in-a-million against the world. "Aw, Dad. I won't be far," I remind him. This is why he'd relented on this place. Besides being a steal—which he loves for the eventual bottom line of the flip—the school I got accepted to was just a few hours away by car. "We have phones. Goodness. And eight weeks to flip this dump." I wonder if the reason he's adamant about his unrealistic timeline is because he's as scared to be on his own as I am to be on mine. I haven't considered the impact of my leaving on him. I haven't allowed myself to ponder it. It's complex and stitched together with a complicated history I know I can't unravel.

He gives me a chuckle. "Don't you worry your head. Your old dad's got it."

"Can we afford help?" I ask.

He sniffs and knuckle itches a spot on his nose, which makes me wonder if he's coming up with a lie. It wouldn't be the first time he's given me just enough truth mixed with a version of optimism riding the line of a lie to keep me complacent. "I'll have to dip into savings."

My eyebrows rise with a question. "Dad. I need the truth."

He raises his hands. "For real. I have a few side gigs lined up already—legit—and I'll offset it with some savings so we can get started right away."

9

I nod. "And while you're working the side gigs? How is this house—which is generous identification by the way—getting done?"

"The hire."

I give him a side eye.

"You and me plus one more. I think we could knock this out in no time." He smiles around his bite, and I have the sense he's telling himself this story as much as he's telling me. "Have I ever steered us wrong?"

I shake my head. He's taken us into some pretty horrible houses, but he's always made it out of them just like he's said even if his timelines haven't always been accurate. There are always unforeseen complications, and I'm one hundred percent sure this house is full of them.

"Dad?"

"Yes, daughter?"

"Aren't you tired of fixing houses for other people? Don't you ever want to find a place of your own?" This is a question I've asked him before, but his answers have been as shifty as the houses we've lived in, taking on characteristics of whatever house it was at the time. I'm expecting him to say something metaphorical about the stained-glass inserts, but he doesn't.

He clears his throat.

"Dad?"

"Home is where you are."

And I'm leaving.

I don't think he understands that this answer makes me feel like

I'm carrying the world on my shoulders, like I've got to hold it up for both of us. I swallow the bite. "What about when I leave for school?"

He doesn't respond.

"Dad?"

"I messed this up, didn't I?"

"What?"

"Being your dad?"

I set my pizza on the paper plate. "What are you talking about?"

He looks at me, his gaze connecting with mine. "I just—I thought it would be an adventure after–" He stops. I know he was going to say, "after your mom left," but can't bring himself to say it. His regret is written on his face even after thirteen years. This isn't because I think he's still in love with her, but her abandonment left both of us as ghostly as the houses we inhabit.

When I was younger, I used to resent the moving, but now that I'm eighteen, I can understand it. I scoot closer to him and lay my head on his shoulder. "Our adventures have been the best," I say, and I'm being honest because they've been with him, even if there's resentment mixed in. I want him to know I love him, but I can't—won't—be a heartbreak, too. "I'm just worried about you when I go to school. You being alone."

This is the first and thickest thread wrapped around my heart. Dad has chosen me every day. He's lived for me. He's been my number one, and now I'm leaving him alone. If I thought too long and hard about it, my breath turns to steel in my lungs. I'd consider not leaving. Dad wouldn't allow it. Going to college feels a bit like abandoning him—like mom. Worse yet, I want to leave so bad, and I'm afraid it makes me just like her.

"What's this?" He wraps a strong arm around me. "Last I checked, I'm the dad. Don't you worry. If all goes well, I'll be right behind you looking for the next place."

Thing is, I can't help worrying about him.

I was five when my mom left us. Indigo Denby—in as much as I can piece together between what my dad has said and what I remember—was a free if unstable spirit unable to be saddled with a husband and a child. A hippie wrapped up the privilege of growing up wealthy, she disappeared, and after a search, was found strung out on drugs (not the first time) and incoherent. Her parents—grandparents who I've had very little interaction with—admitted her to a rehab facility. The divorce papers were delivered to Dad shortly after, and he was given complete custody, her rights as my mother signed away. We haven't heard from her—or my grandparents—since. These are fragile threads I don't understand as clearly since I was only five at the time, but threads that stitch together my experience, nonetheless.

Later, after Dad and I have cleaned up dinner and escaped into our own spaces to get some rest, I wait for the quiet to steal around the house. In the dark of the new room, my lantern glows in the horribly stark space with new shadows and new sounds. I eventually sneak from my bedroom, taking great care to keep my steps from creaking as I move to the stairs. A strange noise reverberates through the belly of the old farmhouse, and I freeze at the top of the stairs, wondering if I should have braved the window and the tree. I hold my breath.

I wait.

My dad clears his throat.

When the silence settles again, I take a step down the stairs. It squeaks. There's a moment when my heart speeds up with fear, thinking maybe I'm going to alert my dad, but I don't hear any movement from his space in the house. I keep going, moving slowly until I'm on the ground floor and out the cracked front door now covered with a plank of plywood.

As much as pizza is a first day move in tradition with my dad, sneaking out that first night is wholly mine. My ritual started at house five. Up to then, my dad and I bunked it in the same room, and his presence gave me bravery. When I turned twelve, there was a shift in me wanting to be brave and independent, to prove I could sleep in my own room by myself. My fear of the new places and my imagination, which conjured all sorts of terrifying creatures stretching in the shadows, did a number on my confidence. Instead of going to my dad, I snuck out into the dark where it felt safer. That night, I found a way to claim some power. After that, I continued to sneak out every first bedtime in a new place. Disappearing into the darkness of a strange place isn't because I want to sneak around. Rather, it feels like one of the only things in this pattern of living over which I have control. Tonight is the last time, I figure, because it's my last move with my dad and is more about the nostalgia of the routine of things rather than the compulsion to control something.

House nine, he caught me sneaking back in.

He was pissed. "Do you understand how dangerous it is?" The panic was clear in his eyes. "Why didn't you just ask? I would have taken you somewhere."

I recognized the disappointment, and I hated disappointing him.

"Why?" he'd asked.

I just shrugged. I didn't know how to put into words the why, not without hurting him. I was being dragged all over the country to fixer uppers by a loving dad, running from the ghost of a drugged-out mom who was too broken to choose us. I had this awful truth of being an outsider—always an outsider—to face the trepidation that pressed in against us every time we started over. I'd been seventeen then, and the sneaking out felt more like a sticking middle finger at the world. A loud "fuck you" to the universe, to every kid that had made fun of me, to my mom, and even my dad on some level.

I didn't think he'd get it, and I refused to hurt him because even if it was a small rebellion, I knew he didn't deserve it.

As I walk down the driveway, I consider that part of the reason I think my dad was so panicked that night he caught me wasn't just because he was scared for me. There is this part of him that probably thought about my mom. The way she walked out into the night and never returned to us, and how he couldn't fix that. My dad can fix anything. Seriously. He's made nine houses look like custom homes. Any problem I've brought home—cuts, scrapes, and bruises both physical and emotional—he's been both Dad and Mom to restore me to normal working order. He couldn't fix my mom, and I'm pretty sure, knowing my dad like I do, he gave it his best go.

As I walk out into the darkness beyond the farmhouse, I wonder if I hide my first night sneak-out from him because I don't want to hurt him like my mother did. I've thought about what it would feel like to just keep walking. The idea took root when I was fifteen—house eight—I thought about just going, finding a place to settle down for good. I was smart enough to know it didn't work like that, which brought me home. It made me wonder if Mom had found it easy to leave us. To leave me. I'd gotten caught up in how much that would hurt Dad, which I knew I couldn't ever do to him, and I wondered how it couldn't have been a part of my mom's thinking. I don't specifically remember the leaving. She was there one day and gone the next. Each time I walk out into the night, I wonder if she weighed us in her decision, and I can't think she did.

When I was younger and asked my dad why she left, he'd just say, "Indigo was a free spirit."

Back then, I imagined her like a bird needing to fly. Now, as I walk toward the streetlights ahead, I don't think of anything so romantic as a bird needing freedom. I just think she was selfish, and maybe—I worry—I'm exactly like her.

I've got eight weeks in this dump since college races toward me. I can hear the sadness and the fear in my dad's voice when he talks about it, but his fears don't change the fact that I'm leaving. It's always been us, and when I look ahead to that eight-week deadline, what I feel is the impending anticipation of freedom weighted with a heavy cost: leaving my dad behind and alone. I finally get to make choices for me. I finally get to make friends. I finally get to stay somewhere—four years—in one place and grow some roots even if my dad jumps around business as usual. As much as I love my dad, I'm looking forward to leaving this vagabond lifestyle for something that's mine, of creating a permanent home. As much as I want my dad to settle somewhere, I don't know that he ever will. The thought makes me bitter, tired, and sad all at the same time. What it boils down to is I'm leaving him and no matter how I try to dress that up, I know I'm just stepping into my mother's skin. And I'm cognizant of how selfish that makes me.

2

The convenience store is lit up like a casino in Vegas. It seems so bright against the dark. On the walk there, the road stretched dark in both directions, I thought of all the ways that my dad would be freaking out about me walking alone in the dark. Not smart. True. His worst fear of me becoming another cold case because I didn't use my fucking common sense.

My dad has spent my lifetime teaching me to be smart. "Don't be dumb, Wells." His lessons have ranged from "You're all you need," to "boys are idiots until they're about twenty-five, maybe even some as late as thirty," to "you are strong and determined, why do you need them?" The last one was always about whatever group was giving me shit at whatever school I was in that year. Moving around sucks the big one (not that I'd know, but be forewarned, my dad hasn't held back in being very frank about sex, the varying degrees of male douchiness, and a woman's right to her own body, which included lessons in self-defense). Walking toward the convenience store, I think I've just failed most of his lessons. This was pretty dumb.

As I cross the lot toward the entrance, I notice a guy sitting outside the store. He's sort of slumped over whatever is on the table in front of him. He takes a sip, and I note it's a bottle of water. The closer I get, I realize he's about my age. His dark, blondish hair, maybe closer to light brown, is straight and longish, hanging around his face. When I get closer and he looks up, I realize he's kind of cute, in a sharp, angular, sullen, skinny kid kind of way. He looks mad, his anger riding his dark brow, but I don't get any bad vibes. No skin crawlies or that feeling in my gut that warns me when something is just a bit off. One of Dad's lessons: "trust your instincts."

The guy looks away, and I walk into the cool air of the store.

Jackpot.

Slurpee Heaven.

Strawberry.

I know I'll have to run an extra mile to make sure this sugar doesn't stay on my already full hips and thighs, but for the sweet sugar rush, I'll take it. Besides, I like running. That started freshman year—house seven—when I got tired of being called "Big Crush" by a group of dickhead boys. I was already taller than most of my classmates, including the boys, and larger too. Dad caught me crying about it, and when I finally fessed up, he insisted those boys were dumbasses with no awareness of beauty. I knew he was trying to help—it didn't—but one thing he said to me stuck. "Your opinion of you is all that matters, Max-in-a-million."

I realized my opinion of me was pretty bad.

After so many years of moving and never setting down any roots, never having a friend that stuck around (aside from Cassie when I was in the fifth and sixth grade—house four was our longest stop), and always feeling like I was trying to fit in somewhere, I didn't really like who I was. I'd always been the big girl kids teased and the one it was easy to ostracize because she was new. I hadn't had a lot of exposure to building self-confidence, even if my dad bolstered those parts of me outside of school. I knew he loved me, but he liked me too. We talked and laughed, worked and moved on to the next fixer upper together. These home interactions didn't always translate to school ones, because they weren't reinforced among my peers. It might have been Dad and me against the world, and he might have been my best friend (even if I knew that first he was my dad, because frick, his rules were annoying), but what was happening at school tugged and pulled at the parts of me he'd tried to lift up.

At fourteen, hearing Dad repeat that it didn't matter what anyone else thought, only what I did, opened my eyes anew. Somehow, I equated his message to taking control over my own ideas about myself and connected it to my first night sneaking out. The way sneaking out felt like me finding freedom and control. I started running the next day—after hearing the lecture about paying attention to my surroundings and should a creeper show up to go to the nearest public building and call the police. I've been running ever since.

With my Slurpee paid for, I glance at the back of the kid—though 'kid' isn't relevant to him any more than 'girl' is of me now. Something about him is recognizable. Not him, so much, but the feelings he's exuding, as if he's alone in the world. That is a language I speak and understand. I mean, I have my dad, but I understand alone in all the other ways that matter. Aside from my first best friend, Cassie, and my first boyfriend during my senior year, I haven't had many close relationships.

Ignoring all the lessons my dad has given me that translate to talking to strangers outside of convenience stores in the middle of the night, I leave the confines of the store and approach moody boy like he's a wild animal in the zoo. Okay, too tentative. I actually just sit down. I don't do much with hesitancy and never have. Hesitancy hasn't gotten me much, and besides, there isn't time for it. Life lessons from my father haven't been about hanging back or blending into the background. His lessons are, "go after what you want."

Do I want this boy? Hell no, but I wouldn't mind helping him smile. Maybe if I pay it forward, I'll receive it in the future, you know? Like Cassie in fifth grade, who approached my lunch table where I sat alone. She sat down with me.

"Hey," she'd said and smiled.

I'd smiled back, and it was like kismet.

I channel that moment when I sit down across from wild-animal guy. "Hey."

He looks at me like I have two heads, his upper lip curling, and his eyebrows scrunching together. He has really nice eyes, a mix up of colors: green, gray, gold, brown. "Yeah?" Even as unattractive as that sneer is, he's actually cute.

"I'm not carrying any diseases," I say and draw an incredibly sweet pull of Slurpee through my straw. Strawberry, my favorite, though in a pinch I'll drink cherry. I hate any other flavor. This delicious goodness is my secret vice. Since I'm always harping my dad about his soda habit, I can't let him know I'm being a hypocrite with this diabetes slushie.

The guy looks around like someone might be pranking him, which makes me smile around the straw. Then he looks down at his water bottle and swirls it around a little, as if he isn't sure what's happening, and the water is the one place where reality exists.

I'm wondering why I haven't done this before. His reaction is super entertaining. Then again, I don't know him, and he could be a serial killer in training or something.

I move the straw around in the Slurpee cup so that I can sip up more of the magical unicorn goodness. It squeaks loudly, and I look at the guy. He's just watching my movements and maybe assessing if I'm safe, which makes me say, "Decide I'm not a serial killer?"

He lifts the water bottle to his mouth, and is it terrible that I think he has a very attractive mouth? God. Upper lip has this beautiful bow shape, and the bottom is full. I imagine he's probably a good kisser and realize I'm being creepy.

"Jury's out," he says.

I like his voice. Full, kind of melodious, like a ballad with one of those amazing kitschy pop riffs, but deep. Not baritone or bass deep. More like a low tenor. I wonder if he sings.

"Why's that?" I ask.

He shrugs his sharp shoulders under his dark t-shirt. "What if I'm the serial killer?"

"It's a distinct possibility." I smirk at my cup.

"Why's that?"

I think perhaps I've insulted him, and it makes my smile widen, not because I've hurt him or anything, but he just seems incredulous about it. "Guy sitting outside of a convenience store on a Monday night, looking all moody. Definitely sending shady vibes. You spike that unassuming water bottle?" I nod at the bottle in his hand. "Use the innocence of water to lure in your victims but in reality, you're just setting the trap?" I smile, this time looking him in the eye, hoping he can tell I'm messing with him.

He doesn't smile, and I have the impression smiling isn't something he does much of. "You're weird."

"I get that a lot." I don't take his assessment personally. He isn't the first one to say it, and I've had a lot of practice with not letting those words have power over me.

I've heard it in most places I've lived. In elementary school, third grade with Mrs. Peterson, Cecily told me that I was weird because I didn't have a mom. That stuck. When I was in fifth grade with Mr. Smythe, Bobby and his goons asked for a school picture, then tacked it up to a bulletin board defaced with the word "weird" written in Sharpie. The day Cassie had sat down at the lunch table, she laid all of the photocopies of my defaced picture Bobby had made; she'd gone and collected all of them she could find. That cemented our friendship. In middle school, I got invited to a party, but it had been a joke. I showed up to the birthday party and was the only girl. I got called "one of the boys" for the rest of the year (and not in a good way). Even my one boyfriend, Michael, had often told me I was "too much." The way he said it at the beginning of us was different from how he said it at the end. How have I survived? I don't know, but my dad, sneaking slushies, and running have been a pretty good combination.

"What do you do in this town for fun?" I ask him.

"Get drunk. You new?"

"Yes. Why aren't you doing that?"

"It's Monday."

"So, a drunk six days a week then. I see. You have standards. So that must be real water." I pause and take another sip.

He looks like boys I knew at my last high school; the ones who skated around to alleyways and then took out their joints to smoke with friends in hiding, or the ones who came to school on Monday bragging about their party life the weekend before. Michael would always talk about that group condescendingly, but I questioned his motives eventually, because he sure was trying hard to practice that hook-up culture in his basement with me. This guy is maybe not the popular jock but known and seen anyway. He's got that I-don't-give-a-fuck-attitude covered up with leave-me-the-fuck-alone-I've-got-this

23

and a dash of wounded-animal vibe.

To ramp up the discomfort, I say, "You don't look like the type with standards."

"Neither do you."

I like the banter. He's a fighter. "Touché, Serial Killer. So, you don't drink on Mondays for other reasons then?"

"I didn't say I don't drink on Mondays. I just said it was Monday. You made the assumption."

I laugh. "Fair enough." I don't say anything more, figuring I've taken this about as far as I can. It's about time to start back anyway and duck into ditches with each passing car. Tomorrow will be a busy moving day.

"So, you're new here?" He surprises me by breaking the silence.

I focus on the Slurpee and stir it into submission. "Yep. Just moved. Only here for the summer."

"Why's that?"

"Why's what?" I take a sip, looking at him as I do.

He watches me. "Only for the summer?"

"The band I play for is going on tour." I enjoy making up the lie, putting on a skin for a moment to see if it fits. Besides, I don't know him and will never see him again. We won't go to school together. Playing around won't hurt anyone and amuses me for the moment. He looks surprised and maybe a little impressed, so I won't be able to hold onto it.

"Really?"

I laugh. "No."

He looks down at his water again. "You're weird."

"So you've said." I stand, ready to move on, mission accomplished. He may not have completely smiled, but he doesn't look as hell-bent on being so sullen. "Well. Thanks for sharing the table."

He glances at the other one. "There were two others you could have chosen."

I lean forward. "But then I wouldn't have gotten to talk to a serial killer." I offer him a grin and maintain my smile as I walk away. This is the most fun I've ever had on Sneak-Out night, and this makes for number five. I've never interacted with a stranger before, and while I might be a little unnerved at myself for doing it, I rationalize I'm leaving for college in eight weeks. Trying on the idea of interacting with a stranger, practicing with the idea of getting to know someone new, and maybe even presenting someone who seemed down with a laugh, all feel like a version of myself I like.

My feet crunch across the asphalt as I head home. I wonder if he's watching me, and figure he probably is, trying to figure me out. That, however, is an impossibility. I'm not that easy. I've constructed lots of layers of insulation to protect this fragile heart.

3

"Max?" Dad calls in the bowels of the house. It's probably swallowed him, and he's stuck between old pipes and old gypsum that's imprisoned him somewhere within the walls.

There's another knock at the door.

"Would you get the door, please?"

He could also be taking a shit or patching up some crack to keep the rodents out.

I straighten from the box on the floor in the kitchen, unpacking only what we need to live for the time being. "Got it," I yell back and wipe my hands on my cutoffs.

When I open the door, I freeze. Standing on the other side is Not-a-Serial-Killer, and he looks even better in the daylight. Shit. Dark blond hair with streaks of sunlight framing an angular face all broody and mysterious looking. It's disgusting really, how someone so moody could be blessed with model looks. Thick brows over eyes that seem to be changing color every time he moves not to mention those thick, dark lashes that make me insanely jealous. I glance over my shoulder and step outside, pulling the door shut behind me. "What are you doing here? How did you find me?"

He leans away from me like I'm about to throw a punch.

For the record, I'm not, but I don't need my dad knowing that I snuck out, that I traipsed down a dark road into the wilds of an unfamiliar town to sit across the table with a stranger. He'd flip (as he probably should now that I've pieced it together like that).

"What?" He looks as unsettled to see me as I am to see him and shoves his hands into the pockets of his jeans. He really needs to stop with that lip pout thing, because my stomach can only take so much fluttering.

Gosh. He's cute.

And tall. Well, taller than me, and I'm a couple inches shy of six feet. My one and only boyfriend Michael—house number nine—had been shorter than me by several inches. Of course, that didn't keep us from enjoying one another's company, if rounding the bases while watching reruns of Star Trek in his basement counts as enjoying one another.

I shake my head to get rid of that errant thought and cross my arms over my chest. "Well?"

"I'm looking for Cal Wallace," he says.

"Oh. Shit." I take a deep breath and relax. He isn't here for me at all. There is both elation at the realization and an inexplicable crash of disappointment in the bottom of my belly that fizzles and smokes. But of course, he isn't here for me.

The door creaks open, and my dad's face appears. He smiles.

"Hey, Dad."

He steps out onto the porch which I don't think has the capability to hold all three of us. "Hi. You must be Griffin."

Griffin.

I now know his name.

"I see you've met Max."

And now he knows mine.

I take a step back, away, and wait for the impending doom of my father finding out about my late-night romp through town.

"Yeah. Just met."

My eyes flash to his, and he holds my gaze a moment. It's only a split-second as if to say, *I get it*, but then, how could he? The crash site in my belly reignites. Then he looks away and follows my dad into the mess of the house. I offer him some filtered water, sarcastic comments where appropriate, and then escape up the stairs into the room. I've cleaned the space as best as I can to make myself feel less like a homeless squatter in an abandoned building and more like a resident in an actual bedroom I'll get to call mine.

I leave the stuff I won't need for the summer in boxes—no sense repacking when I'm leaving for college soon—and only unpack a few things I'll use. Summer clothes I fold and stash in stacked crates that serve as a dresser. Everything about my life feels temporary. As I fold my t-shirts and stack them into the crate I've set up against a wall, I wish that Dad would consider fixing up one and staying. I know he won't. It makes me nervous to think that after flipping this place he's going to follow me. I love my dad like nobody's business, but how am I supposed to break out on my own? I'm seeing this four-year college thing as an experiment in staying. Four years to make friends. Four years in the same place. Four uninterrupted years to grow some roots. My turn to choose where I go. My turn to become the fixer upper, because ultimately, I know that's what I'm ready to do: discover what I want for myself. Maybe that does make me a little bit like my mom.

I'm pushing another box of some winter things into the corner when my dad knocks.

He pokes his head in when I invite him to open the door. "Would you do me a favor?" he asks.

I wait, because it isn't like I'll say no.

"I got this call for a job." He waves his phone at me and presses it against his navy t-shirt. "Could you drive Griffin home?"

I nod and follow him from the room.

Griffin follows me from the house, and I climb into the Rust Bucket.

The door creaks as he gets into the passenger side, and I try not to stare as he settles himself. There's something about the way he moves that I find interesting. It's fluid, as if he doesn't care what his body can do. He isn't quite arrogant, but borders on it, while at the same time carrying around something on his shoulders that seems to weigh him down.

I'm spending way too much time thinking about his body.

I look over my shoulder to reverse Rust Bucket out of the driveway. Once we're on the road I say, "So, thanks for not saying anything about last night to my dad."

"Sure."

I glance at him, and he's staring out the passenger window. "How come you didn't?"

"It didn't seem like you wanted him to know." He glances at me, unsmiling, but not angry.

"I snuck out," I say.

"You still have to do that?"

It's a fair question, and I ponder it. No. I don't, but I also don't want to ask for permission or get a lecture about safety or any other ways that exchange might play out. Dad's love is smothering sometimes. He worries about me, and he isn't really a worrier.

We pass the convenience store where I met Griffin the night before, and I glance at the table where we sat.

Griffin surprises me again by seeking more information and repeating the question in a new way. "You sneak out a lot?"

My eyes slide from the table to him. "No. My dad—he's cool and all, and he probably would have given me the keys—but he worries. I also don't like to leave him alone on the first night in a new house."

"How many houses have you lived in?" He points out a turn I need to take.

"This makes ten."

His eyes grow wide, but they still have a hooded, sleepy quality to them. "Shit. That's a lot. Ten different houses? Not here?"

I move, adjusting myself in the seat. "Nope. All over. What about you?"

He directs me into another turn. "I've been here my whole life."

I refrain from sighing. That sounds perfect. The consistency of the same place, the same people. "That must be nice. You must have lots of friends—the same ones."

He hesitates, and I have a sense there's a story behind the pause. "You too? Friends in lots of places."

"You'd think. It's hard to make friends when you're just passing through."

"Next right." He points out his house, a single-story, ranch-style house. Dad and I lived in one a little like it—house number four. I park on the side of the road.

"Thanks, Max." He pushes open the squeaking door but doesn't get out, looking at me. While I've felt his eyes on me before, fleeting and flippant, this is the first time I feel like his gaze stops and takes up residence. "Is it short for something? Max? Like Maxine?"

I shake my head. "Not that. Maxwell."

"Maxwell." I like the way my name sounds when he says it, as if he's considering all the letters and how important each sound is. "That must have a story."

"Yeah." It totally does, but it includes a story about my mother, and I don't know him well enough, so I don't add to it.

31

He nods and gets out of Rust Bucket onto the sidewalk. "Well, thanks for the ride."

"You're welcome," I tell him and drive away after he closes the door. I coax myself not to look in the rearview mirror, but I can't help it. I totally look. He's just turning away from watching the truck and walking across the yard. I ignore the slight pitter patter of my heart, reminding myself that this place, that guy is temporary like every other place I've lived, and I drive back to a house falling apart.

4

I wake up the next morning to the sound of scritching somewhere in my room. Afraid I'm about to come face-to-face with a rat, my adrenalin bumps up about ten notches, and my heart speeds up as I squint my eyes open. With a deep breath, I'm relieved that the sound is just a branch grating my window with its sharp nails. Now that I'm awake, I get up, shrug into my running clothes, and walk down into the kitchen where Dad is scrolling through the headlines on his phone and drinking a cup of coffee.

He looks up when he sees me. "Morning, Sunshine."

"The tree needs trimming outside of my window. It's scratching up the pane."

"Going to have to replace the windows anyway, but I'll add it to the list."

I nod, bend over into the fridge to find some food to energize my run, and forage an apple we got last night on our first trip to the grocery store in town.

Dad sets down his phone. "Off for a run?"

"Yeah." I take a bite.

"Good routes?"

I finish the bite. "Seeing as this is only day three, I'm still getting a feel for it." I love the stretch of road between the house and town, but roadside running can be risky. "There are some side roads both paved and dirt that look promising."

"Phone. Location services."

"Yes. I know," I say and take another bite.

"Griffin will be out this morning," Dad says, returning to his phone. "I've got an onsite job this morning, so I'll get him started before I go." He picks up his coffee cup and takes a sip.

I don't respond but take another bite.

Dad looks up at me. "That okay? You feel comfortable being out here with him?"

I choke on the apple.

Dad stands up and is at my side, patting my back.

When I can speak without coughing, I ask him, "Are you asking if I think he's safe?"

"Well, I hired the kid, and it didn't dawn on me until this morning that maybe he wasn't safe." He returns to his seat at the table. "I don't know what I was thinking. I met his mom, and she seemed nice, enough. He's quiet, and I'm not sure if he'll work out. He's... green."

"Maybe your desperation to get this house done in eight weeks is clouding your judgment," I say.

He picks up his cup, looks inside, and sets it back down. "You might be right." He stands and refills the cup, then makes a new pot. I never nag him about his caffeine because he loves coffee as much as soda. I'd rather he drank the coffee.

"Did you just say I might be right?" I cross my arms over my chest.

He continues making the coffee. "Yes."

"And that eight weeks isn't going to be enough time to flip this place?"

"Not with a green kid like Griffin." He looks at me over his shoulder. "I might have been desperate, but he also kind of reminded me of myself when I was his age." He pauses, remembering. Then he shakes his head. "I'm sorry, Max. I thought about looking for someone else, but I've got work coming in now. I don't know when I'll have the time."

"Dad." I walk over to his side and wrap an arm around him. "First, I'm not scared of Griffin. He seems quiet, but nice. He was pleasant and respectful when I drove him home." I leave out the bit about the convenience store. "And it's okay if it takes longer than eight weeks. Truthfully, I'm tired of moving." It's true. I'm weary of it, but I'm weary of it for him too. I want him to find a life without me. Maybe find someone to share it with, then I wouldn't worry about him while I'm trying to figure my own self out. Another selfish wish, I figure. "It would be nice to have a home base for college, you know. Like for holidays."

He replaces the coffee carafe, turns the machine on, and then wraps an arm around my shoulders, squeezing me to him. "It may have to be that way for a bit. Maybe I can flip it after New Year's."

"In the middle of winter?"

"We'll see."

We stand side-by-side, one arm around each other, staring out the window for a few more minutes while the coffee pot sputters and puffs as it brews fresh coffee.

"Griffin's fine, Dad. Don't worry. Okay?" I hug him one more time. "I'm off."

"See you this afternoon."

As soon as I'm in the driveway, I go, warming up my muscles before stretching them out. The gravel under my shoes is slippery, but I'm used to varied running surfaces. I started running cross-country my sophomore year—house eight—after I started running and did the track thing my freshman year. Cross Country and Track became the unifying things at each school, and though the faces of teammates and coaches changed, the running never has.

I turn up the main road. It's still and quiet. The sun is only beginning to think about climbing over the horizon. With my music pushing my pace through my earbuds, I breathe and run through the pain of getting started. My dad's admission on my mind, I'm glad he's beginning to be realistic about this flip. He might be a dreamer, but he's usually a realist too. It's where I've gotten my pragmatism.

Something has gotten into him, and I think it's because I'm leaving, except he hasn't said it in those words.

The thing is, Dad and I haven't ever been apart. It's always been us, after my mother left. He's been my rock, and I've been his Max-in-a-million. He hasn't dated (and if he has, I didn't know about it); he's been a constant, and a freaking darned good one at that. But I'm feeling the pressure and the fear of worrying about him when the time comes for him to be alone. I'm feeling the worry and concern for myself too, knowing I'm stepping out beyond our borders into an unknown frontier by myself. I know Dad will always be there, but the idea of him following me makes me feel claustrophobic. What if I keep trying to get further and further away? What if that was why my mom left?

I hate that I've thought this.

I turn up a gravel side road and push my pace to punish myself for the ugly thought. My mom left because she was a user. That's it. My inner voice recognizes the fallacy of this either-or argument, but I don't modify the thought. I don't know her. I don't know her story. I only know what my dad has shared, and I know he's kept the hard stuff back because he hasn't wanted me to grow up thinking poorly of her. But she left, so it's hard not to.

With a shake of my head, I focus on my feet hitting the earth, the sound of the music in my earbuds, the feel of my breath moving through my lungs, and the burn of my muscles as they work. This is what is mine in the moment, and that's all I need to do. Exercise the thoughts. Burn away the fears, the bitterness, the doubt. Focus on the now.

By the time I'm running back up the driveway to the haunted house, not-a-serial-killer Griffin is there, but Rust Bucket is gone, so Dad's left. Griffin stands at the side of the house, looking at his phone, and I wonder if that's his idea of working, worried for my dad and the workload. "So, Serial Killer, is that what you're going to do on the job, today? Stare at your phone instead of work?" I call out to him.

He looks up from his screen and flicks the hair out of his eyes with a toss of his head. "You my supervisor?"

I stop far enough away from him that he won't smell me. After that workout I'm not sure I'm smelling all that great. Then I think it's ridiculous I've even thought about it. Stupid. I lean into a hip to stretch it. "You can be sure as shit that I'm going to let my dad know if all you're doing is standing around staring at your phone." I offer him a smile.

He looks at me, and I noticed that his eyes take in more of me, moving around my shape before he focuses his attention back on his phone. "Don't worry. I'm just making a plan." His eyes flit up and he gives his phone a slight wave toward me. "Your dad wants you to text him."

"Got it." I turn away, stretching my arms as I walk back to the house. I look over my shoulder, and my spine tingles when I see he's watching me. "That—" I say, indicating the porch— "shouldn't be too hard. Swing the hammer and back away."

When I turn around, I smile.

After I've suffered through a shower in the awful bathroom where the water pressure is barely a trickle and the water is the color of rust until Dad gets the plumber out, I attempt to wash my hair, rinsing it with fresh water we've bought even though it will take all day to dry. I dress, then jump into going through the boxes, rearranging stuff throughout the house. It's a useless endeavor. In a few months, Dad will be renovating the inside after he's gotten the exterior where it needs to be before the winter weather hits. I'm only unpacking things that we'll need to live, rearranging things into long-term boxes, and moving them into rooms that won't be renovated for a while.

While I'm reorganizing, my mind drifts to Griffin, who I can hear moving about in the back. I reimagine him standing where he was and me coming up the walk. When he turns to look at me, I imagine a smile. I wonder what a real smile would look like. Then I wonder why I'm wondering. He's cute and all—cute isn't really the right description since he's got a bad-boy edge to him that has his appearance outside the norm of typical cuteness—but I don't need to be thinking about his smile. I'm leaving for school in a few weeks. I'll be in a dorm room with a roommate named Renna (we've been emailing), and I'm pretty sure I'll be looking out for cute guys to check out and get to know. I don't have the inclination to get to know someone here.

That makes me ponder ex-boyfriend, Michael, who I thought was nice (but my dad didn't). We started out as friends, having met during cross-country. Eventually, we started training together, and after some time and some questionable awkwardness, he asked me out. We dated exclusively—if it could be called dating—and by the time it ended, it was a welcome end for the most part. What I can see now in hindsight is that Michael wasn't a very good boyfriend, and my dad was right. Michael was really good at taking, but terrible at giving unless it was unsolicited mansplainations and advice about how I *should be*. We went out on a couple of dates in the beginning, but he always wanted to hang out at his house in the basement to round bases.

The closer my impending departure date loomed, the more distant he became until finally he said, "You're leaving, and I don't want a long-distance relationship. I can't trust it." I couldn't blame the first part—the long-distance stuff. I mean, who could blame him? I didn't want that either. My transient life has always been a complication to any kind of permanent relationship. It had been the second part that got me. Couldn't trust what? I'd asked him to clarify, but he hadn't been able to articulate it, changing the subject to not wanting to be tied down to someone as we went away to college. I still get hung up on the trust thing. Was it a me issue or a *him* issue? I don't have the answer, and I guess I won't get one.

Eventually, I tire of spinning thoughts about Michael, hungry now, and make myself a meal; I make enough for Griffin too, just in case he's hungry.

I'm walking across the yard to invite him to eat when I hear the crash and hustle around the corner. "Are you okay?" I ask before I've even seen him.

Griffin is standing away from the crash site of the porch, hammer in hand, facing me. The heap of the porch, still settling, and the surprise on his face makes me smile.

He seems to remember himself, smooths his face into that robotic mask and says, "Yeah."

I don't laugh because I don't think it would go over very well. I mean, I don't know him or anything, but I know my dad, and I know when the robot face comes out to leave it alone. "Hungry?" I ask instead. "I made some breakfast sandwiches if you're game."

He offers me a nearly imperceptible nod and follows me into the house.

When we're seated across from one another at the table, sandwiches on plates and glasses of water in front of us, I'm hit with how domestic it feels, a permanence I'm not expecting. I frown and glance at Griffin who is glowering at the sandwich which erases my prior thought. "I don't think it's going to hurt you."

He offers me a strange half-smile. It lifts the corner of his mouth (have I mentioned how pretty his mouth is. Oof). "Thanks."

I have to look away from his mouth. I shrug. "Sure. I was hungry and made extra." Which is true since that's how it's been with my dad and me.

He takes a bite—a big one—and I can't look away. I'm both enamored by the way his mouth moves and disgusted by the size of the bite. Then he speaks around it, "That's really good," and I'm wondering where this boy was raised? In a den by wolves? But it's the first time, besides the look of surprise on his face which doesn't really count because it wasn't in my presence, that I've seen his mask flicker off.

"Most things taste good to a caveman," I say with a smile.

He stops chewing, and his eyes suggest he isn't sure what to make of my comment. I take a smaller bite and chew with my mouth closed. He doesn't look away. "Are you saying I'm a caveman?"

"I might be insinuating that. Yes." I grin at him, then shrug. "Serial killer and caveman. That's not a great combination."

"I am neither of those things." He looks down at his sandwich and takes another bite, but he looks back at me, again, and seems to take my measure. Mouth closed as he chews.

I smile and take another bite of my sandwich. He can learn.

"Where's your mom?"

His innocent question—because who is missing in this little twosome—twitches a nerve in my shoulder. I set the partially eaten sandwich on the plate, pick up my napkin, and try to figure out what to say.

"Sorry," he says.

I shake my head, hoping he knows he doesn't need to apologize for my silence on the matter. "I don't really like to talk about her," I finally tell him.

He gives me a nod as if to say he understands, and that makes me curious.

"How about your mom?"

"She's around."

"Cryptic much?"

"She's always working. Got like three jobs. I don't see her much." He tries to make light of it by offering me another one of those half smiles.

"Three?" I think about all the work my dad has done to keep us afloat. Two jobs maybe? Working the flip and side jobs, but he was always home when I was.

"Yeah. After my dad—" he stops himself from saying any more and clears his throat. "She's just trying to make ends meet."

"And your dad?"

He looks up at me, and I know why he understands because of the look on his face. It's a combination of anger, bitterness, and hurt. He smooths it away almost as quickly as I saw it.

"Or is that a little like how I feel about my mom?"

He gives me a nod and takes another bite of his sandwich.

Feeling empathetic of Griffin's non-admission, the way it was written on his face, I tell him, "She left us, my mom."

Griffin freezes, and his eyes shift up from the plate to mine. His mask drops again, his eyes flickering with emotions, but he tucks them away as quickly as they surfaced. He looks a little like a deer in headlights.

I keep going. "I was five. I don't remember much about it. I mean, I do, but it's like I'm not sure what's real or made up anymore, you know? You asked about my name. She didn't want to name me Maxwell. That was my dad's choice after some famous football player or something. Her first choice was Ruby. So, they flipped a coin. My dad won. Ruby is my middle name."

Griffin stands as if he's been burned. The chair he was in tips over and crashes against the floor. He glances at it. "I better get back to work."

His abruptness surprises me, but I nod. "Yeah. Okay."

43

I follow him with my eyes to the sink. He sets the cleared plate inside. "Thanks for the sandwich."

"Yeah. No problem."

He hustles out of the room like it's on fire around him, and I'm left more curious than ever about a boy named Griffin, even as I tell myself I shouldn't be. I have less than eight weeks to go.

5

My gaze slashes sideways to steal a glance at Griffin on the other side of the opening where the window had recently been. His gray, t-shirt-clad torso leans against the wall, his denim covered legs stretched out in front of him, crossed at the ankle. He has an impressive lean. He has the broody-boy thing down, and it's sort of funny, but I don't dare express my amusement at that, not without cutting off any sort of camaraderie we've found since we met. I'm content at the level of interaction we've attained over the last two weeks: polite and friendly if a bit aloof.

Besides, it's too hot to do much more than move my eyes around; laughing would create a Mount Vesuvius of molten sweat on my body which, unless I'm running, isn't welcome. I'd prefer to roll my eyes instead. The hot summer day soaks into the seams of everything, and beads of sweat are currently collecting between my boobs despite one of my dad's old Guns-n-Roses t-shirts I've stripped of sleeves, cropped, and cut out the crew collar for a cooler fit.

A bead of sweat treks over my skin toward my navel. I press a hand against the cotton of my t-shirt to catch it and groan. "It's so hot." I move away from the wall ready to scream. The stifling heat makes me feel claustrophobic, so I grasp the bottom of the shirt, swishing it back and forth to create some air.

Griffin's eyes track my movements. He doesn't smile, doesn't do anything other than observe.

It's unnerving in a way that makes me feel a bit self-conscious, and I haven't felt like that since… mid-Michael days, though I'm not going to fool myself into thinking Griffin is interested in me even if I'd tell myself that lie because I'm physically attracted to him. I'm not easily flustered, but Griffin does it, somehow, and that makes me want to throw something at him. "What?"

He shrugs, bends down to pick up his water bottle, and takes a sip.

I notice the water on his chin, look away as he wipes it with the back of his hand, and move across the room, away from the window because the breeze I'd hoped for doesn't exist. It's a little cooler across the room, or so I tell myself. Plus, I can also openly watch Griffin if I wanted, though I don't. Instead, I look down at my feet and contemplate the grooves in the flooring.

After our breakfast that first day along with his quick getaway,

Griffin has made it pretty clear he isn't into opening up. He's polite, and that's about it.

I sneak a peek at him.

He looks away, which means he was looking at me, and shifts to look out the window for my dad, who we've been waiting to return from the shop. He'd had to grab the window flashing tape since we ran out in the process of replacing the windows on the first floor. He was adamant there was more. "I'll grab it. Stay here," he'd said and disappeared from the exterior side of the house. "I know right where it is," he'd called back as he'd walked away.

That was close to twenty minutes ago.

Tick. Tock.

Griffin resumes his lean. His eyes jump up to mine. "What?"

My turn to shrug.

Okay. So, no big deal. Griffin isn't into making friends. I get it. Certainly, lived the solitary life, though I wouldn't be one to advocate for it.

"I feel like you're judging me," he says.

I shake my head. "I'm overheating. It makes me cranky and when I'm cranky it's best to keep my mouth shut because I don't say nice things."

He looks away.

Thinking back on all the last nine houses where I've lived, even as the outcast, apart from the shortest of stints—six months—I'd found people to connect with to some extent. Usually another outsider. I'd made a few temporary friends. Tamara was the first friend at the first

47

house—Barton Road—and we'd established a first and second grade foursome with Shara and Kim.

Then Dad and I moved to house two—Frilling Avenue—where I spent third grade with Avery.

House three—Downey Street—produced my fourth, fifth and into sixth grade bestie, Cassie. She was the only one I'd actively looked up on Instagram, though our lives and interests have diverged since we were ten. This was the longest stay of all of them and ended in the middle of sixth grade. This not only abruptly ended my best friendship up to then, but it took us to our shortest stay, Misten Avenue—house five—and onto a new school for the remainder of sixth grade. Making any friends that year proved impossible with established friend groups.

Middle school started in earnest at house six—Victoria Boulevard. That's where the "one of the guys" practical joke occurred because I'd thought I'd found a friend group. That was the year I learned about not extending trust until it was earned. Eventually, I met Dillon and Jensen, who taught me a lot about gaming.

Glancing across the room at Griffin, his pouty frown and arms crossed over his chest, I think he'd probably understand that sentiment.

Then high school happened. Making friends in early elementary school hadn't been awful. Little kids are more open. If making friends in middle school was problematic when adolescence appeared on the horizon, social status mattered, and peer groups made collective decisions, making friends in high school was nearly impossible.

I started freshman year in house seven—Holmes Street—and this was when the "Big Crush" started running. Carla and I spent lunches together, though *together* is a very generous description of sitting at the same table. Sophomore year was spent at house eight—Reader Road—and resulted in the invitation to prom with a boy named Ivan who abandoned me at a house party while he hooked up with some other girl. Most of junior year and senior year were lived at Davis Court, house nine. This was where I ran cross country, met, befriended, and dated Michael, then graduated.

While I understand Griffin's standoffish demeanor, I don't have it in my nature to accept it. Even if a friendship with him is temporary—like they all have been—time together is always more enjoyable with people.

"What if I was judging you?" I ask. "Would you care?"

I push away from the wall and walk toward him.

He tenses. "No. I don't give a fuck what people think of me."

I stop at the window and stare at him, eyes narrowed. "Lie. Everyone cares what others think about them." With my hands on the replaced frame, I lean out the window hoping for a breeze. None. But I feel a rough bit of caulking under my skin. "May I see your scraper?" I hold my hand out.

Griffin pulls it from the toolbelt on his hips and hands it to me.

"Thank you, nurse Nichols," I say with a grin, and it's his turn to roll his eyes. I push the edge of the tool across the surface to smooth out the unfinished sill between the old and the new. Then I hand the tool back. "You make a stellar assistant, nurse."

He gives me his usual partial grin that expresses his amusement but rarely reaches his eyes.

Returning to the window, I yell, "Dad?!"

"Does that usually work?"

"Rarely," I say, but don't want to explain that there's this giant ball in my chest of antsy annoyance that I need to expel. Yelling does the trick.

"Then why do it?"

"Because I like the sound of my own voice making that screeching sound." I raise my eyebrows with my point. "Now, you know what I'd sound like when I let the vocal cords loose. It should keep you from attacking, Serial Killer."

He huffs a laugh and looks at his hands. "What? That you sound like an angry crow? A drowning one."

"Are crows angry? Do you have experience with this particular animal?"

Another partial smile.

"What? You don't like that sound?"

"Not particularly." His gaze raises to meet mine, and this time I see a twinkle of amusement, but it isn't in a smile. His eyes. Those nice gold flecks gleam.

"Let me do it again, then." I turn back to lean out the window and yell for my dad a second time.

My dad's voice echoes back, "I'm still looking!"

I laugh out loud. "Okay!"

Picking up my water bottle from the floor, I take a drink. "Is it always this hot?"

"Mostly. We spend summers at the Quarry."

"We?"

Griffin presses his teeth together, his jaw going rigid.

Okay. A sore spot. Whoever *we* is. It makes me think about breakfast and how I'd shared what I had about my mom. He'd gotten prickly.

I change the subject, "What's the Quarry?"

"A lake. There's this rock people jump from. It's a lot of fun."

"That does sound like fun."

"Really? You'd jump? I haven't known many girls to jump."

"Well, Mr. Nichols, you haven't known many Maxwell Wallaces then."

He does another of those grins but instead of giving the smile to me, looks down and smiles at the large splinter of wood he's fiddling with in his hands.

I huff a frustrated sound and roll my eyes. "It's too hot in here. I'm going to go help him look. I need to get out of this house." I stomp from the room.

Surprisingly, Griffin follows.

"Do you spend a lot of time with girls, Serial Killer?" I look over my shoulder at him, and when I see a telling smirk on his mouth, I stop in my tracks and hold up my hand to stop him. I press the flat of my palm against his shoulder. "Let me qualify that. With girls who are friends?"

He looks at his shoulder where I've touched him.

I withdraw my hand and rub the hand over my t-shirt to dissipate the sparks crawling under my skin.

He gives me another shallow grin but doesn't respond.

"Clearly not," I reply, start back through the house, and walk out into the sunshine.

The gravel underfoot punctuates our steps.

"Let's fix that, Mr. Nichols," I say. "Favorite color. Go!" I glance at him with a grin I hope communicates encouragement.

He just looks at me with confusion.

I sigh. "This is how people get to know one another, right? I'm trying here."

"Black."

"That's a shade, not a color."

"So."

"Color."

He makes an annoyed sound but answers. "Green. Yours?"

"Yellow. Favorite food?"

"Food."

"Nope. Has to be specific."

"Says who?"

"Me. My game. My rules."

"Sandwich."

I give him what I think is an incredulous look. "Why?"

"A meal in your hands." He says it like it's obvious, his brows moving toward one another and a hand coming up as if offering a solid bit of wisdom.

"So is pizza."

"Is that your favorite?"

"No. It's–" I stop, thinking. "Okay. Yeah. It's pizza. Favorite book."

He grimaces. "Gross."

I stop at the threshold of the shop. "You don't read?"

"Only when forced."

My eyebrows drift up, and I slow blink. "I don't know if we can be friends." I lead us into the shop, and my eyes adjust to the dimmer lighting inside the room.

"Who said we're friends?"

"Found it!" Dad appears from behind a stack of boxes holding several rolls of flashing tape. "Maroon. Shepherd's Pie, and any book by Tom Clancy."

"Good answers."

"You read?" Griffin asks.

"Absolutely," Dad says, handing off the rolls to Griffin and me. "I'll grab the extra shims," he says. "Favorite scary movie. Mine is Hitchcock's *The Birds*."

"All of them," I say.

"None of them," Griffin says at the same time.

"What serial killer doesn't like scary movies?" I tease Griffin.

"Maxwell! Why did you call Griffin that?" Dad's appalled, and I've forgotten he doesn't understand there was a convenience store rendezvous.

"Just a joke, sir," Griffin covers for me and heads out of the shop, carting his rolls of tape.

Dad gives me a look.

"Just a joke," I tell him and hustle from the shop.

Perhaps we've established a foothold of friendship.

When we get back to the house Griffin looks over his shoulder. "Favorite music?"

"Old School rock bands."

His gaze drops to my t-shirt. "Oh." His eyes return to mine. "Got it."

"Yours?"

"EDM."

I want to grimace, but I keep my face neutral. Party boy. "Don't worry, Serial Killer, I'll help you achieve better taste in music and books."

He scoffs, but I catch a private half-smile.

We finish the first-floor window replacements as the sun slips below the tree line, then invite Griffin to go to dinner with us. He declines, but Dad insists we take him home. Rust Bucket is a tight fit, Dad driving, me in the middle, and then Griffin. My thigh is pressed against his, my feet sharing the space of the passenger floorboard with his. Hyper aware of being this close to him, I attempt to lean toward my dad, but my dad's broad shoulders (yes, my genetics came from Mr. Linebacker) are making it difficult, so I can't keep my right side from grazing Griffin even if I try to hold myself apart. He's also trying to give me room, half of his body climbing the passenger door. It doesn't work. Every time my dad takes that right turn, Griffin gets the full Maxwell lean.

After we drop him home, I slide into the seat he vacated as my dad drives the pickup away. The seat is warm, my right side is warm, my chest is warm. I'm annoyed about it, but then at the same time, it is fun, feeling feels, enjoying the beginning of friendship, even if it's temporary. I enjoy messing with Griffin.

"You're smiling." Dad interrupts my thoughts.

I look at him. "Don't I always smile? I'm generally a happy individual."

He makes a noise that seems like he's making calculations. "No. You haven't smiled like that since you were younger. It's... unguarded." His gaze drifts to me for just a moment.

I snort and look away. "Well. I'll try and refrain from being too happy."

"I like it." He reaches over and takes my hand, then says he loves me.

"I love you too, Dad."

He lets go of my hand and drives us toward our eating destination. "Before that Michael kid. Maybe even before that."

"Michael?"

"The smile. You didn't smile like that even when you dated that Michael kid."

"Why do you call him 'that Michael kid' when his name is just Michael?"

"I didn't like him."

"I know. You've made that clear." I smile again. "I did smile."

"Not like now," he says and pulls the truck into a parking lot outside a diner.

I realize my dad's right. My chest never felt this open with Michael. I feel like my shoulders are back, my heart exposed, and air is moving through my lungs with the ease of the middle of a run. There's a lightness, a moment at the onset of the run when I feel like I could float away. Then, when the endorphins hit, it happens again. That's how I feel, now, and Dad's observation help me realize—I never felt like this with Michael.

I blame it on the impending newness of college less than six weeks away now.

Excitement.

But I also had fun today with Dad and Griffin, even if it was hot.

My heart beats a new rhythm in my chest that I don't really want to think too hard about. I don't know why it's there, a quickening, but I'm not going to complain. With time slipping toward college, along with the new start I'm looking forward to, I know that anything here is temporary, but I'm going to do my best to enjoy this time with my dad and any new friends I can make while I'm here. Even Griffin Nichols.

6

The next couple of weeks move through like summer rainstorms, and I find myself looking forward to seeing Griffin, interested in pushing his buttons to see if I can get a reaction. He's adept at keeping himself buttoned up, but occasionally, he'll release the robot lever. It's usually because I've said something surprising, and his eyebrows shoot up over his eyes, or he suppresses a smile. I haven't really determined the why of his reserve yet, but I have made the assumption it's because he thinks it isn't tough enough. I know. There's no need to remind me ASS-U-ME. I get it, but there are other clues, too, that I'm thinking support this weird way he thinks he's got to be more manly. The grunting and monosyllabic conversation, the way he doesn't share about himself, and the lack of feeling he allows on his face.

What bugs me the most is that I can't stop thinking about him.

Okay. Look, I know this is a bad idea. While I don't have a ton of experience with guys, Griffin intrigues me, but mostly it's because I'm physically attracted to him; he hasn't given me much else, otherwise. And even if I know crushing on him isn't smart, what else have I got to do in the time between now and college? He's hot, and he isn't interested, so I figure I can be an incognito equal opportunity sexist. He's nice eye-candy, and it's safe. I'm not making more of it than I should because there's nothing to make.

We've achieved this semi-cool, we-can-be-in-the-same-vicinity-and-be-sort-of-comfortable place that has the feel of a maybe-friendship, even if my thoughts take me down infatuated roads. Blast off to college is in T-minus four-ish weeks now. Dad here. Me on my own. Griffin Nichols wherever he'll be. It's a nice distraction from my otherwise boring-ass existence. Oh. Wait. That's just my normal existence.

I circle a cabinet I found in the house. Technically, I didn't discover it, but it was pushed against a wall looking like something that needed to be murdered with an ax and burned, but then I realized it wasn't attached to the wall. When I pulled it out, I saw this gorgeous spot of clean wood. Now I've cleaned it up, as best as I can, and it's a beautiful piece that has me thinking about my dad. In all the work he's done over the years, he's remade and created beauty, but he's never taken anything. We've stopped, hit it, and left. Goodness, that sounds like a one-night stand. Forgive me. But maybe that's what a one-night stand is like? I don't know. I haven't had one, though if Griffin… No! Not going there. I'm pretty sure I need feelings to—

Moving on.

Back to my prior thought—the cabinet.

I want to refinish it. For Dad. Put it in this house, and maybe he might see it as a pain to move, so it will keep him here. Seriously, my dad is pragmatic like that. Actually, he'd leave it. He isn't super sentimental. I just want to do something nice for him. He could take all the books he carts around in crates and store them somewhere nice.

The problem is, the cabinet is huge, and I can't refinish it in the house. It needs to be stripped, which will require room, air space, and chemicals that can kill you.

I hear a thump against the siding.

Griffin.

Two problems solved: my desire to see him and this humongous cabinet I can't move by myself.

Griffin is up on a ladder addressing the paint and wood siding of the house. He and my dad have done a lot in the last three weeks: both porches demolished, the windows prepped and mostly replaced (a few special orders to go), the back porch rebuilt, and now they're prepping the siding for replacement and paint. Dad's on a job, so Griffin is solo today, well, besides me.

"Griffin?"

He doesn't respond, though in his white coveralls set up to keep any toxic materials out of his lungs, maybe he can't hear me.

"Griffin? Would you help me with something?" I ask, a little louder this time.

Still no response. He just keeps working, and I'm feeling a little insecure.

"Are you awake up there?"

Griffin looks down from his perch on the ladder. "I hope so. You shouldn't be around this without the gear." He returns to scraping the siding.

"I've been down here talking to you, and it's like you're somewhere else."

"I'm working, Einstein. Remember when you threatened to tell your dad if I wasn't working?"

This makes me laugh. "Yes."

He stops scraping, and I continue staring up at him with a grin on my face. "Did you need something?"

"Yeah. I was wondering if you'd help me move something from the house."

His eyes move over me. "You can't do it with all of your muscles?"

The initial words in my mouth die. My skin grows warm with embarrassment as I return to all of those insults and comments about my body and my size over the years. Darrin Johnson—house eight—had said, "You're built like an NFL linebacker." He hadn't meant it as a compliment. House seven when "Big Crush" was coined. I swallow the memories, remind myself that I just need to love me, and focus on what I came for. "I needed help, but that's okay." I turn away from the ladder and hurry back the way I came, mortified even as I try to release it.

"Max! Max! Wait."

I turn and watch Griffin hurry after me in his white suit swishing as he does. "You didn't need to get down," I tell him.

He stops an arm's length or three away. "You said you needed help. I'm here."

Still smarting from the body comment, I climb the step ladder to get into the front door.

"The house is coming along. In a minimalist kind of way," he says behind me as I lead him through the living room.

I'm able to push away my annoyance a moment to appreciate the fact he's strung several words together and used a word like minimalist. "I don't want to unpack too much. All of this stuff will have to be moved again when you do the inside of the house."

"And what will you be doing then?" he asks.

I turn around and look at him, both wary and intrigued. It's only like the first or second time he's tried to draw me into a conversation since the breakfast sandwich incident, and when he does, I feel like I'm hearing a more honest version of him that he hides behind his facade. "I'm leaving." I look away and focus on a dusty spot I missed on the cabinet, though I know it won't help yet, and swipe at the surface with my hand.

"Leaving?"

"College." I move around the backside of the cabinet to put it in between us. I'm unnerved. First by his innocuous comment that pushed me back on my heels even after all of the self-work I've done to be okay inside this body. Second, because he's actually trying to engage with me, and I'm not sure what to make of it.

"Oh. Yeah. That's good. Me too." He peeks around the cabinet, and our eyes connect.

"You're leaving for college?"

He shakes his head and shifts his gaze to study the wood. "No. I mean, I'm going to community college in September."

"That's good."

He changes the subject. "This is huge. You want to move this?"

"Yes. It's an old china cabinet. Solid wood." I give it a thump with my knuckles, then run a hand over a smooth spot. "I wanted to move it out into the workshop."

"Your dad doing something with it?" he asks.

I bristle at his assumption and swipe my hands together to clear off the grime. "No, Serial Killer. I am."

He gives me one of those half smiles, but it reaches his eyes this time, and I like the way the corners of his eyes crinkle. It makes me wonder what a full smile would do to his already handsome face. "You haven't called me that for a while."

I snort—ugh. Yeah, snort—at him. "You haven't deserved it."

"Well, I'm sorry for annoying you," he says, loaded with sarcasm. "I can help."

He does help me get the hulking cabinet out of the house, which is a major feat given we didn't have stairs and had to make it across the gravel drive to the workshop. By the time we get it there, we're both breathing heavily from the exertion, and I try not to think about what sex with him would sound like. It's an inappropriate thought even if it's interesting and makes me tingle low in my belly. I overheat and smile with nerves that don't belong.

Griffin clears his throat, unable to meet my gaze, which makes me curious, and says, "I'm going. I'll grab some water and get back to scraping. Got to get that side of the house finished today."

So many words.

"Hey, Griffin?" I ask, wishing to keep him in my same vicinity for just a little longer.

"Yeah?"

"Thanks for the help."

He nods and starts for the door but stops before he crosses the threshold. I watch him as he weighs whatever is on his mind. Then he turns and says, "You know earlier. Did I say something that, you know, made you mad?"

That is unexpected. Completely unexpected, and I suddenly feel exposed, as if I'm standing in front of him in the buff. Shit. In my whole experience, other than my dad, and in some instances, Michael when he'd been annoyed, I haven't had many people ask me about my feelings. I cross my arms and shake my head. "It's no big deal."

"Kind of seemed like it was."

Nervous, I sort of laugh to deflect how exposed I feel and make light of it in one of those self-depreciative ways. "I used to get teased for, you know—" I indicate my size with my hands.

"For using your hands to talk?"

My eyes flash to his, and I smile grateful for the humor. "I got teased a lot for my size. Growing up."

His smile fades, and his eyebrows pinch together, then he swipes a hand over his face, the white coveralls making that swishing noise when he moves that seems so loud now. "I'm sorry."

"You didn't know," I tell him, but his apology throws me off balance. I'm not sure I even remember Michael apologizing when we got into an argument.

"I'm sorry people are assholes."

"Thanks. I appreciate that."

He turns back to the door again, and I watch him go, thinking he'll disappear out into the light, but he stops again, his back to me. "My dad," he says. "He's been in prison since I was eight. People used to tease me about that." He looks over his shoulder at me.

I'm shocked, moved even, at this unexpected bit of information. First the information itself has me appalled at my insensitivity, but also the fact that he's shared it, offering a connection, as if he's peeled back a protective layer of the coveralls he's been living in to allow me to see him.

"Shit. I've been calling you a serial killer. I'm sorry."

He laughs. Oh, my lord, an actual smile, and it lights up his face. Holy shit. His eyes—the gold flecks sparkle against the green and gray—light up everything about him. I'm mesmerized.

"He's not a murderer or anything."

With a hand to my chest to still my racing heart, I say, "Still."

"It's okay, Weirdo." He chuckles again, the mirth still on his face as he turns and leaves the workshop to go back to the job my dad has given him.

I'm rooted to the floor next to the cabinet, my hand still pressed to my heart, trying to catch my breath, knowing my infatuation just blew up into something bigger, and that's terrible.

7

When I offered to drive Griffin to a party, I told myself I did it to be nice and to continue the tentative friendship we'd somehow established. Now, though, sitting next to him in the truck on the way to some place called the Quarry with my heart thumping in my throat, I'm not so sure that my motives are purely rooted in friendship. A veil lifted when he offered the nugget about his father, and it seemed to break open an entryway through the wall that Griffin has built around himself. It made me think of my relationship with Michael. Not so much Michael, but me.

Making friends and maintaining them has been difficult. It's about all the moving, but not just about that. Every time I walked into a new school, a new classroom, I held up walls, thickened the existing ones. Being a bigger girl, I'd been teased. Being new, I might make an initial connection, but when the teasing began, it was always harder to keep those connections. No one wanted to sacrifice themselves on the altar of Outcast with the new kid. Protective walls were always easier.

Then Michael happened.

Though we broke up a few months before graduation—the tearing away of all those firsts—first boyfriend, first love, first kiss, first sexual experience, first everything—I'm far enough away to turn around and look at the experience with clearer eyes.

My relationship with Michael taught me a few things. First, I learned that I'm worthy of love. Though not perfect, because as I learned later, Michael's love came with conditions in place. We started as friends, though, and liked one another. Second, I learned the importance of talking through stuff. Feeling insecure was easy, but I'm not one for making assumptions when I have a perfectly good set of working vocal cords to ask the question. This wasn't Michael's favorite of my qualities, since being confronted about his feelings made him angry more than made things better. But when we had a conversation—or an argument—it seemed to clear the fog we'd wandered into. Granted, I've done enough online searches to understand that Michael and I weren't always healthy. I mean, the guy's major complaint was because I'd done something impetuous. Being me, really, which I learned is nonnegotiable; whoever I date had better like me for me. I learned that I needed to be vulnerable, and that wasn't easy. Still isn't. I've got some walls, and Michael broke up with me because of whatever he'd meant about trust. Most of the time, allowing someone to root around in the soft soil around my own roots doesn't feel safe. Michael didn't always make me feel safe because there were underhanded judgements attached. I couldn't always drop the walls. I didn't feel safe to be that open. I'm recognizing this might have been a me-with-Michael thing, not necessarily just a me thing.

When I look at Griffin, I see those walls in him too.

Earlier, in the workshop, we'd shared a moment, and just thinking about it makes my heart puff up with helium and float away. We'd bumped into one another when he stepped closer to help me with one of the doors on the cabinet. His body grazed mine, and every place my body touched his felt like it lit up like the sky during a summer storm. He'd masked up. Of course, I brushed it off to maintain the normal banter we've established, cognizant that a physical response is a norm of physical attraction (even if it is one-sided). I'm not thinking Griffin is physically attracted, but our contact crossed some boundary for him that shut doors. Unfortunately, I haven't been able to shut the door on the electricity that has been tingling my nerve endings and makes my chest ache every time I recall it.

Maybe walls are a universal human response to emotional pain, though.

I glance at him now, helping navigate Rust Bucket where we need to go, and he glances at me.

"Is it weird I'm excited?" I ask.

"You're weird," he answers with a half-smile meant to rile me, "so that would be normal for you."

I give him a mocking laugh. "I haven't done anything since we moved here. This will be my first time out since the night I met you, SK. You're navigating."

"You aren't missing much," he says and returns to staring out the window. "If it makes you feel better, this is the first time I'm going out too."

I glance at him.

"I may not have a car, but I do think it entails watching the road while driving."

"I'm surprised. You seem like the party type."

"Didn't we already establish that?" he asks. "Six days a week and Mondays off?"

"You're making my point. Thank you."

He tells me to make a turn, then adds, "Yeah. That was my MO."

"Was?" I ask, curious. More than I should be, I think, but I can't help myself.

"Things change."

"By choice?"

"Necessity."

"Sounds like there's a story."

"I'm going to skip it." He runs his hands down his thighs.

I look at him and allow him some leeway. "For now."

The radio fills the silence of the cab punctuated by Griffin's directions, and though the song playing is a popular tune, I'm not feeling the ease being with a friend I should have, or so I imagine. I think about his tidbit the other day and figure it's time to offer my own.

"Truth: I haven't really had many friends. All the moving. Hard to hang onto any when all I did was leave."

He resumes his staring out the window. "They're not all that they're cracked up to be."

It's a heavy statement, and I'm jumping back to his earlier admission about friends and the story he decided to skip. I go in with humor instead because Griffin seems to respond better when things aren't so weighted. "I'm beginning to question hanging out with you."

He chuckles like I hoped he would; it softens his edges.

"Okay. Since you're stuck with me, tell me something else."

"I'm getting a car soon."

"You are?"

"I'll only be able to afford a piece of shit, but I won't have to share with my mom anymore."

I reach over and turn down the music. "Where's the first place you want to drive this piece-of-shit car?"

A look—which I shouldn't be observing because I'm driving—smooths out his features while at the same time makes him seem unyielding like granite. "There's this ghost town I heard about—it's an hour or so from here—that I'd like to visit."

"A ghost town? Really? Not like to your best friend's house or something?"

His jaw sharpens, and I know I've hit a nerve. "Yeah. The ghost town."

I wonder if this connects to his mention and subsequent

annoyance around the nebulous *we* he mentioned before—when we were working on the house—or his subsequent prickiliness everytime we talk about *friends*.

"So why there?"

"I–" He stops a moment.

I force myself to keep my eyes on the road. I don't want to spook him or anything since this is the most he's ever opened up about himself since I've known him.

"My brother and I used to play cowboys and bandits when we were little. Our dad watched those black and white Western movies when he was home. Those were his favorite. Phoenix—that's my brother—he was always the villain, and I wanted to be part of his gang, but I usually had to play the sheriff because he wanted me to chase after him and take him to jail." He pauses. "I guess I just always wanted to see one of those towns."

"I think that would be something cool to see," I reply, though I have so many questions running through my mind. You have a freaking brother? Why an abandoned town? What about your best friend?

"Yeah. I think so too. Turn right here."

I turn the truck onto a final stretch of road where Griffin directs me, find a parking spot when we make it into a parking lot, then follow him from the truck across the lot to a path that leads us into the woods. "So, what am I going to see?"

"Probably a bunch of drunk people dancing around a fire."

I hear the smile in his voice. I don't bite at his teasing though, because I haven't had the best experiences with people and parties. "Truthfully, I haven't been to many parties. A couple. So, yeah. I'm kind of nervous."

He makes a humming noise acknowledging my admission. "You act so worldly."

Feeling defensive in conjunction with my nerves, I ask, "Are you making fun of me?"

"No. Just making an observation."

"I may have lived in a lot of places, but I haven't really known people who invited me to stuff." The sound of music drifts toward us. "I went to my first party when I was in eighth grade. A group of kids invited me. I showed up and realized I hadn't actually been invited. They were playing a joke on me. And in high school, I went to one party after a dance and left early because my date hooked up with someone else. Makes me really nervous about college."

We walk. The tall trees obscure the sky. I can see the slices of blue-green water in between the tree trunks, though the sun is going down, so the shadows stretch around us. I glance at Griffin, who's got his hands in his shorts pockets and his head bowed. His t-shirt fits nicely across his back, and I'm wondering if he has more muscles since I met him.

"Parties aren't all that great, but you should definitely walk into them—as a girl—with smarts."

I smile. "That's sexist."

"Yeah. But there are a lot of douchey guys."

"Are you speaking from experience?"

He doesn't answer right away, and I have the feeling he's thinking about what to say, which makes me think my assumptions about him being a party boy were right on. Eventually he says, "Maybe," and looks at me without turning his head. When I don't respond, he adds, "It isn't like I purposefully set out to be a douchey guy."

It makes me wonder if he's worried about what I think. He'd told me he didn't care what people thought, and I knew it for the lie it was, but could he care what I think? I bump his shoulder with mine. "And what constitutes a douchebag, coming from someone who may or may not be a douchey guy?"

I don't realize he's stopped walking until I hear him say my name. I stop and turn around to look at him. My belly does this twisty acrobatic maneuver in my body. I hate that I find him so attractive because it makes me feel weak, but I don't remember ever experiencing that kind of attraction to Michael. Curiosity, sure, but not this level of body talk.

Then, when Griffin says, "I don't want you thinking bad of me," my heart decides to get involved too, nosediving into my body, only I know there's no net to catch it.

I try to keep it light and smile at him. "I call you serial killer, remember. I already do think badly of you."

It's his turn to offer me a mocking laugh, and he catches up with me as we continue down the path.

"I think since you know your way around a party, you can offer me pointers."

He hums again. I like that sound. The vibration of it reverberates in my chest and adds to the already flighty rhythm of my heart.

"Okay. First. Don't get too drunk."

"But a guy can?"

"He shouldn't either. You need to keep your decision-making functioning. If you're shit-faced, you aren't going to be clear enough to. Like, if you do want to hook up with someone, you should be aware of that decision so there aren't any regrets."

"You have regrets?" I don't know if I want to hear them.

"Lots of them." He presses his jaw together, so it sharpens again.

I wait to see if he'll say more, but he doesn't. I'm so curious, and I'd like to demand details, but I'm not sure he'll share. I don't have the energy to face that rejection right now. "So, don't get too drunk so that I can make proper decisions. Check. Next?"

"Stay away from guys—or girls—" he pauses.

"Guys," I clarify.

"Guys who are saying all the right things. Stuff you want to hear."

"I'm not sure what you mean."

"Like the smooth talker who seems to be saying everything that connects with you."

"That just sounds like someone being nice."

Griffin hurries past me, turns, and stops in my path. "This is important, Max."

I'm afraid to look up at him. Afraid that if I do, he'll see that I might be feeling more than friendship, but then it's getting dark and shadowy, so I do.

His face is serious, his perfect pout neutral and kissable. He swings his hair out of his eyes and looks at me like he's taken on a very important role. Like he cares.

"Can you be more specific?"

He hesitates. Swallows. But his eyes, dark in the shadowy light filtered through the trees, stay on my face. His hands are still in his pockets, and his shoulders are broad, but sort of rounded with whatever burden he's always carrying. "First, Max, he'll just be nice, like you're saying. He might grab you a drink, find you a place to sit, maybe offer you his seat. He'll be like a new friend."

"That sounds nice."

"He isn't doing it because he wants to be your friend." Griffin takes a step toward me. My heart jumps against my ribs and grabs ahold, and my lungs constrict. "He wants you to trust him so that when he takes it another step further, he can get what he wants. He's not being nice to you for the sake of being a good human being—he's thinking about it like a business transaction. He'll compliment you." Griffin pauses, and his eyes roam my face. They stall out on my mouth. "Max," he says, his voice different, huskier, "you have such a sexy smile."

I know he's playing a part, and I fight a smile, but I can't help but blush. The part of me enjoying his undivided attention wakes up.

Griffin leans even closer, his mouth so close to mine all I would need to do is lean forward a bit more and turn my head.

Though I hold my ground, the thought of testing the boundary does dance through my mind.

He says, his voice low and rumbly, "I bet every guy here wants to get with you."

I lean back. I know he's trying to show me, but suddenly I'm fighting with his words and his actions. The part of me who knows he's my friend and only my friend goes to war with the female part who's physically attracted and maybe emotionally curious about this other human.

He swallows, and his eyes drop to my mouth again.

I wonder if he's still acting.

When his hand finds my waist, he adds, "I bet you can do a lot with that gorgeous mouth."

He is.

I shove him away. "That's rude."

He takes another step away, hands in his pockets again, shoulders drooped. "Yeah. It is. That was perfect, Max. Stay away from those assholes." He turns and continues down the pathway.

I follow, considering him, his words and actions. My body says there's chemistry between us, or I'm too hopeful for that to make up ideas about his level of interest that might not be there. Hard to know since I don't have a lot of experience to make that determination. My throw-caution-to-the-wind side would like to ask, but I don't have that kind of courage with him yet. I don't know him well enough.

"You still want advice?" he asks.

I glance at him when I catch up to him. "I think, perhaps I've come to the right guy."

"A guy like that will try and talk you into being alone with him somewhere. There are worse slimeballs who force things."

My heart stops beating. "Have you done that?"

He stops and looks at me. "Fuck no. Of course not. That's terrible and illegal. Shit. I can't believe you asked that." He runs his hand through his hair. "Whatever happens between people should be consensual, you know? But there are douchebags out there like that."

"And you'd know?"

He waves a hand. "Did a report on it for health class."

We keep walking.

"There's also the guy that will pressure you until you give him room to keep pressuring you. He wants you to say yes, which is why he'll look for the drunkest girl in the room."

"Don't get too drunk."

He stops and grabs my shoulders so I'm facing him. "And never, ever leave your drink alone with anyone. In fact, you should only get your own drinks—don't take a drink from someone else."

I tilt my head to look at him.

"Give me a little credit. I would never do that. I wouldn't want to get–" he pauses as if he's realized he's going to share something personal, but he looks down at his feet– "with a girl because she was so drunk, she couldn't decide. I think that's awful, and I would beat the shit out of someone who did that, but I've heard stories, though."

"So, you have principles then? When hooking up?" I ask the question, and it isn't like I'm a prude. I mean, I had sex with Michael a couple of times, along with a bunch of other sexual experiments. It was both of our first times, so I wouldn't characterize the experience as exceptional and, of course, I'd be lying if I haven't had thoughts about sex stuff with Griffin. He's hot. But I'm not into the idea of hooking up for the sake of hooking up. No judgements from me if he does that. I'm pretty sure I need feelings and reciprocation for my own enjoyment.

"I guess so." He starts walking again.

"Like only drinking six days a week." I'm smiling when I say it.

"Yeah. I have some rules."

"Can I ask what they are."

"You can." He doesn't say anything else.

"Will you tell me your rules?"

He stops again. He looks left and then right, as if he can find an escape route from sharing, but then he levels his gaze on me. "I don't get too drunk, though I've broken that rule a lot, but I haven't gotten with a girl when I do. I don't get with a girl who's too drunk either because I want her to be able to say what she wants. I want what happens with a girl to be mutual. I always use protection because I'm not about that long term stuff."

"So, you just hit and run?"

He looks down, and I can tell he's hesitant, his jaw working over itself again. "Historically, yes."

"No girlfriend."

He shakes his head. "No."

"How many girls have you been with."

"A few."

"Vague." I measure his honesty with my instincts, knowing that what he's told me isn't wrapped up in a pretty picture but rather one that it would be more useful to hide if he were playing a game. The knowledge that he's been honest about it bolsters why he interests me. "Okay, SK. I appreciate your candidness."

"Speak English."

I chuckle and shake my head. "I am, SK. Honesty." I lead us down the path.

"You're not disgusted?"

No. Sure, it makes me feel more cautious. He seems to have the emotional capability of an inanimate object even though I know this isn't true, he's just hiding from something. His number of partners isn't my business and who am I to judge his journey—not if he's telling me the truth which I sincerely hope. Griffin's never come across as a liar. I don't tell him these things. Instead, I opt for humor because Griffin speaks humor better than any other language. "Want to know my rules?"

"What?" he asks.

"Stay away from guys like Serial Killer."

He grins. "Smart."

I ignore the way my stomach nosedives at the sight of his smile and walk with him into a throng of people in the vicinity of a bonfire. We meet a jerk that knows Griffin, whose eyes sweep over me and give me gross vibes. A douchey guy. I ask Griffin to help me find a bathroom, and he leads me to one.

"I'll be out here."

There's a joke in there, but I leave it alone. Besides, the idea of him waiting for me constructs a world in which I have a friend. Someone to wait for me, to care. The idea churns inside me with a mixture of discomfiture—this is all temporary—but also pleasure at the idea of something being permanent.

I walk into the restroom, where there's a group of girls using the mirrors. They are pretty in the Barbie Doll kind of way, the ones I avoided in school because their derision about my size was always so cutting and hurtful.

I duck into a stall to escape their watchful gaze.

"Did you see Josh?" one of the girls asks.

"Yeah. Did you hear that Tanner isn't going to parties anymore?"

"Who said?"

"Well, Josh is here with Ginny Donnelly and Emma Matthews. When I asked them where Tanner was, they just shared a look and said, 'not here.'"

"Trouble in paradise?"

"I heard they aren't together anymore."

I flush the toilet and leave the confines of the stall to wash my hands.

They give me a cursory glance and keep talking.

"That was only a matter of time. Matthews is a fucking prude. You all heard what Keller said about junior prom right?"

They do a weird cackle together like what they've said might cast a spell.

"I was hoping he'd come with Griff tonight," one of them says, and I can't keep myself from looking at her. She's pretty. Blond, sleek, made up, fit but not athletic looking. The kind of body that comes with good genes. I bet she is—was—popular (I'm not sure how old she is, but definitely somewhere in my age group).

I can see them huddle up through the mirror, and it makes me think of Ashley Barns, house six, and her fellow eighth grade minions. She'd instigated my arrival at Mason Kristy's birthday party, telling me that Mason had given her my invitation to pass to me. She'd handed me an invitation, and I'd been gullible enough to believe her (in my defense, it looked legitimate). I'd arrived at Mason's to discover he had only invited his basketball teammates (I had not been invited), hence creating my "just one of the boys" nickname.

Their snickering laugh draws me back to the sink. I turn off the water and look for a towel to dry my hands.

"Is Griff here? I thought you two were getting together."

My breath catches in my throat, but I finish drying my hands, wondering if this is the same Griffin? How many Griffins could there be in our age group? In this town?

She laughs. "Why would I get with Griff if I had the opportunity to get with Tanner? That's like choosing a Nissan over a Tesla."

They all laugh, and one of them says, "Jesus, Bella."

I force myself to swallow, adrenalin suddenly making me tremble, worried they are talking about Griffin, who's standing outside. I leave the bathroom, walking around the concrete wall, and grasp it to keep from tripping. I can still hear their words, and if I can, so can Griffin.

"It's true. What does Griff offer anyone? The only reason anyone ever put up with him was because he's Tanner's friend."

"He'll probably end up in jail like his old man."

Oh. Shit. Rocks drop into my stomach.

They laugh.

I stall on the gravel, where I see Griffin leaning against the wall. When he looks up at the sound of my footsteps on the ground, the mask is back. Only now, I can see the hurt behind it in his eyes, confirming the worst—he's heard it all. Those awful words slam straight into my heart, and the pressure of tears threatens to find a way out.

He tries to recover with a half-smile, but it doesn't work and my heart swells in my chest. I understand this kind of hurt. I've lived it over and over.

"Griffin." I lean against the wall next to him, but he won't look at me.

The girls file out of the bathroom and pull up short at the sight of us. Of Griffin. Their titters drift into silence, and one of them mutters, "Oh shit."

The pretty blond one, the mean one named Bella, says, "Griff?"

He pushes away from the wall. "Hey."

She stumbles around trying to find words, wondering if he heard but can't exactly ask. So, she deflects and changes tactics. "You didn't text me back."

"I was working."

"I'm glad you're here," she lies.

"Too bad I'm not Tanner, though, right?"

My eyes flit from bitch number one to Griffin, who just scored a point in my book.

She steps toward him, and I can see that she does feel bad, or maybe just regretful for getting caught, but instead of owning it and apologizing, her sharp eyes find me. "Who's your friend?" They graze me up and down as if taking measurements. My gut churns with anger. Anger for what she just did to Griffin, and anger for all the ways girls like her have hurt others, hurt me.

I push away from the wall and lace my fingers with Griffin, not particularly concerned if he cares. If there's anything I know about girls like her, it's that they don't like to compete for attention, so I play the role. "I'm Max." I look at Griffin with a look as adoring as I can muster (which isn't super difficult considering how attracted I am to him) and say, "Babe, are you ready for that swim?"

Griffin tips his head to look at me, and I see his gratitude—my gamble has paid off. "Sure," he says and leads me past them.

As we pass, I give Bella the once over with as much disdain as I can and say, "It wasn't nice to meet you," then, loud enough so they can hear, say to Griffin, "Who the fuck were those bitches?"

Though we've left them behind, he doesn't try to pull away from me, and I can almost feel the wheels turning in his head. He leads me down to the water's edge. We stop there and stare out across the water that's now dark because our spot on the earth has left the sun behind. In times like these, of which I've experienced a few, I draw on my reserves of trying to shift his thinking away from the lie. So, I do what I wished someone would have done for me.

"I'm sorry." I let go of his hand.

He crosses his arms over his chest. "For what?"

"For what happened back there."

"You didn't say it."

"Well, if I crossed a line?" I pull my shirt over my head because swimming sounds perfect to wash away the shit we just walked through.

He watches me, then looks away. "You didn't."

I offer him an overdramatic sigh, loud and breathy. "I'm relieved. I wouldn't want you getting any ideas, SK." I laugh and peel my shorts over my hips and down my legs.

He smiles and looks down at the gravel, which maybe feels more like he's trying to not look at me in my swimsuit, and that feels pretty good.

"Come on, SK. Let's swim." I step into the cold water and make unattractive noises of disdain about the temperature but keep going. The water closes around me the deeper I go and conceals me, wraps me up in its embrace. I love it.

"That defeats the purpose of going to a party and meeting people," he says. I hear him wade into the water behind me.

I glance over my shoulder. His torso is bare. He's sharp and angular but defined in a masculine way that makes me want to touch him. I look away, my head growing hot and the flush spreading down to my neck. "If the rest of the people are anything like the people I've already met tonight, I'm good."

He laughs—a real one—and that sound does something to my insides, the heat radiating lower. "There are probably some good ones."

84

I dive into the water to cool off what's happening inside my body when I look at him. When I come back up, he's within arm's reach, but I keep my distance. "You're 0-for-5, SK. It's not looking good."

Then he laughs again. "Well, as a fake serial killer, I don't have a lot to offer in terms of friendship. You probably should branch out." His words sound heavy again.

"That's a huge red flag." I send a handful of water his way to put him back into the good mood. "You check all the SK boxes."

He grins at me.

We swim about, chatting about all the places I've lived, and Griffin shares he likes gaming, so I tell him about learning to game with Dillon and Jensen, but despite our meandering superficial conversation, I'm worried about him. He seems to be drifting even though he's engaging with me, a feeling rather than something I can concretely identify. It's in the way he's struggling to make eye contact, or the way he loses his thought. "Are you okay, Griffin? What they said was really shitty."

"Truth hurts." His hands move about in front of him as he treads water.

I don't like what he's said, but I suppose I can understand the sentiment. I offer him a noise as I consider similar insults hurled at me, and my father's lesson, *you have to accept you; that's all that matters.* It makes me wonder who Tanner is and if he's connected to Griffin's earlier comments about friendship.

"What?"

"Who's Tanner? Or is this the story you skipped earlier?"

"The same."

I don't let him out of it this time. "Well?"

"He was my best friend."

"Was?"

"We got in a fight. The night before I met you. Haven't talked since."

I swim back toward the shore, moving slowly but wanting to know more. "What was it about? The fight?"

"Something stupid."

His answer makes me wonder if that's true. If it were really something meaningless, how could you not talk to your best friend? Then again, I'd thought Michael had been my best friend. We'd fought that last time and said things that were hurtful. He'd left me with unanswered questions, but I'm not sure that is the kind of friendship Griffin had with this person named Tanner. It seems more like maybe what I had with Cassie though there's a big difference between elementary school friendships and high school ones. I feel like I would still try to talk to one of those kinds of friends, but then I realize that not everyone operates using the same guides. Dad has always taught me to face things head on. Not everyone has a Callum Wallace.

"If it was stupid, how come you haven't fixed it yet?"

"I don't think it's like your cabinet."

Clearly, I've said the wrong thing because Griffin—by the sound of his voice—has put the wall back up between us.

"You might be surprised," I offer. Maybe thinking a relationship can be fixed if it's meant to be makes me an idealist, and maybe it goes back to my mom. She didn't try, and while I love my dad, and cherish the relationship I have with him, I do wish she'd tried harder. I wish she'd chosen us.

"At what?"

I watch him swim past me. "I just think that if a relationship has strong enough roots—trust, honesty, respect—then a fight won't damage it beyond fixing." I follow him back to shore, where he's shoving his feet into his shoes and tugging his t-shirt over his torso.

"I'm going to get a drink," he says, but it's more like a growl, and I've got the sense that he's phased into a werewolf under the moon.

"Griffin. Wait," I say and attempt to put my own clothes on, but it takes so much more time drawing on dry cloth over my wet skin, putting on shoes. Luckily, the bonfire illuminates his path to the keg, and I follow him. When I finally get there, Griffin is tipping back a cup and handing it back to the guy manning the keg, who hands him another full cup.

"Griffin," I say and lay a hand on his arm.

He draws away from my touch and finishes the next cup. "What? You can't fix me like a cabinet. No matter how much you try to strip away the layers."

I take a step back at his anger. "I didn't mean–" I start but stop. Had I thought I could fix him? Had I been thinking of him as a fixer upper? *Look beyond the surface.* Maybe some part of me considered it, but then I know it doesn't work like that. Too many lessons from Dad to teach me that it can't. My mother is proof.

He drains another beer.

"Griffin. Stop," I tell him, more worried than anything else.

87

He glances at me. "You aren't my mother."

Now, I feel the pearl of anger in my own belly and narrow my eyes at him. "No. I'm your ride. And you're about to break one of your rules because it will fuck up your decision making."

He turns to the keg guy and asks for another as he slaps down more money.

"This won't solve anything," I tell him.

But he drinks the next cup all the way down and says, "Another."

His cheeks are red, and his body is loose, his shoulders drawn back instead of held forward to protect himself, and his face isn't as tense. Despite those changes, his anger is more aggressive, not in a way that scares me, but one that seems self-destructive.

"Dude," the keg guy says. "You should listen to your girlfriend."

"She's not my girlfriend," he says.

"I'm not his girlfriend," I say at the same time.

"Griff?"

I whirl at the sound of a new voice. There's a redhead next to a new character in Griffin's story and another girl, dark-haired with big eyes, standing next to her. She's partially turned away from us.

"Fancy meeting you here," Griffin says in a voice I've never heard and takes another chug of his cup. He stares at them over the rim.

"Bro. What's happening?" the guy asks. He looks as concerned as I feel. His face swings my way. "Hey."

The redhead looks at the dark-haired one and grasps one of her hands.

Griffin glances as the dark-haired one and then back at the guy.

"You'd know if you texted."

"Dude, I've been travelling with my family. You know that. What the fuck happened with Tanner?"

"I don't want to fucking talk about it."

The redhead holds her hand out to me. "Hi. I'm Ginny. And this is Emma."

And I'm thinking about the names in the mouths of those girls in the bathroom. Josh. Ginny. Tanner and Emma. Griffin. I look at her again, and she offers me a smile, but it doesn't reach her eyes; she looks like she'd rather be anywhere but here, and I'm feeling that too, but I acknowledge both of them. "Hi."

"That's Max," Griffin says, and his voice sounds looser. "That's one of my bros, Josh. Used to be," Griffin says and drinks again.

"I heard about you earlier," I say.

Josh glances at Griffin, and then at me. He maintains his smile, but it's slipped from his eyes. He glances at Ginny. "I hope it wasn't bad."

"Just some girls gossiping in the bathroom about some guy named Tanner and Emma." My eyes slide to the dark-haired girl, who has an arm curled around her torso like she's protecting herself.

The girl named Ginny crosses her arms. "Let me guess, Bella's crew." She rolls her eyes.

"Ding. Ding. Ding," Griffin sings.

Josh wraps his arm around Ginny's shoulders. "Don't worry about them. You either, Emma. Can't sweat the small stuff."

"Or small minds." Ginny glances at the other girl.

"Right." Josh presses a kiss to Ginny's temple.

"You two are together now?" Griffin asks, but the way he says it sounds awful. "Seems all my friends are hooking up with the long-term shit. Tell me, Emma? How's Tanner?"

Emma's eyes narrow.

"He hit that and leave?" He smirks at her.

Emma turns and walks away. Ginny goes after her.

"What the fuck, Griff?" Josh's voice sounds like the snap of a wet towel. He's pissed, and he hasn't given me the vibe that's his usual operating system, considering he's been trying to engage this version of Griffin.

"Griffin. Stop," I tell him.

His eyes slash to me, and I can tell he's ready to burn everything to the ground.

But Josh steps in. "Are you coming to Danny's swearing in?"

"I wasn't invited," he says.

"Yeah. You were. You're just being a dick."

"I haven't talked to him either. And–" he holds his hands out– "I've never claimed to be anything else."

Griffin is exploding and about to leave a shit ton of collateral damage.

"We should go," I say, grasping at the only thing I have left to control what's happening.

"Go," he says.

"I'm your ride."

He scoffs. "Yeah right." He takes a sip of his drink.

The sexual innuendo is clear, and it hurts. "Who are you?" My throat burns with tears climbing the tissue with claws, but it just makes me angry. I shake my head. "I don't need this shit." I turn to Josh. "It was nice meeting you."

I stomp through the crowd away from Griffin and all the crap people he introduced me to even if Josh, Ginny, and perhaps Emma seemed sort of normal. My anger grows with each step, and I feel sick with it. Sick because of who he became. Sick at his words even if they weren't only to me; he was an ass to everyone. *The Truth,* he'd said to what those bitchy girls had said behind his back. Sick because he slid right into their version of him as if it were a prophecy. Sick because I felt something for him. Sick with myself for allowing myself to go there.

I fling Rust Bucket's door open. It creaks loudly but it moves slow. It isn't satisfying, so when I get into the truck, I slam it shut and lay my head on the steering wheel, breathing heavily to keep the tears—now threatening to fall—in my eyes. When I feel somewhat in control, I start Rust Bucket. It decides to take a few key turns to start. I slam it into reverse and back up, then drive around the stupid loop, wishing I could cut through the lot illegally by climbing over curbs that would just break the truck. When I swing around back toward the entrance, Griffin is in the headlights.

I stop even though I'd like to drive around him and leave him there. After manually unrolling the stupid windows of the stupid truck, I say, "Get out of the way. You don't need a ride, remember?"

"I'm sorry," he says.

"You aren't. You're lying."

"I am. I am sorry I am who I am."

And I can tell this horrible statement is the truth of how he feels about himself, and it breaks my stupid, bleeding heart.

I sit behind the wheel, Rust Bucket sputtering. Griffin stands in the headlights, hands at his sides, his head bowed. I take a deep breath and slump into my seat. I can't leave him stranded even if he deserves it. "Get in."

Griffin walks around the passenger side and climbs into the seat. He shuts the door. "Thanks."

I push the truck into gear, and it grinds like the frustration I feel. "Don't talk. I don't want to hear your voice."

He listens and doesn't say another word, just stares out the window. He doesn't say anything when I drop him at his house or when he gets out of the truck. And like an idiot, I look at the rearview mirror as I drive away and watch his shadow watch me.

I stop at Custer's Convenience, but even the strawberry Slurpee doesn't bring me joy like it usually does. Instead, I just feel hurt and empty, which I think is utterly ridiculous. Griffin Nichols deserves no such attention, but even as I tell myself that story, I recognize it for the lie that it is. Griffin Nichols has somehow opened a door into my heart and set up shop there. It's stupid. There is nothing long-term about this stint. It's a post-it on a giant bulletin board, a single photograph in my life's photo album that I'll look back on and think *remember that summer.* I've got less than two weeks until I leave for college. I need to fix my gaze on what's coming, and that alone. That is when my new life begins, and it doesn't include jerks like Griffin.

He told you.

Shut up! I tell my dumb inner voice.

8

I open the door to my bedroom, and it creaks on the hinges louder than the knock that called me over to open it. I expect my dad, but Griffin is standing outside, looking like a lollipop I'd like to lick. He's wearing worn jeans that hang on his lean hips and a black t-shirt that stretches across his shoulders. With his arms outstretched, he leans against the doorframe, one hand on each side of the jamb, taking up all the room and sucking up my oxygen.

"Max." He says my name like it weighs a ton, and the kaleidoscope of his eyes flashes against my face like a warm caress and stops at my lips.

I glance about the hallway landing and whisper, "What are you doing here?" No Dad in sight, but then maybe he's already left for his next job. I try not to fixate there, not with Griffin standing outside my bedroom, and all of me straining toward him even though I know it's a terrible idea. He's in no emotional space to choose me, not to mention all of the compromising of what I deserve. But does it always have to be about all that? Can't I just explore the physical call pulsing through my body?

"Can I come in?" he asks. "I need to talk to you."

"I don't think it's a good idea," I tell him even as I want him in my room. Even as much as I want my hands all over him.

"Please?" he asks with a half-smile, and I feel like he's read my mind.

I ponder it and look down at the floorboards.

"You aren't following the rules," he says.

I twirl, and Griffin is already in my room. I don't ponder how, only cognizant of the tug of war my heart and body are playing. "Neither did you."

He stares at my bed, the box springs and mattress directly on the floor. My multi-colored comforter with a mandala design in white hidden because it's been rumpled in the sleep. "I'm sorry, Max." He only turns his head to look at me, his body still facing my bed, and his hands occupied by whatever he's holding.

I step toward him. "'Sorry' isn't enough, Griffin."

"Will this help?" he asks, turns to face me, and offers the item.

I step closer still, close enough to reach out and grab what he has. It's a tiny purple flower.

"I picked it for you."

I spin the delicate blossom between my fingers and think about my mother. One of the last times we were together, she'd taken me on a drive, and we stopped in the country to pretend we were mice. We'd played in a field filled with these flowers. "How?" My eyes flash to his.

"I see you," he says.

I shake my head. "No. No one ever sees me," I reply, and he closes the distance with a step.

His hand wraps around the back of my neck. "I see you."

I don't wait. I don't think. I grasp his t-shirt and rise up to meet his lips with my own because I want to. I need to. For me.

His hands are in my hair, and his tongue tastes like cinnamon.

I moan and say against his mouth, "I'm still mad at you."

He smiles and kisses me again, deep and thorough so that my blood is moving like a flash flood in my system.

I don't know how—it's like I've turned a page—we're lying entwined on my bed. I'm on my back with one of Griffin's legs nestled in between mine, pressing against the part of me that is hot and needy. My brain is hung up on the conflict of last night instead of focusing on him, his mouth, and his body. "Talk to me. What happened?"

"You want to talk?" His nose moves against the skin of my neck, and his teeth nip at my skin. "Now?"

I arch against him, hanging onto his back, but I can't let it drop. "About last night."

"I'm sorry," he repeats and gives me another kiss. This one bends my mind away from the past and knocks me into just the moment, holds me prisoner there. Makes it difficult to breathe and not tear the clothes from my body and his.

"I see you," he repeats.

My instincts flutter.

I want to be seen.

Unbidden, I think of Griffin's advice: *beware a guy who will tell you what you want to hear.*

I pull away, and it isn't Griffin with me anymore. It's my ex-boyfriend Michael hovering above me, his black silky hair hanging around his face, his mouth frowning, his brown eyes full of censure. "This just isn't going to work, Max. I'm not choosing you, and I don't trust you, but we can still fuck."

I push him away, kicking, but my feet are caught in my bedspread. "No!" I scream, and my eyes fly open. I'm in my room, alone, breathing like my lungs are coming out of my mouth. The comforter is wrapped around my legs. I fall back against my pillows and will my heartbeat back into my chest.

A dream.

"What the hell," I mutter out loud at my ceiling and shove both of my hands into my hair. I feel unresolved, and if that dream is any indication, I'm all over the place. I sit up in my bed and recall the dream. Griffin. Michael. The flower. I can't make any sense of it, so instead, I get up and get ready for my run, instead.

Once on the road, I push myself and think about Griffin the night before. My anger at him offers me fuel, and I burn through it to find a calmer place. Despite being angry and hurt by how he acted, I can't get the dejection of him standing in Rust Bucket's headlights out of my mind. I think I understand. Last night, he was that wounded wild animal I've always compared him to. While he presented a front to the bitches and their awful comments about him, the moment he was confronted with his feelings, he lashed out. He ran and tried to hide. As much as he deserves my anger, I can also empathize with him. I understand the hurt, the fear, and the running.

My words come back to me: *if a relationship has strong enough roots—trust, honesty, respect—then a fight won't damage it beyond fixing.* I'm not going to lie to myself and claim that Griffin and I have any sort of roots, but what kind of person would I be if I make claims like that and then don't live them? Cal Wisdom. "What kind of person do you want to be, Max-in-a-million?" or "Do what you say. Nothing worse than someone who says one thing but acts the opposite." I certainly don't want to be a hypocrite. But Dad's also offered me the knowledge to recognize my worth, to speak plainly, and to face things head on. I decide the next time I see Griffin, if he's not being a jerk, I'll talk to him about it.

Feeling clearer, I return home. Dad and I flow into the rhythm of a normal Sunday. Breakfast. Working on a project.

The sound of tires rolling over the gravel of the driveway pulls me to the doorway of the workshop. A small, blue SUV parks, and Griffin gets out as my dad walks toward him. This is sooner than I anticipate seeing him, and it simultaneously fills me with joy and trepidation. Griffin offers Dad a handshake and a half smile. Though I can't hear them, I think based on their common body language side by side, facing the vehicle, that they're talking about what I guess is Griffin's new car.

With a sigh, I leave the shelter of the workshop along with the escape of working on the cabinet and walk across the lot.

My dad claps him on the shoulder and turns away to work on Rust Bucket. "His new wheels," he says with a smile as he passes me.

"Nice car," I say to Griffin.

"First place I drove."

"Where? Your ghost town?"

"No. Here. To show you."

I look away. I don't want him to know how much that statement affects me. I also don't want to acknowledge that fact. It can't impact me. I refuse it because I'm leaving—but he thought of me. First. No one, besides my dad, has ever chosen me first. Not even Michael, not really. His family was first, followed by friends. Then me. When I look back at Griffin, after finding a neutral space for my face, he's leaning against the car, his gaze on the keys in his hands.

"I'm really sorry about last night, Max."

I suppress the fantasy part of my dream. Of him saying those words and kissing me. "Do you know what you're apologizing for or are you just saying it?"

"For being a jerk."

"I need you to be more specific, Griffin."

"The drinking."

The obvious answer which is frankly lazy and a cop-out. Cal's taught me to consider my feelings, the why of them. "We get caught up, don't we?" he said once, "in the passion of our feelings. The immediate, but we don't always stop to consider the reason behind them. Why do we feel that way? Why we act the way we do?"

Sure, I was angered by Griffin's drinking, but that's the surface; underneath is the way he behaved. The way he eviscerated the people who care about him and how he used his words to hurt everyone around him. Maybe that was exacerbated by the alcohol, but it wasn't the alcohol speaking. That was all Griffin.

I shake my head and give him an incorrect buzzer sound. "Nope. Thanks for playing. Nice car. Nice chatting." I turn back to the workshop.

"Wait."

I hear his feet on the gravel and stop.

"Honestly, Max. I'm not very good with words."

"You being terrible with words isn't an excuse to be a dick. Your words do a pretty good job hurting people." I start away again.

"I didn't mean it like that."

I turn back, tilt my head, and study him. He looks apologetic. His shoulders are rounded again, his mouth and eyes dressed with worry, like he's afraid he's broken something, but there's also the absence of his usual robot mask. This is Griffin, not a version he's offering me, and it hits me that perhaps he's never had to do this before—face his shit. Maybe the alcohol wasn't a lazy answer for him because he doesn't have a Callum Wallace to help him see things on a different level. "And how did you mean it?"

"I meant that I know I say shitty things that hurt people—what

I'm not good at is figuring out how to use them to fix things. Not a lot of practice."

Now, I turn to face him fully, annoyed. "I don't have time or patience to teach you, Griffin. You're a man already and need to own your shit. You're old enough to know how to treat people. But since you tried to teach me some life lessons, here's a free one for you." I hold up a finger for him. "One of the things you should do is follow your own rules about drinking and decision making." I hold up a second finger. "Two, you shouldn't treat your friends like they are the opponent, use them like verbal punching bags, but then treat the enemy like they are somehow better than you. And–" I hold up a third finger– "you shouldn't make jokes at your friends' expense. It hurts."

He has the decency to look abashed. "I'm sorry, Max. Really. I am. Let me make it up to you."

And with that, I figure his shame is real. I take a deep breath to cleanse the swirling vortex of emotions inside me and allow the relief inside, but simultaneously, I'm confused. This is temporary. Right? Why would I be so emotionally connected to it, I wonder. That might suggest whatever I'm feeling isn't temporary, and that can't lay a foundation.

"Apology accepted, SK." I turn and leave him, needing to figure myself out. Being around him confuses the issue. I can't seem to find the balance necessary to recalibrate my future vision. I feel like I'm walking a tightrope that's stretching out in front and behind me without a starting point or a destination, and I'm getting ready to topple over into an abyss. "But I don't want to look at you right now."

It's a lie I tell both of us.

"Does that mean you don't want to go for a drive?" he calls from behind me.

"I'm busy," I say without looking back, and walk back into the shop. The moment I'm out of his line of sight, I duck and lean against the wall, closing my eyes. My heart knocks against my chest. I listen for him to start the car and drive away, my eyes still shut as I will my hands to stop shaking.

"What was that about?"

I jump at the sound of my dad's voice, my eyes opening, and my hand going to my throat. "Oh. Shit. You scared me."

He's on the other side of the workshop, standing in the doorway that leads to the garage where he's pulled Rust Bucket in for an oil change. He wipes his hands with a blue mechanic cloth, then crosses his arms. "What was that about?" he repeats.

"What?" I ask and busy myself at the toolbox, completely unsure what I'm even looking for. I'm so unsteady.

"With Griffin."

"Nothing," I say.

He makes a humming noise. "Nothing, huh?"

I find the bravery to look at him. I'm not lying. There's nothing between Griffin and me even if my feelings are more involved than they should be. I shake my head. "What would it be? We're just friends."

My dad glances at the door near me as if recalling Griffin outside, then back at me. "In my experience, Max-in-a-million, a young man makes an effort to come out to show a young lady his car, there's more than just friendship on his mind."

His words do something more in me than I think he intended. If this is a warning, it doesn't do its job. Instead, I feel a flare of bright hope, which is ridiculous. I'm leaving!

"Believe me," I tell him, "I think that's the last thing on Griffin's mind. I don't think I'm his type." I think about the Bella girl who is 180 degrees from me. Sure, I omit the part about how I've been thinking of Griffin that way, but it doesn't matter what I think. Not really. I'm content to just be his friend. That was always the way it was supposed to be. I'm leaving. I'm leaving. I'm leaving.

"That so?" Dad asks. He's rubbing his hands again with the cloth.

I give him an affirmative sound.

He just stares at me a moment, nods, then disappears into the dark doorway.

I'm left wondering what that was all about and remind myself I'm leaving.

9

The deluge hits while I'm running the next morning, and by the time I get home, I'm soaked.

Dad's on his way out as I'm walking in. "I texted Griffin. We can't paint today, and I don't have time to get something else together for him. If he shows up—because he didn't answer—would you let him know?"

I nod, kiss his cheek, and escape to the bathroom to shower away the rain.

Griffin knocks at the back door as I finish making myself a pot of coffee. It's still pouring outside, and the cloudy sky is dark and oppressive. He's soaked.

"Dad's not here. You can't paint in this."

With his hair, dark and dripping, his blue t-shirt is plastered to his frame, he looks alluring, and my belly tightens noticing the ridges and planes of his form.

He looks about as if to confirm it. "Yeah. Okay."

"You're soaked." My dream—kissing, hands running over bodies—flashes in my mind. I turn away, leaving the door open so he can choose to follow and internally fan the blush heating my skin, berating myself for even going there. *I'm leaving. I'm leaving. I'm leaving,* I chant to myself as I disappear into the house to get him a dry towel.

I hear his steps against the wooden flooring. "Did he leave me directions?"

"He said he texted you." I walk back into the kitchen, toss a towel at him, and retrieve a cup of fresh coffee.

"Maybe he forgot?" He sets down his coffee cup and looks at his phone. The cracked screen doesn't look functional.

I can't keep my eyes off of him even though I know I should. This limited-term relationship isn't conducive to the flutters I experience inside my body when I see him. "What happened to that?"

"Stupid choice."

This makes me want to laugh. "You're full of them."

He ignores my comment as his phone pings. He reads the new message and waves the phone at me. "I guess I have a day off then."

"Big plans?"

"No."

I don't want him to leave, spoiled by having him around for the last seven weeks. Granted, he was on my shit-list, but I've made it my mission to forgive him. Besides, I'm too short on time to waste it being angry. An idea surfaces: I could use a driver, since Dad is busy. "Would you like to demonstrate how sorry you are for Saturday and be my chauffeur?" I set down the mug of steaming coffee. "And think carefully before you say 'yes,' because I will not allow you to bitch about it after you agree.'"

He shrugs. "Sure.

I grin because I'm going to have so much fun with this. "Remember what I've said, car-slave."

He gives me a partial smile. "Yes ma'am."

After getting my wallet and a jacket, we trudge back out into the rain and get into Griffin's car. It has a clean scent of a newly purchased used car with a hint of lingering smoke, but it's nice.

"What are we doing?" he asks.

"You are taking me dorm room shopping."

His eyes widen.

I point at him. "No complaining."

He zips his lips, locks them, and throws away the key. "Would you mind if I run home to change into dry clothes? Before we go?"

"By all means," I say with the air of a queen.

He scoffs at me and drives us to his house. Once he parks the car in the driveway, he hesitates, then turns his head to look at me. "Want to come in? I won't be long."

"Sure."

I follow him from the car, up the front steps, and into his house.

My heart skips about in my chest, cognizant that I'm walking into Griffin's house. "Is your mom home?" I ask. "It would be fun to meet her." Though I really just want to know if I'm walking into an empty house. With Griffin. I fantasize about the possibilities of that even though that's all they are.

"She's at work. And Phoenix is out job hunting, I guess." He says this last bit like it tastes bad and unlocks the front door.

I follow him in.

We enter directly into a cozy living room even if it's lingering several decades behind in decor. It's got all the dressings: a sofa, a chair and coffee table, a TV. There are homey touches with mix-and-match things hanging on the wall: a stock print of a farm landscape, another of flowers, another of a wheat field. There's a trio of matching mirrors hung in a line down the wall, and through a wide, cased opening I can see the dining table and a large, sliding-glass door to an overgrown backyard.

"Want something to drink?" Griffin swipes his hands over the damp fabric covering his thighs as if he's nervous.

"No. Thanks. I'm adequately hydrated." I offer him a smile.

He nods, waiting a beat as if he's trying to figure out what to do. "Make yourself comfortable," he says, apparently deciding to just get to changing his clothes. He disappears through a hallway between the dining room and living room to the right.

I peek through the cased opening. A kitchen, and a door to what I figure is the garage. The dark hallway leads to the rest of the house. There are frames along the hallway walls, and I wish I could venture in to look at them, but I don't. Instead, I return to the living room, and sit on the chair to wait.

Griffin's house reminds me of the house on Downey Street. Dad and I lived in house four at the time I was friends with Cassie. Sitting in Griffin's living room makes me wonder how things might have been different if Dad and I stayed on Downey. Would we have decorated the house with farm landscapes and mirrors? Would my school pictures be hanging in the hallway? Would Dad have a significant other? Maybe I'd have a stepmom. Would Cassie and I still have been friends? Griffin—who's lived in this house his whole life by his own admission—has lived a life of permanence, and for a moment, I feel envious of it. I know being fixed to a place doesn't guarantee the perfect life. Nothing does that, but as I sit there waiting for Griffin, I can't help but feel like I've missed out on something.

"Ready?" I hear Griffin's voice, then he appears.

My heart plays hopscotch in my chest when I see him. In dry clothes, his hair is now dry and sort of wavy, and his heather green t-shirt he's wearing with the word *trouble* stamped in the center does something beautiful to his eyes.

He pats the back of his blue jeans riding his hips. "Wallet," he says and pats his front pockets, slipping a hand inside. He pulls out his keys and holds them up. "Keys."

"Got everything?" I ask.

He does a little spin as though he's checking. Then he faces me again with a grin. "Yep."

We retrace our steps from the house back to the car.

"Where to?" he asks.

I direct him to the Triple B: Bed, Bath and Bigbox at the edge of the city about thirty minutes away. He's a good driver—calm, cool, and collected—which tells me something about him that I like even if it shouldn't matter. When he parks the car, it isn't raining, though the clouds still hover in the sky outside the store.

"I'll even drive the cart," he declares, then jumps on one and sails past me.

"Perfect." I withdraw the list I've made. "Bedding first," I call after him as he rides the cart through the automatic doors. I draw my eyes away from his butt which looks delectable in those jeans.

He stops just inside the doors. "I'll follow you."

"I don't know where I'm going."

"Me either. We shop at the CheapMart."

I lead us through the maze, ignoring the impulse to just watch Griffin, and admonishing myself to focus on the task. We start in the kitchen section, which is unnecessary for my dorm room though I pick up an electric teapot to examine. Then I set it down since the budget is tight, especially with the renovation dipping into the savings.

"Max."

I stop and look at Griffin.

He holds up a huge mixer. "Do you want one of these for your dorm room?"

"What am I going to do with that in a dorm room?"

He slides it back into place with a pyramid of matching mixers and shrugs. "I don't know. What's it for?"

"Baking."

"Who bakes? I thought that was like only in the 1950's or something." He leans over the handle of the cart and moves toward me.

I laugh.

This makes him smile wider—a real one—and the gold in his eyes sparkles.

"You could bake," I tell him.

"I don't have one of those."

"You don't need one of those."

His chin drops, and I home in on his lips. As I recall my dream, the air moving through my chest cramps up and grows heavy.

"I don't know, Max. Triple B seems to suggest that I need one of those to bake."

I roll my eyes and look away before I do or say something stupid. "Come on." I lead him through the maze. When we finally stumble upon a sign that points to "bedding," I turn in that direction.

Griffin pushes the cart behind me, but I hear him stop. When I turn, he's stopped at a display bed. He sits down on it with great flourish, his hands moving about on the bedspread, feeling it, and touching the pillows.

My cheeks warm watching him, and the heat travels down my body as I recall the dream. I hustle back to him. "Griffin. Stop." I glance around in case a worker is about to yell at us. "Get up."

He moans. "I'm so tired." He flops onto the display sprawled like he's at home.

"You're going to get us kicked out."

He stuffs one of the pillows under his head and grins at me.

I tug on his shirt sleeve. "Griffin. Get up. That's decorative."

He's enjoying himself; his smile tells me so, and I feel like this might be the first time I've ever seen unmasked Griffin for this long. This is Griffin, the real one, who's allowing himself free rein. It's heady, addicting, and I think I might be floating. I want more.

"I think you should try it to see if you like it." He wraps his hand around my wrist and tugs me toward him.

As he pulls, I lose my balance and awkwardly roll over his hip until I'm sort of lying next to him, my legs draped over his body. One of his hands is on my waist. My mouth is open with the surprise, and he's smiling like he's just managed the biggest joke of all. I close my mouth, fight a smile, and say, "What are you doing?"

"You should test out the product. I think it's scratchy."

His face—boyish and impish at the same time—is endearing. I can't help but laugh, lost in the fun of the moment. When I open my eyes and look at him, I start to tell him, "You'd wash it first, so it isn't scratchy," but my words fade into nothing because his smile has faded too. Our eyes search one another's faces, and I can't seem to get my breathing to resume its natural rhythm.

I feel seen.

My heart echoes its rhythm in my ears.

Then, because the moment has gone on way longer than it should, I move. Do an ungraceful maneuver to get up and away. "Bedding," I say and chance a quick glance in his direction, breathing too quickly.

He sits up, stands, and wraps a hand around the back of his neck. "Scratchy. Not very good. That's why it's important to test it out."

"Sheets," I mumble and walk in that direction.

After getting everything I need at Triple B, we stop for a bite at a Mexican restaurant Griffin likes. It's dark with walls painted a lemon yellow, and art in black frames hang, highlighting each booth along the wall. Sombreros and rainbow ponchos hang along with other trinkets set about the place. We're seated in a dark booth across from one another. The waiter drops waters and a basket of chips with salsa while we look at the menu.

Griffin takes a chip.

"Thank you, Griffin," I tell him, reminding myself to stop watching his mouth like a weirdo. "For today."

He offers me a grin. "No car-slave or SK?"

I fiddle with the sharp edge of a chip. "You know I'm joking." I lift my gaze to meet his. "I need you to know I mean it, so, Griffin."

"You're welcome," he says. "You should try the salsa. It's good."

I do. "It is." I finish my bite. "Is this where you bring all of the girls?"

"No." He puts his hands into his lap. "I've never brought a girl anywhere." When he looks up from the basket of chips, and I think he's blushing. He can't meet my eyes.

"Right," I say. "No girlfriend."

He moves again, and I have a feeling he's going to put his mask back on, but when he takes a chip and chances a glance at me, I still see the unguarded Griffin.

The waiter arrives to take our order.

"Are you excited for school?" he asks after the waiter leaves, then takes a sip of his water.

"Yeah. I guess."

"State?"

"Yeah."

"It's so far."

This observation hangs up in the closet of my mind by itself, and I consider it, wonder why Griffin would say this. Why would he have thought about how far away I would be at school? "Not very. It's only a few hours drive from here." I push a chip through some salsa.

"Why 'I guess'?" he asks.

"I'm worried about my dad."

"How come?"

I'm not sure how to articulate it, so I shrug. "It's just been him and me, you know?"

The waiter returns with another basket of chips and refills our waters.

After he leaves, Griffin asks, "The whole time? He hasn't ever dated?"

"No. It isn't easy for him to trust people. The whole wife leaving thing."

"He hired me."

"He did." I smile—so grateful—and take another chip at the same time Griffin reaches for one. Our fingers brush. We pull away simultaneously, and Griffin waits for me to take a chip before getting one himself.

"He wants to flip the house quickly so he can find another fixer upper near the college."

"You don't want him to?"

I set the water glass back on the table. "I want him to have his own life like I'll have my own."

He nods. "My mom has worked so hard since my dad went to prison. She had to hold everything together for my brother and me."

"Exactly." I unroll the napkin around the utensils and then reroll it to keep my hands busy. "I wish he'd stay here. Of all the places we've been, this is the first house that feels like it fits him. It's got everything he needs. He's also been getting a ton of outside work which doesn't always happen in the places we've been. And there's you." I venture a look, glancing up from my napkin.

"Me?" He looks skeptical.

I reach for the water glass again. "Yeah. He likes you. He wouldn't be alone." I take a sip.

Griffin stares at his water cup, swiping away the buildup of condensation. I'm struck with how insecure he looks, as if it's unbelievable that someone would like him, which makes me think back to his drunken comment at the Quarry: *I'm sorry I am who I am.* That commentary, along with those awful comments made by those jerk girls, makes my heart expand, wrapping itself around him.

I change the subject to keep Griffin from slipping back into his mask. "Are you ready to start school?"

"Registered. Books bought. Parking pass. It's just down the

street."

"You'll be commuting?"

He nods. "I considered moving to the city, but I don't have the cash for that yet. Plus, I like working with Cal."

"Know what you want to major in?"

He scoffs. "No. I don't even know why I'm going. You?"

"Not yet. Maybe business. I'm good with money."

"That's good."

"What do you like?"

"Puzzles," he says, then takes a sip of his water. He sets it down a little too hard, and it sloshes. "Oops." He wipes the spillage with his napkin, then sets the napkin down and moves things around again. I wonder why this conversation has seemed to make him nervous.

The waiter returns with our food, interrupting the conversation and resetting it. He warns us the plates are hot.

Griffin reaches out to touch it.

"What are you doing. You'll hurt yourself?"

"I want to see how hot it is."

I scoff at him and reach out to push his hand away from his plate, then pull back from touching him as if I've touched the hot plate.

He doesn't touch it.

"Puzzles?"

"I liked woodshop in school. Like how you have all these pieces and parts and you put them together to make something new. I didn't do very well in it, though. I didn't do very good in high school actually."

"Why do you think that?"

"Because I didn't. I was bored and distracted by other stuff. I was too worried about what someone might think of me to try."

"Wait. *You* were worried about what people thought of you?"

His eyes sort of roll. "Okay. Yes. I did." He pauses and twists his water cup in its place on the table. "Not all of us are so lucky to have someone like Cal to guide us."

I'm struck by the envious tone in his voice and transport myself to sitting in his living room feeling envious of the place. Here he is feeling envious of me.

"You have your mom," I say.

"My mom has been too busy working three jobs to be around. I know she loves me and everything, but she's just absent." He takes and finishes a bite and sets down his fork. "She's always nagged me and Phoenix about going to college. I think that's why she kicked him out because he wouldn't go. She finished high school and all but has regretted not going to college because then maybe she wouldn't have to work three jobs. She could have been with us more."

"You're going."

"Yeah."

"What is it?" I ask.

"It feels like something I should be ashamed of."

And it hits me. His nerves. He's insecure.

"Why is that?"

He looks up from his plate. "I couldn't do the four-year college thing."

"Who cares about that? In the end, you make it through your two-year degree and onto a four-year one. You'll have a piece of paper that means the exact same thing as someone who went straight to a four-year school. A degree." I push around some of the rice on my plate.

"I don't even know if that's what I want."

"Maybe this is cliche or whatever, but your journey is yours—college or not, you have to create the best version of you."

He swallows and offers a little smile. "You just sounded like your dad."

I blush, pleased.

When we get back to the house, Griffin helps me carry in the packages, and though there's really no reason for him to stay, I ask him if he wants to see what I've finished on the cabinet. He follows me out to the workshop, and I turn on the light.

The cabinet is clean, all of the old finish removed, and the naked wood gleams.

"Wow," he says. "It's amazing, Max. It looks completely different. Perfect, really. Brand new. Your dad is going to love it."

His compliment feels awesome. "He already does, he just doesn't know it's for him yet."

Griffin's phone buzzes, and he looks down at it. "It's your dad. He says we won't be able to paint this week. Supposed to rain—he's got that plumbing job to finish up, and because you're leaving on Sunday, he's got to help you get ready Friday and Saturday." He looks up, and I wonder if that's disappointment I see on his face. "He gave me the rest of the week off."

I am. "Oh." I reach out and touch the cabinet to ground myself.

"What are you doing tomorrow?" He returns his phone to his pocket.

"Packing."

"Can you take some time off from that activity?"

"To do what?"

"Go for a drive with me? I mean, I tried to take you on my first drive, and you refused me."

I grin and scrunch my nose at him. "Your first drive was here."

"Technically, yes, but I came to get you. And I still haven't gone."

"Okay, SK. I'll go on a drive with you."

He smiles and nods. "I'll call in the morning." He turns, as if to leave, then turns right back around. "I don't have your number."

"Was that a ploy to get my number?"

"Smooth right?" He grins and winks.

I swallow and look down at my phone, wondering if Griffin is flirting with me, wanting that to be true but not true at the same time. The possibility that I'm misinterpreting is far more likely which would be so disappointing.

I'm leaving, I remind myself.

"It would have been if I felt like touching your phone, but I don't want to cut up my delicate fingers."

I'm leaving.

He programs my number into his phone.

"What did you name me?" I ask.

"Max."

118

"Text me so I have yours."

He leans over to watch me save his info. "What are you going to name me?"

"Serial Killer." I laugh and ignore how good he smells, clean and spicy.

After he's gone, the silence of the house presses against the chaos of emotion swirling like that giant whirlpool Odysseus faced in *The Odyssey,* like Scylla and Charybdis are about to draw me down into the depth and crash my boat. I look at all of the Triple B bags and suddenly miss him, which is weird and dangerous. I'm leaving. I haven't known him very long, so it seems impossible, and I've never really missed anyone other than Cassie and maybe Michael because how could I without anyone to really miss? For a moment, I think about what it might be like to stay here. I fantasize that Dad stays, and I have a home to come home to, and to call, and to choose. Then I shake my head of the thought. College is where I'm going to make that happen. Wanting something that permanent here is futile because Dad won't stay either.

The more buried realization, however, isn't the idea of home. Instead, I wonder who would ever choose me? No one except my father ever has.

10

"I made a playlist," Griffin announces when I get into his car, dripping with rain.

"On that monstrosity you call a phone? Are your fingers bandaged?" I grab his hand to inspect his fingers.

He jerks his hand away. "Wow."

I laugh. "Seriously, you should get that fixed." I look out at the slate-gray sky. "Is this a very good idea?"

"It's supposed to clear up at the Bend. And my phone still works," he says and backs the car away from the house. "Just push play."

"I'm not touching it. It's going to sliver my delicate fingertips with broken glass."

"Don't be such a baby. I can't. I'm already driving." He glances at me with a smirk.

"Fine." I make a production of gingerly pressing play. The opening guitar riff of AC/DC's "Highway to Hell" rips over the car's speakers. I look at him wide-eyed and smile. "Oh my, Griffin. What is this? Are we headed toward the afterlife?"

"It is a ghost town." He grins. "The playlist is from all of the band shirts you wear."

He's noticed.

Without taking my eyes from his, I unzip my yellow rain jacket and spread it Superman style to reveal my bright yellow AC/DC shirt.

His eyes widen.

"Have you been spying on me? Do I need to add stalker to the list, SK?" Warmth moves across my skin as Angus's guitar riffs through the car. I have never felt more seen.

I see you.

I shake my head of the dream and refocus on the moment.

"What? No." He looks away, flustered. "Completely coincidental, but if I was truly a serial killer isn't stalker inclusive?"

"You make a good point." I stop and remove my jacket. It's too warm now, and I'm kind of freaking out about his gesture, overthinking what it might mean, coaxing myself not to make more of it than it is. He's right. I love my band t-shirts—though I haven't actually been to a concert—because they started out as my dad's tees, mementos of his life before me. I remember my mom used to wear them, or that's what my dad said once when he gave me one as a little girl missing her mother.

As much as I'm sure Griffin doesn't intend for me to make a big deal about this, I can't let it pass me by. "Seriously, Griffin, this is the nicest thing anyone has ever done for me." As soon as I've said it, I know it to be true (gestures from my dad notwithstanding), and the realization that the statement includes all the months I spent as Michael's girlfriend makes me realize how one-sided our relationship truly was. Me giving, and Michael taking. I allowed it, and it's sort of an open-handed palm push to my face. My dad had been right.

Griffin's brows dip as he turns his head for just a second to look away from the road at me. "I think it's time for some better friends."

I clear my throat, trying to dislodge the emotions that have clogged up there, and blink my way back into the moment. "Well, since I've mostly forgiven you for the Saturday debacle–"

"Wait. Mostly? I thought that's why I was car-slave. This nicest-thing-anyone-has-ever-done-for-me playlist should have put me in the clear."

I can't help but smile. "Almost."

"What now?"

"Here's the thing, SK—I have traced your emotional degradation on Saturday to one moment."

"Would you please speak English."

"I am. Is this Def Leppard?!" I turn up the radio as notes to "Hysteria" roll through the car. These hair bands give me life, mostly because they remind me of one of the only memories I remember about my mom and dad, of them dancing together to the power

122

ballads when they played. I would run in between their legs and get to stand on their feet.

"T-shirt."

I smile at him and sing along to the song, reaching toward him with Academy Award winning theatrics. "Oh Babe..." When I open my eyes, Griffin's eyes are on me, offering a look I don't recognize from him, but I'm reminded of the day before, the flicker of what passed between us on the display bed in the Triple B. My face heats, but I don't know if it's from embarrassment or awareness. I break the connection and look away, afraid to find out.

"Saturday?"

"Right. Sorry. I was thinking about it, and I think besides the obvious restroom-side-chat, your mood soured when we talked about this character named Tanner."

His jaw sets, just like I figured it would. "I don't want to talk about it."

"Which is why I think you should."

"Did you plan this?"

"What?" I press a hand to my chest, and he glances at it, then flicks his gaze back to my face as I bat my eyelashes. "Me? No. How could I have known we'd be stuck in the car for–" I pick up the phone and attempt to read the time on the navigation app– "an hour and fifteen-minute car ride?"

"Yesterday. When I told you."

"True." I grin at him.

"I'm beginning to wonder if you're the serial killer."

"A serial killer of bad moods." I snicker at my dumb joke and think about my dad. "Griffin, you should really talk about what bugs you."

"I already told you about him. We became friends when we were fourteen. We got in a fight."

"Superficial, SK. I want the details." I remove my shoes and put my feet up on the dash, wiggling my toes. "The moment I mentioned the importance of your friendship, you freaked out."

"It's more involved, and I don't really want to get into it."

I stare out the windshield at the road as he drives. The rain has stopped. My mind is spinning about the friendship he's avoiding, and I can tell that it means way more to him than he wants to admit. I just don't understand why. What's so hard about that? It's pretty clear to me that he needs to figure this out. It's more of a feeling than a certainty—and maybe a mixture of Cal Wallace wisdom.

The bigger—and more personal—question is why I care?

I'm leaving.

"Are you mad?" he asks.

"No."

"Why are you so quiet and moody all of the sudden?"

I turn my head back toward him. "I'm doing an impersonation."

"Of?"

"You." The opening of the song *Easier to Run* by Linkin Park trickles through the speakers into the car, and I can't help but smile. "Oh. This is your song! Just listen to the lyrics."

Chester Bennington's voice rhythmically chants the moody tune. I glance at Griffin, who's about to break his jaw as Bennington sings about running over facing the pain.

"That's what you did on Saturday when I got too close, SK."

His knuckles are white on the steering wheel. "That isn't fair."

"Isn't it?" I glance at him. "I'm not trying to be a bitch, Griffin. I'm trying to be your friend."

He's silent so long I feel like maybe I've lost him. I stare out the window—maybe I shouldn't have pushed him, and maybe my lack of filter will snap the friendship we've found. It did with Michael, or at least that's what he'd said: "You're freaking lack of filter pushes people away, Max." But I can't seem to stop it. Anything less than authenticity feels like a lie.

"Fine."

I snap my head to look at him, surprised, and without thinking about it, reach out and place a hand on his arm. "Griffin?"

His gaze slides from my hand to my face. "Yeah?"

"I won't hurt you."

"You're leaving."

My breath stops up in my chest. At first, I think of Michael—his reason for our March breakup was because I was leaving. Griffin has voiced my mantra: *I'm leaving.* He's absolutely right, and I know he's talking about me going to college, but there's a layer he isn't saying underneath the words. His dad is gone. Tanner and the rest of his friends are gone. He isn't talking about me going to college at the same time, which means whatever friendship we've built isn't temporary for him. Whatever we've built over the last seven weeks means something.

My heart picks up speed, unsure what it all means, but cognizant that he's assigned me a permanent place in his sphere, which makes me feel insecure and hopelessly happy simultaneously. I am leaving. I'm looking to the next step in my journey as the thing that's going to finally feel secure and foundational, and yet, this moment seems to be screaming at me. *Listen! This is important.*

I look at him, needing to see the concrete form of him to process what he's said to understand the way it's bouncing about inside of me. My gaze stops on my hand resting on his arm.

Is he admitting that me leaving will hurt him?

I can feel his skin under my own, the heat of him, and I know that the feelings—the friendship ones—pulsing through my blood are real. Perhaps, even though I'm leaving for college, and Dad will eventually uproot and move to the next place, it doesn't mean Griffin can't stay a friend? Would I want that? Yes.

"Physically, maybe, but I'm not going to stop being your friend just because I'm a few hundred miles away at school. Especially now that I know."

His eyes flick to me before returning to the road. "Know what?"

"What having a good friend is like." I take my hand from his arm and fist it before threading my fingers together and resting them on my knees. My skin burns with awareness, though it isn't just because of the physical attraction; it's more than that. Heartstrings I didn't know I had have been tugged and knotted up with Griffin. A friend. A real one. And even as I think it, I remember Michael's words: *I don't trust this.* He was supposed to be my friend, which leads me to add, "You just have to be willing to trust me."

"When I was fourteen, my brother left," Griffin says, surprising me by talking. "My mom kicked him out, but I didn't really understand it. I blamed her first, and when he didn't come back, I blamed him because he left me behind."

"Like your dad?"

He nods and says, "I met Tanner my freshman year. Before that, I was mostly alone because people were always talking shit." He runs a hand through his hair again. I notice his fingers. They're long, and his hand has that masculine veining that makes them look strong. "Tanner and I had homeroom together, and this teacher—he was such an asshat—was picking on Tanner. The thing was, everyone who went to school with T knew that his big brother had died of cancer, and his family hadn't ever recovered from that. So, when this teacher started giving him shit, I jumped in. We both got kicked out of class and somehow became friends."

"Like brothers," I say.

"Yeah. I guess. We both sort of became the brother that the other was missing."

"And the fight."

He offers a heavy sigh.

"I can't think any worse."

With a slight shift of his head, he looks at me. "You might."

"Trust," I say again, surprised and grateful he's extending it.

"We had this agreement called Bro Code that we made during our sophomore year. It was me and Tanner and Josh—you met him the other night."

"With Ginny and Emma?"

He swallows, and I note the regret, a haunting that hovers over his features. "Yeah. And Danny. My friends."

"Bro Code? That doesn't sound great."

"You can probably guess."

"Like a bros before hos thing?"

"Yeah. And some."

"So how does that lead to the fight? Tanner take your girlfriend?"

He shakes his head. "No girlfriends in Bro Code and Tanner would never do that. No, he fell for this girl at the end of senior year, right before graduation."

I put together the puzzle pieces. "Emma?"

He sighs. "Yes. I wouldn't let up about Bro Code. I wouldn't listen to him when he tried to tell me he felt differently about her. I just accused him of breaking the code."

"Did he?"

"In my head, I thought so, but now, I don't think so anymore."

"What do you think now?"

"That I was just–" he clears his throat and adjusts in his seat– "afraid."

"Of what?"

"Things changing. Losing my friends. Ironic right?" He offers one of those partial smirks that looks more like self-hate than humor.

"So that was the fight?"

He shakes his head. "Ultimately yeah, but it happened because we got drunk, and I said some shitty stuff to him about his brother. Then

I told him we weren't friends anymore."

I pluck at some threads on my yellow and black socks. "Do you miss him?"

I figure he'll close up again, but he doesn't. He says, "Yeah."

I take my feet off the dash and turn to look at him. "You should tell him."

"I think it's more complicated than that."

"Why? It shouldn't be. You care about him. If it's real friendship, then it shouldn't be more complicated than working it out." I know I believe this wholeheartedly. I've grown up with Cal after all, but I consider my mom, who didn't even try, and I suppose that's why I think it might be so important to figure it out.

"Is that what you do?"

I start to open my mouth, then close it. I suppose I did with Michael when it came to the small stuff. "I haven't had many friends. Not like you and Tanner, anyway, but if it were someone who meant a lot to me, I would."

"I don't know if it was a real friendship." He stops, and I'm not sure he's going to continue, but he adds, "When Bella said what she said the other night about me—"

I groan, annoyed at that bitch and her rude-ass comments, feeling protective of Griffin.

"—I believed it. And I think I have for a while. Tanner's a good guy. I'm not, though. I'm not a good friend. And maybe I've always wished I could be more like him."

On impulse, I reach over and cover Griffin's hand resting on the

129

stick shift. I can't take away the way he's feeling, but I figure I can show him that he isn't alone. It isn't a lot, but at the moment, it feels like everything.

We continue down the road with the playlist Griffin made, offering a mood. The melody of Linkin Park's *Somewhere I Belong* swirls through the car, and Griffin doesn't remove his hand like I anticipate. My heart beats out a new rhythm I think I'm supposed to recognize, but it's a distant cousin to the one I met with Michael so long ago. This is a heartbeat vibrating the threads sewn up in this new friendship that I can't lie and claim is temporary anymore even if I'm leaving. It's echoing a feeling that scares me, the vibration luring the fear to ensnare what might be good in its web. She reminds me that this will be another goodbye, and if I allow the threads to remain, it will tear open another hole. It's safer to sever the connection.

When Dad and I got here, I'd assumed I could avoid anything like this with only eight weeks. My history reinforced this belief that I could avoid any sort of lasting relationship. Except now it's clear that isn't the truth. And being afraid of saying goodbye and leaving a relationship behind isn't a good enough reason to avoid it. I can hear Cal ask, "What do you want?" I want this friendship. I want to follow my own advice and commit to it. Even if this is about friendship, a seed has been planted in the soil that doesn't feel like only friendship anymore. I avoid looking at Griffin. I'm sure he'll be able to see all the feelings blooming in my heart.

11

I wait near the car outside of the visitor's center while Griffin goes inside to get our pass. While he's gone, I fuss with my clothing, straightening it along with the feelings that are off kilter inside me. While my brain insists that maintaining the line of friendship is imperative for the sake of my own well-being (I'm going to college soon, for goodness' sake), my heart isn't acquiescing to the warning at all. My body is so freaking tuned up, strings tight, being near him. I'm unbalanced and annoyed with myself because it's ridiculous. Griffin isn't interested in me like that. He wouldn't be. No one besides Michael ever has been, and I suspect that "interest" was just about physical exploration of which I also benefitted. Besides, even if Griffin were open to the idea, I'm leaving.

When Griffin reappears, I've talked myself into tempering my natural inclinations to blurt my impulses, which I know will scare him away, and match the smile he gives me.

"So," I say as I follow Griffin down the hiking path. He's got a backpack on, and unfortunately, my eyes slide to the nice way his jeans sit on his hips, the pockets elongated, roving over his butt, and curving toward his thigh—I blink. Stop.

"So, what?" He looks over his shoulder.

"I've given some thought to your rules." I quicken my pace to catch up, so I stop looking at his ass.

"Why's that?"

"Well, I feel like perhaps they are limiting you."

He turns his head to look at me, his perfect eyebrows doing this dance over his eyes. "They're for parties, Max."

"Right. But if those are the only rules you're living by, you know, I think maybe you need to expand. Especially because of what we talked about on the way here."

He grabs onto the straps of the backpack and continues forward. "Okay." He sounds skeptical, drawing out the word into multiple syllables.

"I have decided to share my rules with you."

"I wasn't aware you had rules."

He's right. I don't. I'm making this up as I go. "I definitely have rules."

"Wasn't the whole purpose of me sharing my rules because you hadn't been to parties? If you have rules, I didn't have to share mine."

"Oh. These aren't for parties." I've trekked ahead of him and toss glance over my shoulder.

"What are these rules for?"

"Relationships."

"Because you've had so many?"

I turn, walk backwards, and give him an appalled gasp even if he's right. "I beg your pardon. I've had a boyfriend. You haven't even had a girlfriend."

"You had a boyfriend?" He looks down at the asphalt. "When was this?"

I turn back to the front and keep walking. "Yes. Last year."

"How long did you have this boyfriend?"

"Seven months, give or take. So, your objection is irrelevant and overruled."

"Did you just lawyer and judge me at the same time?"

"Yes, I did." I snort. "I'm going to school you on my rules."

We reach a fork in the path, and Griffin halts the conversation to pull out the map. After making a decision about which way to go, we continue on. Griffin continues looking at the map as we walk through the deciduous trees away from the river. Tall grass lines our path. I love the sound of the birds bantering back and forth and the sizzle of bugs as they make their living around us.

"It says here that resources dried up and that's why everyone moved away," he says.

"Isn't that why most ghost towns become ghost towns? They lose what keeps them alive?"

He puts the map back into his backpack. "It isn't because everyone mysteriously dies, and then the town is haunted by the remaining ghosts? I thought we were going to like a massive, haunted house."

"That sounds more imaginative."

He chuckles. "Okay. So, your rules."

"Yes. My rules. First rule, you have to trust."

"Okay. Trust. Got it."

"Do you?"

"I trust you."

"Because I coerced you into it."

He smiles, a real one, then looks away. "Well, I allowed myself to be coerced, by you. If I didn't trust you, I wouldn't have shared." He pauses a beat. "I haven't shared it with anyone else." His eyes find mine, then skitter away.

Stop, I tell my heartbeat. "Rule two is that you have to talk."

"I talk."

"About real stuff."

"What isn't real about ghost towns?"

I stop, and Griffin bumps into me, and then catches me, his hands grasping my arms. He offers an apology, lets go, and we continue side by side.

"Griffin, you know what I mean." My arms tingle with the remnants of his touch.

"Okay. Okay. Talk. Next."

"Third rule. You have to be willing to share the hard parts of yourself."

He turns, his whole body now facing me as he walks sideways, and his eyebrows are high on his forehead, his eyes wide. "The hard parts, Max?" He wiggles his eyebrows at me.

Shit. I walked into that. I can't help but laugh and playfully swat at his arm. "Griffin. I didn't mean it like that."

He dodges my second smack. "You said 'hard.'" He laughs.

"You're a child. I meant, the difficult stories, the things that are harder to share about ourselves."

"Hard," he says with a smile.

"Griffin."

He shoves his hands into his pockets. "Fine. I get it. Be willing to share. How many more rules are there because this seems like a lot to remember?"

"Really? Because you had four and I'm only on three. Trust. Talk. Share." I count them off on my fingers.

He mimics my finger counting. "Trust. Talk. Hard." He skips forward to avoid my playful wrath.

"Stop it." I chase after him, catching him from behind, and wrapping him up in a bear hug.

He chuckles, covering my hands with his, and I let him go.

"Share," he says, glancing at me.

"Rule four: Allow others the space to mess up."

His eyebrows draw together. "Huh?"

I tilt my head. "Case in point: Saturday night."

He nods. "Oh. Got it."

"And the last rule."

"Thank God. My limited brain capacity just can't take anymore. It's just too *hard*."

"Griffin, you're obnoxious."

He laughs when I lunge at him again. "Go. Go. Sorry!"

"Rule five: forgive."

He settles and sobers, walking along the path near me, studying his feet with what I can only guess is pondering. After a few moments, he stops. "I think for someone who says they haven't had many friends, you have some smart rules."

I search his face to see if he's joking, but he doesn't appear to be teasing me. "Well." I continue walking. "I recently had the opportunity to test them out on this really unruly guy I met." I can feel him smile even though I can't see him, and I refuse to look. I don't want to confuse my decision to focus on friendship. "Plus, I have Cal."

"I bet you had a chance to practice them with this boyfriend. Was that *hard*?" He runs past me laughing. I give chase, then catch and release him. He laughs, and I roll my eyes.

When we make it to the edge of the Bend, I'm struck with how silent the ghost town is. The breeze—which is more prominent in the dry scrub of grass land where the town sits—is strong and pushes through the abandoned wooden buildings, making things creak and howl. The wood is aged, a gray patina silvering the surface, and dust coats the windows, which I'm sure are additions to keep thieves and vandals out. We seem to be the only ones who have ventured out today; the town is empty except for us.

I continue down the main street and feel the hush of voices, pressing in against me even though I know that is impossible. When I notice I'm only hearing the sound of my own footsteps, I turn and look at Griffin who's stopped. He looks sort of pale, his mouth uncharacteristically thin with unease.

"What is it?" I ask.

"It's creepy."

I can feel the pall of this place, too, and recall him telling me about playing cowboys and bandits with his brother. "Is this what you imagined?"

"I thought there would be a boardwalk."

It's a strange observation, random, but it makes me wonder about it. About where he's gone. He's looking at the spaces between the buildings, and I have the impression there's way more happening inside of him than he's saying. That alone makes me curious, but this isn't something I feel like I could ask him, and I know for sure he won't tell. I bite down any words that might cause him to retreat and ask, "Do you still want to go?"

He nods and continues forward until we're together once again.

A drop of rain splashes on my arm, and I look up. The clouds are building above us; the storm we left behind now catching up.

"I don't know that we have a lot of time before the rain hits."

"We're already here and walked all this way. Might as well look around," I tell him.

I climb up the stairs to one of the buildings and peek in a window. Griffin is next to me, and our shoulders brush as we peer inside. It's a house or something, everything frozen in time as if the owners will just come back and pick up where they left off. We move on and pass a steepled church and an overgrown cemetery marked with wooden crosses.

I think about those people—the buried—their families moved on. I think of my mother and my father and me moving. "They were left behind," I say. "It's so sad."

"Couldn't exactly take them," Griffin says, but I hear a layer in his words that makes me wonder if we're talking about the same thing.

More drops fall, splattering my exposed skin.

We stop and peer into a saloon. It looks like the house. Dusty tables and glasses, tables with unfinished card games, wood warped with time.

"It's so quiet," I say.

"It's hard to believe that people are just gone, left everything like this. Abandoned."

The raindrops begin in earnest now, plinking around us.

I glance around for cover since there isn't much in this general vicinity. When I spot an open building that looks a bit like a covered bridge, I point to it. "There."

By the time we get to it, the rain is falling without reprieve, with no hint it will let up anytime soon. We might be stuck. I glance at Griffin standing at the opening, his back to me, and I'm thankful because I'm blushing, imagining what could be done while stuck.

Stop, I tell my imagination.

"It could be a while," he remarks.

"It's okay." I remove my yellow coat and sit on it, leaning against one of the walls, grateful the wind is pushing against the building rather than flowing through it.

"You sure?" He turns from the doorway and watches me. "We could make a run for it. I know you had plans."

I sit down and look at my phone for the distance. "I don't mind waiting."

"It's going to be muddy either way," he says.

"Packing isn't going anywhere. Besides, I'm an expert."

He turns away from the opening and joins me by pulling his jacket out of his backpack and setting it next to mine. He sits on it. "I packed some food."

His thoughtfulness makes me smile. "You did? I'm impressed."

He pulls them out of his backpack. Several sandwiches in baggies. "They're smashed. Sorry."

"Still food," I say and take one. "Who knew you were so resourceful. I may have to change your name."

"To what?"

"I'm going to be thinking about it," I tell him and take a bite of the peanut butter and jelly he's made. "What does your name mean anyway?"

"Griffin?" He finishes his bite. "It's a monster. You know the one with the lion body and the eagle head and wings? When I asked my mom why she named me after a monster, she said she wanted something to match my brother's name."

"What's his name again?"

"Phoenix."

"The bird that dies and rises from the ashes?"

He nods. "She claimed something like the Griffin is revered. As a monster."

"Well, you know the internet never lies." I bump his shoulder with mine.

"Online it says, 'ferocious monster.'"

I can tell this bothers him. "That plus serial killer and car slave. They all kind of work." My joke sort of splats onto the dusty ground around us. "You could have a name like mine that means 'great stream,' and get teased for having a strong urinary flow."

He turns and looks at me with a smile, one of those that just touches his eyes, sort of, as if he's holding back and might not want to. "Great stream, huh?" He stops, and I can feel his joke coming before he even says it. "Is that before or after being *hard*?" Then he laughs, a loud one that's free and fun, so uncharacteristic of him, his eyes shut, and his head tipped back. This is Griffin. Unmasked.

I roll my eyes, but really, I feel that laugh in my bones as if he just added marrow to the soul of me. As if I would do anything to make him smile and laugh like that all the time.

12

I fill the day before I leave for college with things to keep me focused on my goal. The alternative is grappling with thoughts and feelings about Griffin, the anxiety of leaving my dad, and being alone at school for the first time. Disquiet about Griffin and worry about Dad hover about my edges, threatening to push me into the abyss, so I run. I pack. I present my dad with his cabinet (which he loves, getting all misty-eyed). Except despite my best efforts at keeping my mind and body occupied, I can't avoid replaying all the moments of the trip with Griffin, overthinking each word, tone, look, movement. I wish I had one of those girl best friends like they portray in TV and movies where you bounce on a bed during a sleepover and swap secrets. Perhaps it would help me figure my brain and heart out about Griffin, but I don't, and talking to my dad about this is a big nope.

By the time afternoon rolls around, I can't keep myself from texting Griffin. I rationalize that I'm leaving, he's my friend, and since Dad and I are having pizza, he should join us. A good-bye party I'm throwing myself. I've never had one before, so I do it. I haven't seen him since our hike, and he's coming over. It isn't until after I've sent the text, and he's agreed that I second guess my impulse. Bad idea! My nerves are pointy slivers, sharpening themselves on the underside of my skin. My brain is twirling around like a dancer, pirouette after pirouette. I'm dizzy with it. Nervous and wishing I was just walking down the dark road toward strangers without cares.

Which makes me wonder why I'm feeling this way. A couple months ago that is what I'd done. No cares. No worries. No second-guessing myself. I'd sat down with Griffin—a stranger then—without concerns. Insecurity is filtering my feelings, and I hate it. This isn't because of something Griffin has done, but me, and I can't identify the shift. He wants to be my friend. I'm still leaving for college. The endgame is still the same. And though I can recognize that my feelings for Griffin are discombobulated and foolish, they shouldn't be impacting my overall vision.

But I'm watching for him out the window like a puppy anxiously awaiting playtime, annoying myself because I am. It's stupid, and I can't seem to stop. When his car pulls into the drive, I'm throwing open the door, making sure I don't fall over the ledge onto the ground because the porch is gone, and hopping toward the car as he gets out like a damned golden retriever.

He looks so good in those jeans that fit him just right and a heather gray t-shirt that reads *I'm not for everyone*. He leans forward into the car to grab something, pulls out a box and a mylar balloon that reads *Good Luck*, then closes the car door with his hip and offers me a smile—one of those subdued ones—as he walks toward me.

My stomach does this stupid ballet move my brain was doing earlier that makes me almost sick, but a good sick. Maybe that doesn't make sense. I feel as though if I don't touch him, I might fall over but through the ground, falling for infinity. I lift my hair off the back of my neck to cool off, suddenly overheating.

"Am I late?" he asks.

"No. Pizza hasn't arrived. You won!"

"I didn't know it was a competition."

"Life is a competition, SK. Come on."

He holds up the box. "I bought you a cake." He hands it to me.

"That's sweet. Literally." I look from the cake decorated with thick frosting flowers to him and grin.

"Clever."

"Kind of big for the three of us." I lead him up the step ladder outside the front door and stall to catch my balance since I've got a cake in my hands.

Griffin's hands are suddenly on my waist, heavy and warm. "You good?" He steadies me, but nothing about my insides is steady. I'm thinking about his hands and how much I like the weight of them. I can't even answer him. If I can't catch my breath, how am I supposed to catch my words?

I make a noise and continue up the ladder, pausing at the threshold of the door to wait for him. When he makes it to the top, he clenches his hands, then wipes them on the back of his jeans, the balloon moving in matching bursts with the rest of him.

"I picked that one because you never know," he says. "Maybe that's what your dad will eat when he gets back."

I swallow, all the worry I have for my dad rising up like the tide inside me. He's going to get diabetes. He'll drink too much soda and eat horrible food. Maybe I shouldn't go.

He reaches out and touches my elbow. "Shit. I'm kidding, Max. I'll make sure he's eating good."

"Promise?"

He nods and holds out the balloon. "I got this for you, too."

I need a moment to compose myself because I want to throw my arms around him and devour him. I resort to sarcasm. "I bet you think you deserve some applause for it, too."

He grins. "Maybe."

I snort—very unattractively, I might add—and lead him into the dining room. "Griffin's here, Dad."

He lights up when he sees Griffin, and for a moment, I feel like perhaps things will be okay. That maybe Dad has found someone to keep him company. I know he likes Griffin. "I'm glad you're here. This one's been moping about." But then I also feel slightly jealous of both of them, feeling like I'm going to be missing out and lose status in this

144

triad. It's ridiculous. Leaving was what I wanted.

"Dad. You lie."

He wraps his arm around me, squeezes me to him, and plants a kiss on my temple.

"All packed?" Griffin asks.

"Yes."

"Nervous?"

"Yes."

"Excited?"

"Yes."

"I'm not," Dad says. And my heart aches.

Griffin helps me set the table, and we joke around while we do. He's incredulous that we're using actual dishes with pizza. "You know that pizza is really a finger food, right? All the water wasted washing the dishes."

"But salad isn't a finger food."

He moves around the table, putting forks at each place. "It could be."

Dad sets the salad bowl on the table just as there's a knock at the door. He goes to collect the pizza, and Griffin and I continue around the table.

I lay another folded paper towel at a place setting. "That makes you a caveman."

Griffin steps closer as he puts a cup at each spot. "Is that your new name for me? I thought I might have earned something nicer."

I take another step, and as I fold the last napkin and set it down on the plate, we're standing side by side, shoulder to shoulder, staring at the table. The sound of his voice makes me want to look at him, but I can't. I know he isn't looking at me either, but my arm is hanging by my side. It brushes against his, skin to skin, sending a shockwave straight to through my chest that makes my heart palpitate. I swallow.

"You think you deserve a nicer name, SK?" I ask, and I might be trying to keep it light, but the sound of my voice is so airy it seems heavier somehow.

He hasn't moved. Just stares at the table like I am, the back of his hand now touching mine, and my breath locks up like it's thrown in a box and buried in my lungs.

Then his touch is gone, but the electric glow remains.

Griffin folds his arms over his chest and looks at me, the spell broken. "I hoped."

My dad walks in with the pizza, "Here's the pie. Let's eat!"

We drift in opposite directions and take up spots around the table.

Dad says a prayer, and we dig in.

The dinner conversation is easy and includes lots of laughter. After we stack things up, we play cards, and Dad tells stories about our adventures. When he gets to sharing my quirks, I feel embarrassed, but Griffin seems to like it, asking questions to learn more.

"I think that's enough 'embarrass Max' for one night," I say, standing. I take the cake from the table and return it to the counter.

"I don't know why you think it's embarrassing," my dad says, leaning back and resting his hands on his belly. He yawns.

"Dad? You just told Griffin I color code the grocery list."

"I'm sure it's helpful," Griffin says with a smile.

"It is." Dad stretches. "Before I forget, Griffin would you do me a favor while I'm gone taking Max to school?"

"Sure."

"Would you come out to the house to check on things. I don't trust those doors."

"You got it."

"On that note, this old man is sleepy." He yawns again. "I'm going to leave you young ones to the cleanup." He stands.

"We got it," I say.

Dad leans over and kisses the top of my head. "Night, then."

I watch him disappear and listen to his steps echo in the stairwell as he climbs the stairs. I glance at Griffin, suddenly so grateful that he'll be here and that my dad won't be alone.

"Thank you," I tell him as we finish clearing the table.

"Sure. No problem. I don't mind helping," he says.

"No. I mean for being there for my dad." I hold out a damp cloth for him.

He takes it, his fingers brushing my hand.

"It's for the table," I tell him.

I watch him walk back to the table and lean over to wipe it. Looking at him is too hard, so I turn away.

"He's going to be okay," Griffin says.

"I know."

He stands next to me at the sink. "Then what's up?"

I fill the empty salad bowl with water. "It's just me."

"What?"

"I'm scared to leave him." I chance a glance at him, but then look away because I can feel the threatening tears.

Griffin wraps an arm around me and pulls me closer against his side. "You're going to be great. I know it."

"What if I'm not. What if I can't find any friends? What if I can't find my way around? What if I flunk out? What if I miss my dad so bad that I sink into a horrible depression where I never shower and my roommate plots to get me removed?"

"All of those things are improbable." He squeezes me with reassurance. "You're one of the weirdest people I know."

"That doesn't help."

"Sure it does. Weird is good. You're original and fun and kind. You care about people. I mean, if you could care about me—a fake serial killer—and get me to talk to you, then surely you can get normal people to like you. And you're one of the smartest people I know. As for the roommate and depression and stinking up the place, I'm not sure a girl who color codes a grocery list is bound for not showering."

I wrap an arm around him and rest my head against his shoulder. "Want to hear something really weird?"

"You mean something normal since everything you say is weird."

"I'm going to miss you."

He takes a split second of silence, tensing up under my arm, and then relaxes. "Definitely weird."

I pinch his side. "I'm being serious."

He squeezes me against him again. "I'm going to miss you too."

I turn my face to look at him, to tell him how much meeting him has meant to me. At the same time, he turns to me, and his mouth brushes my cheek, near my mouth. It surprises me, and, based on his wide eyes, I think it was accidental. My fingers touch the spot where his lips have left a brand still burning. I want it again, for real, and without considering anything else, I reach for him. I take his face between my hands, draw him back, and press my mouth to his.

It's only a moment.

A moment for my heart to choreograph a new beat and dance. A moment to accept the heat that exists there, the softness of his mouth that I knew would feel good to kiss. A moment to acknowledge that this new beat has only been waiting because it's always existed. Then it crashes and burns because Griffin steps away.

My eyes open, and he looks stricken.

His mouth opens, and it seems like he wants to say something but doesn't know what to say. His hands are fisted at his sides, and I see my impulse for what it was—a mistake. I crossed a line he didn't want. I misread everything. Always fucking up, ruining things, and forgetting that people don't want me.

"Oh," I sputter. "I wanted–"

"I'm sorry," he says at the same time, our words rolling together like clouds in a stormy sky.

I clamp my mouth shut. It has never mattered what I wanted. His thoughts are locked up behind his teeth too. The mood now awkward and neither of us sure what to say or how to extricate ourselves from the mess I've made.

I swallow and just jump into the swampy mire like I always do. "I guess I hoped–"

"Hoped?"

"That maybe you might be–" I stop and turn away, face the sink and the dirty dishes and consider that perhaps it's symbolic somehow. I forgot. It doesn't matter what I want. "Forget it." Embarrassment swirls inside me like the suds in the salad bowl. I offer him a smile in an effort to go backward, but it's impossible to retrace those steps and take them away.

"Max–"

"It's okay," I say, covering the words he will say that might crush me. "I get it."

"Get what?"

"I'm not your type." I can't look at him, afraid that something I hadn't known I would want could be irrevocably ruined.

"Max. No. That isn't–"

"Please." My embarrassment is solidifying into something else, something more dangerous. "Don't say something you don't mean."

"I'm not. It's just I care about you."

His words careen around in me, finding a place to settle, except that I've developed calluses around my feelings to shelter me, and they can't find a place to land. I look at him. "What? I'm confused. You care about me. You just don't want to kiss me?"

"You're my friend."

"So, let me get this straight. You have four rules about sleeping with nearly any girl that moves as long as she isn't drunk and is willing.

Is there another rule you skipped telling me?"

He runs his hands through his hair and steps back, leaning against a chair at the table. "No. I don't sleep with girls I care about." He shakes his head, hearing the way that sounds.

"You think that's supposed to make me feel better? That it sounds better? And who said anything about sleeping together?"

His hands return to his sides. "I just don't want—"

"Yeah. I get it." I turn away from him, hearing Michael's criticisms again: *You're so much, Max.* "Me. You don't want me. It isn't you, it's me, right?" I dump the dirty water into the sink and rinse the bowl.

"Max—"

"Just. Please, don't." I smack the clean salad bowl into the drainer and swallow the tears. I don't want him to see. "I think you should go." And my voice fucking catches on the tears waiting there.

"Max. Please don't do this—" he says.

I spin on him, the embarrassment now anger, the tears filling my eyes. "Go. Please." I know it's against the rules I made the day before, except I can't face them at the moment. I'm embarrassed and ashamed, and I rationalize that maybe it's better this way, like tearing off a bandage.

I'm leaving.

Griffin backs away, his face looking more like the first day I saw him outside the convenience store, and it makes me feel awful. Except I did this. I ruined it just because I can't seem to control myself. And he's so fucking good at following his rules, he listens because I've asked him to go.

151

When he's gone, with my face in my hands, I let the tears fall, angry at myself for lowering my guard and forgetting the goal. But that is a lie I'm telling myself. The truth is, I'm more broken hearted that I messed up, crossed a line, and got to see what Griffin wanted. I got to see that what he wants isn't me, and it's horrifically painful even if I remind myself it would have only been temporary. Despite all the logic I can use to wrap up the ugly package in the safety of what's immediate and what might be long-term, I felt myself imagining there was more between us. Worse yet, despite knowing the pining isn't fruitful, I wish I was someone different—someone that he might want. The awful realization is how weak that makes me feel.

13

"Dad?" I ask, breaking the silence after we've been on the road for over an hour. The city is long gone. I know we still have at least another two hours to get to the campus where I'll be attending school. Farmland scattered with trees stretches around us, peppered with livestock. Every once and a while a river or creek curls into view to say *hello*.

"Yes, Max-in-a-million?"

"How did you know you wanted to be with mom?" I ask. I expect him to dodge the question since speaking about my mom and the circumstances around her abandonment aren't areas he likes to explore. Feelings? What feelings? But he surprises me.

"It was sort of a whirlwind."

I don't say anything afraid he might shut up about it, and I really need to hear this. I need to understand his thinking even if I'm doing the leaving, and though Griffin and I weren't really a "thing," I'm feeling left behind.

"We met at a bar, which I don't think is probably the healthiest place to find a partner." He glances at me with a smile and tilts his chin as if offering a small snippet of wisdom. "Kind of just fell into seeing each other. She knocked my socks off."

This makes me smile. "How's that."

"She was just so–" he pauses, looking for the right words– "free and alive. Different than me."

"You're alive," I tell him.

"I do have a pulse." He chuckles. "I mean… I thought I was a risk taker, but your mom was just fly by the seat of her pants. I was drawn to her."

"How old were you?"

"Early twenties, I think. Maybe just twenty."

"And she got pregnant. With me."

"Right. Pretty soon after we started dating, I think. Six months or so, I wanted to do the right thing. I loved her. And I wanted to be your dad, so I asked her to marry me."

"How did you know, though?"

He takes stock of what I've asked him, eyes on the road, but I can see him thinking. Then he says, "I'm not sure. Do you think it's possible to really truly know?"

"What do you mean?"

"You could have a good feeling, right? Follow your instincts and jump into a relationship with someone, but you're only one side of the equation, right? You got a-whole-nother person who's on the other side of the equal sign. A person you're trusting to have the same level of feelings. And if they don't–" he pauses a moment with a heavy sigh– "well, a one-sided equation can't work."

I'm equating this to Michael and Griffin but say, "Is that why you haven't ever had another relationship?"

He clears his throat and shifts in his seat. "Wow. What's with the questions?"

"Just curious. Will you answer it?"

He glances at me again, and whatever he sees on my face makes him acquiesce. "I didn't want to complicate our lives with another person," he says. "And I wasn't willing to split my time. You were and have always been my priority. When your mom left, I just couldn't do that to you again with someone else. And I'm not sure I could do it again, either. I loved your mom."

"And she broke your heart." I look out the passenger window.

"Yeah. She did." The tires against the road become the soundtrack for several seconds. "But Wells," he says, using my serious nickname, "nobody's perfect. Your mom and I didn't take the time to really get to know the truth of one another before we jumped in. There were things about her I didn't know. There were things she didn't know about me, like I can be a stubborn jerk."

"No. Not you." I offer him a smile.

"And I see, now, the pitfalls that existed. Hindsight is like that. I've moved on and forward, and I am content."

"You think you'll ever date again? Now that—"

He clears his through. "I'm not opposed to it. I'd need to meet the right person." He takes a measured look at me. "What's going on, Wells?"

I don't want to tell him about Griffin, so I just shrug. "I'm off to college. What if I meet Mr. Right?"

His brow creases, and he presses his lips together as he focuses on the road. "I don't like thinking about that. Someday, someone is going to sweep you off your feet and your old man will be left in the dust."

I reach over and lay my hand over his. "You'll always be my dad. And I'm not sure I'll ever find anyone as good as you."

"You will. Of that I'm sure. And you're so amazing, I'm pretty sure who you pick will be amazing too, because they have to get through all your old man's lessons." He chuckles.

"I think you should date," I tell him and return to staring out the window, thinking about Griffin.

It's too late to go back to thinking I only like him as just a friend. I mean, I do, but I have weightier feelings for him that he doesn't share. That's okay. I'm not entitled to his feelings and given my shallow pool of friends—Griffin—I feel like a jerk. I'd been wrong, not him. Yet, I'd treated him like he had been. I'd been the one to kiss him, and maybe I misread signals—it didn't mean I should have taken without his permission. Double standards and all that. Reflecting in the aftermath of my swath of destruction, it had been my embarrassment leading me by the nose rather than reason. I should have been a better friend.

I resolve to text him soon to apologize. I'd rather have him in my life as a friend than not at all.

"Penny for your thoughts?" Dad asks many miles later.

"Just thinking about you and the house," I say, which is a partial truth. I'm thinking about Griffin checking the house and feeling disappointed that I finally found a friend who I maybe lost with my idiot impulsivity.

"What about it?"

Of course, he'd ask that. I spin it. "I like it there. You were right about it being a great house."

He gives me one of those you've-said-I-was-right chuckles. "See."

"I think you should consider staying." There's no sense in filtering that.

"I don't know. Most of the savings is getting dropped into this place. I'll need to flip it to recover."

"Or live in it and start a business there. Stay. Meet someone. Now that I don't have to be your priority..." I allow the meaning to drop in on its own.

He scratches his eyebrow. "I thought maybe I'd move up closer to you."

I don't have it in me to tell him I don't want him to because I don't want to hurt him. I'm pretty frank about most stuff, but the possibility of hurting him catches my tongue.

"You don't want me to."

And yet my father knows me.

"It's not that," I say, even if it kind of is. "It's that I wish we had a place. You know? Somewhere to call home and return to. Feels like we've lived in lots of places, which is cool and everything, but there's no roots."

"See. I did mess up."

I knew he'd feel worried that he hadn't been good enough. The apple never falls far from the tree, I suppose. His insecurity is mine. My mom left him. No one chooses me. We've got one another. "No. Of course not. You've been the best dad." This is no lie. "What if I go study abroad next year?"

His face looks a little panicked. "Are you planning on that?"

"I've thought about it, but then, where do I come home too?" I ask. "Or what if I worry about you being all alone so I don't go." A little guilt trip. I'm not proud. "All I'm saying, is maybe consider it, okay?"

After we've checked into his hotel, he drives me to the dorms so I can check in, then helps me cart plastic totes up the stairs with other people moving in. We find my dorm room a few floors up.

"There are boys on your floor," Dad says.

"Everything is co-ed."

"Is a boy your roommate?"

I laugh. "No. I told you, remember. Renna is her name."

The door is propped open when we get there, and though I've been emailing with Renna, and we followed one another on social media, I didn't expect her to be so petite. She's tiny and rounded in

158

nice ways. Her blue-black hair is straight, sleek, and long. Her skin is smooth and dark. She smiles at me, dimples in both of her cheeks. "Hey, girl!" She bubbles over and throws her arms around me. "You're so tall!" But she doesn't say it with accusation but rather awe. "I wish I was tall like you. This Filipina is vertically challenged." She giggles.

"Nice to meet you in person, Renna."

"I hope it's okay that I took this side," she says, walking over to the bed where sheets dangle from being left to attend to something else.

"Of course. First come first serve," I say. "Renna, this is my dad, Callum."

"Cal," my dad says as he sets down the totes and extends a hand to her. "Nice to meet you."

"Nice to meet you, Mr. Cal."

"You can just call me Cal."

She makes an emphatic sound in her nose and shakes her head. "My grandmother would skin me. Uncle then?" she asks.

My dad smiles. "Uncle it is." He glances at me. "I'll go for the next round."

I watch him leave the room and decide I'll join him on the next trip.

"I'm so excited!" Renna says, then continues to chatter stream-of-consciousness about what's on her mind. If my filter is a loose fit, her filter doesn't exist. "I can't wait for you to meet him." She takes a breath, and I realize that I lost track.

"Who?"

"My boyfriend, Carlos. Didn't you hear me?" She grins. "It's okay. Granny says she tunes me out most of the time because–" and she's off again, which I find strangely comforting. "Do you have a boyfriend?"

"What?"

She reaches across the bed she's got pushed up against the wall opposite mine. "A boyfriend?"

"No."

She turns and flops on top of her bed just as my dad returns with another set of things from the car he rented for the trip. He didn't want to chance the Rust Bucket's long-distance chops.

"Here. There's only a couple more things," he announces.

"I can grab them," I say.

"No. This is what your dad is for. Stay and get to know your roommate. I'll be right back." He disappears again.

"No boyfriend or girlfriend, then?" she asks, reminding me where we left off.

I shake my head, but Griffin's beautiful face comes to mind. I shake it away. "No boyfriend. Not since last year. We broke up because of college," I say, referring to Michael but still fighting the image of Griffin and his smile. I need to banish these thoughts right away.

"That's okay. You're gorgeous. You'll have all sorts of people hitting you up. Carlos and I have been together since senior year–" She chatters as she unpacks and hangs her clothing in the wardrobe. I listen, content to hear the story of meeting Carlos and their secret love because Granny forbade boyfriends. Then getting the lowdown about getting caught and Granny finally relenting. How, now that Carlos can visit, Granny treats him better than Renna herself. By the time the story is finished, my dad's been back, we've made a plan for dinner, he's left, and I'm nearly done making my bed and moving boxes around into their spots.

I sit on my bed, do a little bounce and look at Renna.

"What kind of guys do you like? Maybe Carlos knows a guy."

This makes me grin even as I consider Griffin. Meeting new prospects might be exactly what I need to dissipate this one-sided crush. "Well–" I look up at the ceiling and consider her question.

Renna bounces—because she doesn't seem to walk anywhere—to her bed and sits across from me, focused on what I'm about to tell her.

For the first time in my life, I hope beyond all hopes, that perhaps I have found that TV and movie version of a girlfriend ready to listen to my woes. And maybe, just maybe, I can tell her all about Griffin and she'll have the right advice.

14

I finally text Griffin after a week at school. By this time, I've been through freshman orientation, have met Renna's boyfriend, been introduced to some of his friends and have even gone out with groups of people that include Renna, Carlos, and new acquaintances we've met on our floor. No one has said anything rude about how I look. No one has treated me like I don't belong, and for the first time, I'm feeling like I fit in my own skin. Somehow, I knew that this was what college would be like, a light at the end of a tunnel. A place where my impulsive, sarcastic, unfiltered self is exactly the right fit, and before I just hadn't found the correct puzzle to fit into.

I text him:

> Thanks for watching the house
> for Dad.

It's the first thing I can think to write that won't wound my pride. When he doesn't answer, I feel like I've messed it up.

Renna talks me into going on a double date with Carlos and one of his gazillion roommates, Adrian. We go bowling, which besides the shoes and gutter balls, is fun. Renna and Carlos are hilarious together, and I keep wanting to turn to Adrian—thinking he's Griffin—to share in the joke. Adrian seems nice enough. He's got a kind smile that reaches his whiskey-colored eyes and heavy, dark eyebrows that are very expressive, but I have no chemistry with him.

My awareness of the idea of chemistry is new.

While Michael and I explored a physical relationship, besides the mechanics of our exploration, after kissing Griffin, I'm realizing chemistry was forced with Michael. There was no sizzle like I felt with Griffin, and I've decided that some form of the sizzle is going to be important for me moving forward in any relationship. Adrian seems interested. He's attentive and smiles a lot. He laughs readily. If these were the only things to base chemistry on, then maybe, but when he reaches out and puts a light hand on the small of my back as we leave the bowling alley, or later, while we all eat after, the slight touches on my arm and my shoulder feel more like an invasion of my space than something exciting, the sizzle glaringly absent.

A day or two later, I try texting Griffin again:

> Are you alive?

> Dad says you're coming to work so, I'm making assumptions that you're still on the straight and narrow—no SK activities.

> It's okay here. So far. I'm still showering.

I reread it over and over waiting for his answer and realize I've deflected with humor like usual, avoiding what I really need to say. He still doesn't answer, and I officially start to worry that perhaps what happened has ruined things forever. I feel that fear like it's sitting on my chest, but I wait, hoping that maybe he just needs more time.

A few days later, a guy from my Bio class, Timothy, invites me out to coffee. I agree, because why not? Coffee. Timothy is interesting. He's one of those people who talks a lot in class discussions. He's intelligent, and I figure college is all about meeting new people. He's handsome in a different sort of way. A very put together guy, from his styled and gelled blond hair to his perfectly groomed beard. His eyes are bright blue and sparkle as he talks.

We sit across the small round table from one another sipping from our mugs. It's outside, an umbrella offering us shade from the fall sunshine, and for the last forty minutes, Timothy has jumped from his major to his love of science to his horrible experience with a writing professor to his love of hiking. I sip my latte—almost gone—not having to say much of anything at all because Timothy likes to hear himself talk. He does a lot of it. This makes me think of Griffin and how economical he was with his words. How I knew that when he was sharing, how important it was to tune in. A bit like my dad.

I watch Timothy's mouth move, hidden underneath that beard which makes me think of a trimmed hedge or a rounded bullnose trim used to edge walls. I think about Griffin's lips, recall his beautiful features. Beautiful? Yes, an apt description, I think. His eyes that changed color like a mood ring, or his smile that was hard won and the essence of what Griffin hid underneath all of those layers.

"Max?"

My name from Timothy's unfamiliar voice draws me back.

"Sorry? I missed that."

"Obviously. I was just asking what you thought about Professor Lobel's assertions about Darwin?"

I refrain from rolling my eyes and smile. "Oh. No wonder I zoned out." I chuckle.

Timothy looks like he's tasted something terrible. I can't tell by his bearded mouth, which is suddenly turning my stomach because he's got a droplet of his coffee in it. I note the condescension in his eyes which have turned cold.

"A joke," I clarify. Griffin would have laughed with me.

"You don't like to engage in academic discourse?"

I smile again, shifting in my seat so I'm not facing him directly. "Sure. Sometimes." I take another sip of my coffee and feel like, somehow, I'm lacking in Timothy's eyes. While that might not normally be confidence building and would have crushed me in high school, what's nice is the new clarity that I don't really care how I look in this guy's eyes. I don't care about him or what he thinks of me. "I enjoy many kinds of discussions."

"So, you're just into things like pop culture?"

I feel my eyebrows shift high over my eyes, surprised by what feels like an unwarranted attack of my intelligence. "Well, Tim, I like lots of things, pop culture among them." I set down the cup.

Timothy makes a condescending noise. "It's Timothy. Not Tim."

"Yeah. Okay." I glance at my phone because I need to extricate myself from this encounter. "Oh. Look at the time. I have another thing." I wiggle the phone at him, then gather my things. A part of me thinks I should say something courteous like *this was fun*, but it totally wasn't, so I say, "This was enlightening." Which is a truth; Timothy is a jacked-up version of Michael and the kind of person I'm realizing I'd rather avoid.

As I walk out, I'm relieved to leave and decide to text Griffin again, this time with the apology.

> Griffin? Are you okay?

> I'm sorry about getting mad that night.

> It was unfair. You were right. I shouldn't have kissed you or put pressure on you.

I'm sorry (see I'm following my rules.

Rule numbers 2 and 3. Don't say Hard).

But he doesn't text back. At first, I feel angry because he isn't responding to my apology, but then I consider I should follow my own rules and allow him the space. A couple more days and my worry amps up. It's only Dad's mention of Griffin being at work that keeps me from freaking out. I expected him to respond and have decided that maybe I should just take the hint. That whatever friendship I thought we had maybe didn't have equal expectations, like Dad's equation analogy.

The next weekend, Renna begs me into going out with her and Carlos again, but I insist I find my own date instead of them fixing me up with another of Carlos's friends. I've invited Ben from my Humanities class who I've gotten to know because of a group project. While he's cute, I figure going out and making new friends is always a bonus.

"You look cute," Renna tells me.

I look down at my skinny jeans and off-the shoulder black sweater. "I think I look like I always do."

"See. Cute." She smiles. "You ready? Carlos texted they're waiting downstairs."

When we walk into the lobby, Carlos and Ben are deep in conversation. Coincidentally, it turns out that Ben and Carlos know each other from some weird baseball connection.

Renna and Carlos kiss when they see one another.

I glance at Ben, and he makes a face at me.

I smile and think of Griffin.

We end up at a trendy spot where the food comes in baskets and the beer is on tap—not that I can legally order it yet. The light is low, the TVs are rolling sporting events, and the crowd is rambunctious. We sit in a booth, and I scoot into the inside across from Renna and Carlos. Conversation flows, easy and fun. Ben is fun. He has a nice sense of humor. He listens as much if not more than he talks. He has yet to mansplain something which, especially after Tim-Timothy (and what I learned dating Michael), is something I abhor. Ben is easy on the eyes, too. We're about the same height. He has curly, dark hair that he's often pulling back off his face, and the movement shows off his expressive, dark, brown eyes, as well as his nicely formed biceps. He has a ready smile that carves a dimple into his left cheek and though he has some scruffy facial hair, I actually like it.

After dinner, we go to a movie. In the dark, as the movie flashes forward, Ben takes the risk to hold my hand. I allow it. While my heart flutters in my chest at being touched, at the reality of Ben's attentions being more than platonic, there's a heaviness of angst attached to my own feelings about it. Ben's touch doesn't create sizzle, but I don't hate it either. It's just I can't help but compare the feeling—or lack of it—with the energy Griffin's touch kindled.

"I had fun," Ben tells me after, when he walks me into the lobby of the dorm room.

Renna goes with Carlos to his house, so I've been left with the room on my own.

"Me too. Thanks for agreeing to hang out with me."

He smiles, cutting that dimple. "Maybe we can do it again."

"Yeah. Sure." I agree, though there's a reluctance tugging on my insides somewhere.

"What are you going to do now?"

I have the anxious thought that I think Ben would like me to invite him up. I listen to that inner voice and don't. "Homework. Always homework. I have a huge test next week." I take a step away from him.

He nods and takes a step back, away from me. "I'll see you in class?"

"That you will."

I watch Ben leave the lobby, grateful that he didn't try to kiss me. Grateful that I didn't have to try and figure out how I might feel about it. Even as nice as Ben is, I can't shake Griffin from my thoughts.

The following day, after reflecting on my irritation that Griffin has made such an impact on me, I determine that I must be struggling to move forward with anyone because I need to close the chapter with Griffin. I'm incredulous about it because it's one-sided. He really has nothing to do with my feelings. He doesn't have any for me! I figure if I can just define the friendship or end it, I'll find clarity, but Griffin is being stubborn. I imagine him sitting at that table outside of the convenience store, his face stoic and tough, so unhappy and closed off. Then I juxtapose that moment with his playful side on our hike to The Bend. I resolve to try one more time and accept the outcome if he ignores it.

> If you don't answer me back this time, I'm going to spam your phone with emojis. Would you like to test me on this?

Griffin texts me back and relief washes out the tension I'd been carrying in my shoulders.

> Maxwell Wallace. Don't. Griffin

> Don't what? Text?

> No. Spam me with emojis.

I grin, imagining his serious face.

> Where you been?

> Working (because some of us have to work) and getting ready for school. How's school?

> Still showering. Ready?

> For what? Showering?

> School.

> I guess. Making lots of friends?

> It's good. I have. Been on a few dates even. Did you talk to Tanner yet?

His text takes longer this time, and I assume it's because I've brought up Tanner.

> No comment.

> SK…

> Maxwell?

> Fine. I won't push it.

> Push it. LOL.

This makes me grin again.

> I have to listen to this lecture, but please don't go silent again.

The three dots pop up and stay that way a long time. Then they disappear, and I wonder if he's formulating a response. When his response comes through it's a single word: *Okay.*

That's it.

A single word for three dots and a disappearance. I'm sure he erased what he'd planned to say, and I wonder what it was.

After another week of texting dumb stuff like memes and gifs, I send him something real: *Good luck for your first day of school.*

> So far so good.

I'm in writing. I'm terrified.

Where do you sit in class? Front or back?

Writing is one of my favorites. I didn't realize you were so easily terrified, or I would have used it to my advantage.

I usually sit the middle. You?

The back.

Move forward, SK

How come the only thing writing teachers talk about is the thesis?

How else are they supposed to get you to focus on your point?

What if I don't care about the question? Like there is no point??

No point? There's always a point.
You just have to find a way to turn it to what you do care about.

For some reason, this makes my heart jump and trot inside my chest. I care about Griffin. Too much, and perhaps this friendship—or the in-between place we've found here in texting—isn't good for me? Maybe it gives me too much hope, too much wonder to hold onto.

> What if you don't know
> what you care about?

My heart hitches forward and runs when I read his response. I assume he's talking about writing, but I read it like he's talking about life in general. Maybe about us. I know that's a dumb assumption, and I hate that my heart has led me there even as much as I'm addicted to it too.

> I think it's something we discover. Like
> you have to put yourself out there in
> order to figure it out.

> Like your dates?

My belly buzzes. Is he jealous that I've gone out on dates, or just asking as a friend? I chant friendzone in my head, but my heart feels the hope, and reply:

> Yeah. How will we find out what's
> important if we don't try?

He doesn't respond right away, but a few hours later replies on a completely new topic avoiding the last one:

> My dad got out of prison.

> Did you see him?

Yeah. He showed up at my house. I told him to fuck off. I tried to use your rules, Max. I did. Rule #4, but I just couldn't.

Maybe you're just not ready. I think that's okay.

He goes silent again, then sends me a funny gif of a dancing dog the following day. I want to tell him that I miss him, but it scares me that I want to. It scares me that if I do, I'll be left exposed again. It scares me because I get Dad's unequal equation. I know I feel more than he does, and even as I try to shut it down, I'm struggling. It scares me that my head is turned in a direction wholly temporary from the existence at school I thought I'd wanted, and if that's the case, what does it mean about what I always wanted?

Carlos makes a trip home, and Renna and I stay in for a girls' night. We watch movies on my laptop and paint our toenails. We confer about sex and laugh about our horrible first times. She tries to put in a plug for Ben.

"He's nice," I tell her.

"I think he likes you." Renna shakes a bottle topcoat she's going to add to my toes. "He told Carlos that he thinks you're feisty and it's sexy."

I blush. No one has ever said that my feistiness was a turn on or that I was sexy in any way. "He did?"

"Is there someone else?" she asks.

I figure that the only way to find a space to get over Griffin and my one-sided infatuation is to talk about it. "Well, there was this guy over the summer." So, I tell her the story. She listens, which I find amazing given her propensity to chatter, but with regards to being in the moment with me, she's all in. When I finish, she's putting the finishing touches on my last toe.

"Don't move!" she says when I go to adjust, then fans my freshly purple toes. "Sounds like he's important. And if you're still texting—and he's texting too—you're important to him. Do you want to wait around for him to figure out what an awesome person you are?"

"I'm not sure it's a matter of him thinking I'm awesome. He treats me like a good friend."

"Right. I guess I mean to notice how awesome you are as more than a friend?"

I know she's right. In some ways her wisdom settles my decision to continue being open to dating, but I know that my heart is wrapped up in the hope of Griffin. I'm not sure how fair it is of me to keep dating anyone when my heart is drawn in a different direction. "That's a good question," I tell her. "I just feel like maybe I'm not being honest. If I date someone like Ben who might be interested in more from me, and I'm not there."

She finishes the finger she's painting, then looks at me, her dark eyes thoughtful. "I think that's kind of the purpose dating though, right? Enjoying the company of someone else without all of the strings? An opportunity to get to know someone else. To learn who you are in relation to someone else?"

"And what about all the physical expectations?"

Her face scrunches up. "Dating someone isn't an obligation to do something physical."

"I know." I do, but the pressure makes me nervous.

"Do you? No one should ever pressure you just because you went out, you know?"

"Of course!" I think of Cal and his words of wisdom. I also think about Griffin and his rules, one of which is never wanting to do something with a woman who isn't into it too. "I guess, I just wish that I knew where Griffin's head was at, but I don't want to scare him away."

"So, we're back to the original question: are you willing to wait?"

I concede that I need to let go, but I also recognize that his friendship is important to me and the hope that maybe we could be stronger than letting go. "Yeah. I think so."

She nods and starts on her own nails.

A few days later, Dad tells me that Griffin brought over dinner to eat with him. I text Griffin about it.

> Thank you for hanging out with my dad. Bringing dinner. Sweet.

>> Sweet and Sour (it was Chinese food).

> Har. Har.

>> Hard. Hard. LOL.

I just wanted to say thank you. It means a lot that you'd go out of your way to hang out with my dad.

I enjoy hanging out with your dad. He's cool. No problem.

The house is looking good. We're almost ready to demo the inside.

Demolition is good stuff. Don't get electrocuted.

Chat later.

Hot date?

No. Hot homework.

Ugh.

Do your homework.

I am. BTW, I went to my friend Danny's swearing in. Tanner was there.

!!!!!

Did you talk to him?

Not about the thing. But he wasn't rude or anything.

Not even after?

> I left right after it was over.

> Proud of you for trying, SK.

He reads it but doesn't respond until a couple of days later when I'm at a party with Renna and our crew, including Ben, who I didn't invite but has struck up a friendship with Carlos.

> Thanks, Maxwell. I miss your positive vibes.

I attempt to text him back but am jostled by the people in my sphere, so I keep drafting a response and erasing and drafting and erasing. I'm pretty sure Griffin is seeing the three dots acting all indecisive on his screen. I try to find a quiet spot in order to focus my thoughts on the text I want to send, and my FaceTime rings. It's Griffin, and my heart expands while flopping around in my chest. I press the accept button on my phone. Griffin's still handsome face appears, and my heart dives into my belly seeing him. The last time was that night a little over a month ago when I kissed him, and though I knew I missed him, I didn't realize how much until he's giving me one of his partial smiles.

"Hey!" I greet him. "Sorry. It's really loud here."

"You're at party?"

I nod. "You okay? I can find a quiet place to talk."

He shakes his head, pauses a second. "I'm fine. I'll let you go."

But I don't want him to let me go. "No. Don't. Wait." The realization is initially heavy because I care about him so much and wonder how much I'm compromising who I am because of it. This doesn't feel like a compromise of myself however, but a compromise of my heart because it's one sided. Then I'm struck with the question: is that true? Maybe my heart knows something, and it's taking Griffin's longer to catch up? I think about what Dad said the day Griffin came to show me his car, about the sizzle when Griffin and I touch, about that kiss that perhaps was just me, but the feeling it created still moves through me like lightning. Maybe that is why I can't let go—there's something in the foundation of me that recognizes something the rest of me isn't.

Suddenly, Ben is next to me, jostling against me and declaring loudly, "There you are, Maximus. I found her!"

I don't like this nickname, but I also don't want to correct him. He's drunk, it wouldn't matter, and that feels more like a compromise than the feelings I have for Griffin.

Griffin's sort-of smile fades to no smile, his face turning granite hard.

"Who are you talking to?" Ben asks. It's clear he's been drinking, his cheeks bright red.

"My friend," I tell Ben over my shoulder and turn my body away from drunk Ben to focus on Griffin. "Sorry," I say to the phone.

Ben hugs me from behind, his arm wrapping around my shoulders and his forearm crossing under my chin. The action feels possessive and makes me annoyed. I don't think Ben would do it if he hadn't been drinking. "I want to say 'hi,'" he says, putting a chin on my shoulder to try and get onto the screen.

Griffin shifts on the screen. "I'll talk with you later," he says. "You're busy." The call disconnects.

I shrug out from under Ben, angry. "Hey. Stop."

Ben looks surprised.

I shake my head, pissed off at his display, then walk out of the party and text Renna to let her know I'm walking back to the dorm. Then I try Griffin back because that was who I'd felt the most interested in talking to, but he doesn't answer.

I text him:

> Sorry we got interrupted. Drunk people suck. Just left, so if you still wanted to talk.

He doesn't respond.

As I walk, I weigh my feelings. Other than the ill-fated kiss, being with Griffin has never made me feel less than. Ever. He hasn't tried to change me. Renna's question repeats in my head: *Do you want to wait?* Truthfully, if Griffin asked me to wait for him to figure himself out, I would. In a heartbeat. And that isn't about him. It is about listening to the way I feel when I'm with him. While Ben's behavior just now made me feel like something to stake claim to, which in some respects might feel like a compliment, it didn't for me. Instead, his possessive move made me feel like an inanimate object. Griffin hasn't ever made me feel that way.

After the kiss, Griffin admitted he cared about me, and he'd been terrified at the prospect of ruining our friendship. I wonder if maybe he's trying to preserve what we do have, and knowing where Griffin's been, what he's experienced with his family and friends, remembering what those asshole girls said about him, I can imagine he might feel tipsy about relationships, including friendships. Allowing Griffin space to figure out what's important to him and what he thinks about stuff is just as important as me figuring out my own feelings. While I know that doesn't mean he will ever feel more about me than friendship, I'm not sure it matters, really. I know where I am. I feel like I know who I am. And those two things will guide me to figure out what's forward no matter the outcome.

By the time I walk into my dorm room and sneak a look at my phone, there is a new text.

> You don't have to apologize.

I wanted to talk to you.

> It looked like there were other people who wanted to talk to you.

Well, you know me, irresistible.

> Yep.

I'm not sure how to answer. Eventually, I just deflect: *You okay?*

> Yep.

> Okay.

> **I'll talk to you tomorrow. Okay?**

> Okay.

I'm disappointed, but take a deep breath, resolved to accept Griffin as he is in the now, even if that means just friendship.

The next day, I text him:

> Happy Birthday!

He doesn't answer.

15

I walk down the steps from Freid Science building, feeling happy, and anticipating my jog. I'm looking forward to talking with Griffin, since we've sort of gotten into a rhythm of checking in once a day. I anticipate it more than I should, but being his friend makes me more content than not being his friend. I've stepped into a sweet rhythm at school, and for the first time feel like the outside beat of life moving around me matches my actual steps.

As I start across campus, someone calls my name. I stop and turn.

"Maxwell?"

I freeze. I may be eighteen, but suddenly I'm five.

It's a woman I recognize, and my body bursts into cold flames.

"Oh my god! It is you." The woman saying my name rushes forward and puts her arms around me for a one-sided hug.

My mother.

She smells mostly the same: like sweet lemon and a tinge of wildflowers.

My muscles won't unlock.

"Oh my god." She holds me away from her but doesn't let go of my arms as she studies my face. "I've been looking for you. I hired an investigator. I mean, my parents did, but here you are!"

My tongue loosens the concrete. "What are you talking about? You left."

"Well, yes, but–" She lets me go and steps back to study the rest of me.

I blink. "What are you doing here?"

She glances about as people move around us to and from class. "Is there somewhere we can talk?"

"I–" I don't know what I'm feeling. Confusion at the fact my mother is standing in front of me. Wary because she's walked away. I don't trust her or the rush of trepidation in my muscles. Fear because I don't understand what's happening and why she's standing here. Guilty because I wish my dad was with me. Her being here would hurt him. "I have a class." It's a lie, but I need to collect myself.

"Maybe for dinner."

"I have a library thing." I need time to think.

"I just. I needed to see you. To talk."

"You left."

She looks down at her hands, then shoves them into the pockets of her gray coat. We have the same color hair, but her hair isn't straight. Her eyes aren't exactly blue, but they aren't gray either. I have my dad's eyes. She's wearing a full-length skirt and her turtleneck peeks from the coat belted around her waist, stylish and expensive. She's smaller and shorter than me, waifish, and I couldn't be more different. Another set of traits I got from my dad. I am my father's daughter.

"I would like the chance to explain."

"Seems like you walked away from that right." I surprise myself with my strength because I'm not feeling it. When I was younger, all I wanted was for her to walk back through the door. Here she is, and I'm pushing her away.

"You disappeared. I couldn't find you. I came back."

"What are you talking about?" This doesn't sit right, as if she's saying something sinister.

"I did leave. I did." She shakes her head. "I made some mistakes, and my parents helped me get back on track and figure things out." It's a ramble from one thing to the next and difficult to follow.

"A hospital?"

"Sort of. A recovery center." She nods as if punctuating it. "I wasn't healthy, and I knew I needed to get better."

"You didn't come back after, though. Dad waited."

She swallows. "I made choices. Yes. Gave up custody with the divorce. And it was a long, twisted journey trying to get better."

Part of me—the detached human part—can understand her struggles to some extent. The daughter part, who watched her mother walk away and never return, wants to tell her to stop with her excuses, to own that she could have made different choices somewhere along the path. "Are you? Better?"

She looks up. "Yes." She smiles. It's bright, and I think I see the spirit my father referenced for a fleeting moment. She grasps my hands, and I fight the urge to pull away. "And I tried to come back. Your father stole you from me."

I do yank my hands from her grasp.

I turn and walk away, leaving her on the sidewalk.

I hear her steps as she chases after me. "Please, Maxwell. Please. Just let me take you to dinner. Let's talk."

"I'm busy."

"Here." She shoves a piece of paper into my hands. "I'll be in town until the day after next. I'll wait for your call. Please."

I keep walking and crush the paper in my fist. *Ohmygod. Ohmygod. Ohmygod.* Ohmygod is the chant fueling my steps across campus. *Ohmygod. Ohmygod.* When I make it back to my dorm room, I'm a mess, unable to wrangle my thoughts. I can't find my balance. While usually my dad would be my first call in an emergency, I can't call him about this. The first person I want to call is Griffin. I text him: *I need you.*

He doesn't text me back, but my phone rings immediately. "Hey. What's wrong?"

I burst in to tears at the sound of his voice, and despite my best efforts, can't seem to quell the tears coming out in great gusts like the outer bands of a hurricane. "I. Need. You."

"What's going on?" he asks.

I can't put words together. My hands are shaking, my insides trembling, and words tumble out amidst sobs that make it impossible to convey what happened. Her words: *Your father stole you.*

"Are you safe? Shit."

"Yes," I say.

"I can be there. Do you need me to come there?"

"Yes."

"I'm on my way." He disconnects the phone, and I dump my phone on my bed to cry.

When Renna walks into the dorm room a bit later, she's talking. "I can't believe some teachers. The comments on the paper are shit. How are we supposed to get better if we don't get specific feedback?"

I'm cocooned in my bed, the comforter over my head.

"Max? Are you okay?"

"Sick," I say and certainly sound it, my throat raw from crying and my head pounding. Heartsick is a thing, I figure, so I'm not lying.

"Oh. I'm sorry. Can I get you something?"

"No thanks."

"You sure?"

I make a noise of affirmation.

"Maybe I should stay with Carlos? In case you're contagious?" she asks. "Or I can stay. I don't want to abandon you."

"Go," I tell her without turning around. "I'm just going to sleep."

My phone beeps, alerting me that I have a message, but I don't check it until Renna is out of the room. I figure the moment she sees my face she'll know I've been crying, and then she'll stay; I'm not ready to process this with her, yet. When I listen to the message, it's Griffin. "Fuck. Max. Do I need to call 9-1-1? I'm on my way. Call me back."

I text him because I can't talk. *Safe*, I type, and then send him the address.

Somehow, I fall into a dreamless sleep, one that numbs all the feelings stripping my flesh from my bones. It's dark there and deep like a pit where I'm hanging out at the bottom. Waiting. Until suddenly there's a noise drawing me back up and out. My phone is ringing, and I open my eyes, returning to the present from the dark nowhere. I'm dizzy and spent, but I find my phone on my bed.

"I'm almost there," Griffin says.

I tell him where to park and get up, attempting to pull myself together.

Once I'm downstairs, I wait in the alcove and wish I'd worn a jacket, having forgotten it's October cold outside. When Griffin's car parks in the guest spot, I walk outside to meet him. When I see him, the tears pool, pulling from the deep well of my emotions. He's here. He's here, getting out of his car, his tall form, wider and stronger. I can't hold the tears back as they start again, but this time with relief. I tighten my arms around my center to hold myself together, and when I finally reach him, I collapse into his embrace.

"What is it? What's happened?" His arms wrap around me, one of his hands cradling the back of my head, and the warmth of his body seeps into mine. He nestles his head near mine, holding me tight, and dropping his chin so that his mouth is near my ear.

"I didn't know who else to call," I say into the fabric of his sweatshirt, my hands holding tight to the fabric at his back.

"I'll always be there for you, Max." His arms constrict tighter, holding me together.

"Thanks for coming." I pull away, stepping back to look at him.

He has on his serious face, but I'm not sure it's masked. His mouth is a line, lips pressed together. His eyebrows are bunched over his eyes, shaped with concern and maybe something like the night after we kissed. Fear?

"What happened? I'm kind of freaking out."

I swipe at the new tears on my face and take his hand in mine. "Let's go inside. It's cold."

He removes his sweatshirt. "Here. Put this on first."

I give him a partial smile. "You came from work?" I slip the hoodie over my head. It smells like him—a hint of spice but mixed with laundry detergent, bath soap, and sunshine. It smells and feels like home.

"Yes. We were working on the roof." He follows me from the lot.

"Does Dad know you're here?"

"I told him I was helping my mom."

I look at him. "Thank you."

I don't say any more, just lead him through the dorms until we make it into my room. When we walk inside, he stops and studies it, his eyes flicking from item to item: the rock posters that were gifts from him to match my t-shirts, the fairy lights, the desk, and the bed.

Then his gaze lands on me. "What happened?"

I climb onto my bed and invite him to sit with me. He does,

scooting back so that his back is against the wall, and his legs hang over the side of my bed. "My mom."

"What about her?" he asks.

"I don't even know where to start."

"Try at the beginning."

His words make me smile. While I knew I missed him, seeing him, sitting here with him, talking with him makes me realize how much of a gaping hole there's been that I've been trying to fill. "I walked out of class and there she was. I know I haven't seen her since I was five, but it was like no time had passed. She called my name, then said stuff about my dad. I didn't know what to do. What to think."

He sits forward. "Wait. What? She's here?"

I nod. "In town."

"Why? What does she want?"

"She said she's been trying to find me." I look down at my comforter and pick at a loose thread. "She said my dad kept me from her."

"Whoa. Like kidnapped?"

My throat closes up again, and I drop my face in my hands to hide the fresh tears. "Not those exact words."

"But—" He grasps my hands, pulling them away from my face. "Tell me."

"I know she had a problem, but that doesn't mean she's lying. What if what she said is true? I just got so upset and confused."

"Not that it really matters now, but your dad had custody of you, right?"

"Yes. But what if she's right? What if that's why we were always moving because he didn't want her to find us?"

"Maybe it wasn't about keeping you from her, but instead protecting you? I'm sure your dad has a good explanation if you let him explain."

I lay down on my back, exhausted by it all, stretching out, and draping my legs over Griffin's. Staring up at the ceiling, I consider it. "I don't know how to tell him. I'm afraid to hurt him or make him think I'm accusing him of something. I know he'll be on his way here when he finds out."

"But you've got your rules."

I lift my head and look at him.

He gives me a smile and pats my leg. "Why don't you just start with what you told me?"

"What if I don't like what he has to say?" I lay back down, comforted by the weight of Griffin's arm resting on my leg.

"But you love him. Trust. Talk. Share. Accept. Forgive. Remember?"

"You were listening." The thought makes me feel warm, and he's right. I do love my dad; maybe that's why this is so painful. "My mom invited me to meet with her to talk."

"What did you say?"

"I ran away."

"I essentially told my dad to 'go to hell,'" Griffin says. "When he showed up."

"How come?" I ask.

191

"I just got so angry." I feel his fingertips pluck at something on my legging. "He didn't write to me. Not once. And there he was asking me to go to breakfast. Do you think I should have listened to what my dad had to say when he showed up?"

"I don't know. Maybe he wants the chance to apologize?"

"What if there's more to the story with your mom."

I sigh and sit up, drawing my legs away from him. "You're right."

"What was that?" He holds a hand to his ear.

I move across the bed toward him, situate myself so we are side by side, and bump his shoulder with mine. "Don't get used to it."

"Oh. I will."

I lean my head on his shoulder. "Thanks for being here, Griffin."

"Not SK, or some other nickname?"

"No. Not today. Just Griffin, the hero." I take his hand from his lap and thread our fingers.

He's silent a moment but doesn't pull away from my touch. Then he says, "I'll always be here for you, Max."

I try not to read anything into it and focus only on his support. Though we're sitting in comfortable silence, I'm hyper aware of him. Griffin, having driven hundreds of miles to be here for me. Griffin, sitting on my bed in my dorm room. Griffin, with me, alone. I shift my energy toward something friendzone related, so I don't embarrass myself because, right now, the comfort of feeling his hands and mouth would be a welcome distraction. But I recall being rebuffed and know I don't want to go down that road again with him, not if it's something he doesn't want. I need him as my friend more.

"I feel bad you drove all this way. It seems sort of small now."

"I'm not," he says. "And I don't think it's small."

I move away from him, stand up. "I'm supposed to be at a study session—which I wouldn't have made it to, anyway—but since you're here, maybe we could go eat?"

"What about your mom?"

"Not today. Tomorrow."

"But–"

I shake my head. "No. You're here. She can wait. She's been waiting thirteen years. I can't deal with calling her until I have some food. I'll be too hangry."

He smiles.

"See. Let's go eat."

"Then you'll call her?"

I nod and hold my hands out to help him from the bed.

"Okay." He takes my offered hands and rises. I look up at him, and he swipes a lock of my hair off my cheek, his fingertip grazing my skin. "Let me take you somewhere to eat."

16

I steal glances at Griffin, driving us to a pizza place I like. He's here. With me. In my freak-out, I hadn't considered he would come here, thinking only about needing the comfort of my friend's voice, but here he is without question, without irritation, without judgement. Besides looking good, like he always does, he looks more relaxed, more settled in his skin. Perhaps that's a reflection of time because I feel that settling as well in many ways.

The dark pizza parlor is weekday crowded, which is comfortable and still allows for us to be able to talk. I scan the room and don't know anyone. After arguing about paying for pizza, which he won't let me do, I lead him to a high-backed booth covered in red vinyl. Framed newspaper clippings adorn the walls, and a red frosted sconce offers ambiance in addition to the colorful stained-glass chandelier overhead.

"I feel like I owe you," I tell him, settling in on one side of the table.

Griffin sets down the pitcher of soda—I capitulated for the sake of the moment—and sits across for me. "That's dumb."

"Wow. Thanks, Griffin. You just called me dumb."

"No. Not you. That you feel like you'd owe me. There's a difference."

"Why is that dumb?"

"Because what are friends for?" He seems to stall on the word friends, then kickstarts himself by pouring us our drinks.

"So, tell me about your dad." I take one of the hard, red, plastic cups and wrap my hands around it. Talking about anything besides my mom and thinking about my dad is preferable.

"We're not here because of my dad," he says and takes a drink from his own cup.

"Right. But let's talk about it anyway."

"Can we not?" he asks.

I tilt my head. "Friends. Rule number 2. I want to hear about it."

"For you? Or because you're trying to make me work through something?"

This makes me smile. "For me. Yes. It's all about me."

"It's different than with your mom."

"How do you figure?"

"Because your mom left. My dad though–" He stops and stares at his cup a moment. "He's a selfish prick."

"Why? Because he went to prison?"

He looks at me, focuses. "Yeah. And he was fucking around on my mom."

This is new information, and I feel the surprise on my face.

"He has another family. Married to my mom but had another woman tucked away and shares a kid with her—a girl. She's a couple years younger than me."

"Have you met them?" I wonder about my mom. Is she remarried? Do I have partial siblings out in the world?

He shakes his head.

"How do you know, then?"

"Phoenix. I was around twelve or thirteen and was begging to go visit Dad. My brother was so pissed off, and I didn't understand until he said something about Dad's secret family. Then it all kind of made sense. His absences, his indulgences, his disconnection from us. He was a liar."

"Whoa. I'm not sure what to say to that."

"There's nothing to say to that."

"Max?"

A voice I recognize draws my attention away from Griffin. Ben is standing at the end of our table, and my back tenses. The friends he's with, Carlos not among them, move past him toward a different table somewhere in the parlor. I've seen him in class, but I've mostly been avoiding him since the party and his drunken handsiness. His dark eyes drift to Griffin, and I notice the countenance of his normally gentle features harden. When he swings his gaze back to me, it softens again, but I also think maybe there's a vein of hurt running through him.

"Hi Ben." I offer him a kind smile. While I've been avoiding him, it isn't because I don't like his company. I haven't wanted to send him the wrong message.

"What are you doing here? I missed you at the study session. Renna said you were sick."

His tone—sort of possessive, like the arm draped around me as I spoke to Griffin on the phone—grates against my patience.

"I'm feeling better and needed to eat. This is my friend, Griffin."

Griffin offers him a tight "hey," and leans back in the booth. He sort of spreads out in the seat, widening himself and staring directly at Ben. I find it fascinating. The only time I've ever been around Griffin interacting with anyone our own age was that night at the Quarry. He'd been such a jerk to his friends, but his body language was a lot like this: appearing relaxed, but the hint of a predator underneath, waiting. Another mask. It's clear he isn't a fan of Ben by the set of his jaw and the cool gaze.

Ben does the same, mirroring Griffin by adjusting his shoulders, but he holds out his hand. "Hey. Nice to meet you."

Griffin takes it. "Quite a grip, Ben." The sound of his voice isn't complimentary—very Griffin.

Then Ben looks at me again, and his gaze—filled with questions and hope—makes me retreat. I put my hands in my lap and lean forward against the edge of the table.

"Are you going to that party this weekend?" Ben asks.

"I haven't decided." And if he'll be there, I will probably avoid it; I don't want to mix things up further. *He thinks you're sexy*, Renna had said, and that means he's physically attracted to me. I don't feel anything physical for him, especially when I'm sitting across from Griffin and feeling like a twinkling star in a dark sky.

"You should. It would be cool to see you there. We can dance again." Then he looks at Griffin and sort of sneer-slash-smiles. "Maybe Griffin would like to come, too."

The sarcastic way Ben has said it is condescending and rude. I lean back and offer him a condescending smile of my own. "Yeah. Maybe. And maybe not."

His smile falters, and he looks down at the table. "I'll see you in class." Ben glances at Griffin one more time before disappearing from the end of the table.

Griffin watches him leave.

I lean forward. "What was that all about?"

Griffin's eyes return to me, then crash land on the table. "You going to that party?"

"I don't know. You think I should?" I don't really care what he thinks I should do. If I want to go, I'll go, but he's confusing me, and I want to hear his answer. Then, because he's Griffin, he doesn't offer one and just shrugs. "Well, that isn't very helpful. Maybe I will."

Do I want him to be jealous? Yeah. I do. I want him to know that there are other guys who like me. I want him to look at me like Ben does. I want to grab him by the t-shirt and shake him and say, "Stop running!" But I don't.

"That guy likes you."

I know that. Renna and I have talked about it, and I don't have those same kinds of feelings for Ben. I am interested to know why Griffin has made that assessment within a couple of minutes. "He does?" I lean out of the booth to follow Ben with my gaze and then look back at Griffin like I'm enamored with the idea. "How do you know?"

His jaw sharpens. "I'm a guy. I can tell."

"Oh?" I press a hand to my chest, pretending to be an idiot. "How do you know? Was it the way he looked at me?"

Griffin seems oblivious. "Just a feeling." He just tilts his head and raises his eyebrows over his eyes.

They call the number for our pizza order over the sound system.

"I'll get it," Griffin says, then stands and rushes away.

Like he's running.

I watch him go, admire the way his t-shirt fits around his form. He's more filled out. His movement is purposeful, and there isn't anything extra about it. I look away. Watching him makes me think about what isn't mine and wish circumstances were different. I consider his behavior, the way he and Ben seemed to talk without saying a word, as if Ben thought Griffin was his competition. I wonder if Ben's reading cues I want and am missing. Is Griffin competing with Ben?

By the time we return to the dorms and Griffin parks in the lot,

I'm tense with the nerves of making that phone call to my mother. "Will you wait while I call her?" I ask.

"Sure."

I get out of the car and with a shaking hand retrieve the crushed paper in my pocket, then stare at the number for a while, contemplating. Once I cross this bridge, there's no going back, and I know that whatever happens will involve my dad. That scares me, knowing how much he once loved her, and how her return will dredge up those feelings he seems to have moved beyond. But this isn't about him, not completely.

I dial.

She picks it up immediately. "Maxwell?"

I pause, take a deep breath. "Yes."

"I was afraid you wouldn't call."

"I wasn't sure I would."

"I'm glad you did."

There's a stretch of silence. I'm not sure what to say to her.

"Would you be willing to meet me?" she asks.

I agree, and we set a time to meet the following day. When I hang up the phone, I take a breath, then turn to catch Griffin's eye. He's asleep in the car, his arms folded over his chest. His body leans against the door, his head against the window.

I text Renna to let her know I'm better, and Griffin is going to stay over.

What? THE Griffin?!?

I'll tell you everything later.

> You can't get out of it.

I lean back into the car and put a hand on Griffin's shoulder. "Griffin?"

His eyes open, and he sits up, rubbing his face. "Sorry. All squared away?"

I nod. "Come on. You're not driving home right now."

"I'm good," he says.

"I'd never forgive myself if something happened to you. Come on." I look into his backseat. "You got anything clean back there?"

"A workout bag." He grabs it and follows me to my room.

I go through my supply tote, find an extra toothbrush, and direct him to the bathroom, where he showers while I struggle to compose myself. Griffin is staying over. Griffin is sleeping in my bed. I glance at Renna's. I could ask her, but it just doesn't feel right. Honestly, I don't want Griffin that far from me.

He clears his throat as he emerges.

My chest tightens. His hair is wavy when it's wet. Darker. He's wearing athletic shorts and a fresh t-shirt. I want to jump on him. I don't. "All set?"

"Where's your roommate?" he asks, glancing at her bed.

I stand in front of him. "Her boyfriend's." I reach up and move a wet strand of hair off his cheek. "She won't be back tonight."

He swallows. "I should text my mom. Let her know I'm safe."

I nod and step around him to shower. I hurry. When I finish, I'm trembling with adrenalin as if I've just run a race. I don't know why. Nothing will happen, but the want is still there. I vow to keep my hands to myself. Griffin made it clear what he wants: *friendship*. Besides, I won't cross lines he's set just like I wouldn't want any boundaries I've set crossed.

When I walk into the space from the bathroom, Griffin is sitting at my desk. He looks as unsettled as I feel, hunched over his phone, instead of sprawled out in sleep.

"I thought you'd be asleep already." I'm glad he isn't.

At the sound of my voice, he looks up. He stalls. His eyes move over my curves, assessing, as if his gaze were his hands, wishing. His eyes stop on my hair, where I'm squeezing out the excess water with a towel.

He looks away and runs his hand over his thighs while clearing his throat. "I wasn't sure where to sleep. Figured you might have a blanket for me to set up on the floor."

I drape the towel over the edge of my hamper. "I'm not making you sleep on a hard concrete floor, Griffin. Get in the bed."

His eyes shift to me again, slightly wider.

I smile at him. "Don't worry. I'll be the perfect lady."

He offers a nervous laugh that skitters like a skipping stone over water. "Yeah." Then he pauses. "You want the inside, or should I take it?"

I slide past him and climb in, pulling the covers back, and settling in near the wall. I hold the covers open, and he sits down, his back to me. He turns out the light, and I feel him move, his warm body sliding in next to me. It's a twin bed, so our bodies touch, and my heart races ahead of itself thinking, hoping for more than it should. He's facing the opposite direction, which gives us more space.

We lay in the dark for some time, my brain spinning with him so close. I want to reach out and lay my hand against his back, but I don't. I want to ask him to turn and face me. I want to lean forward and kiss him and see where it takes us, but I don't.

Instead, I say, "Griffin?"

"Yeah?"

I swallow, trying to find my voice and working through the words I want to say to find the words I should say instead. "Thank you for being here."

"Of course. I'm like Batman. Just flash the bat signal, and I'll be there."

I huff a little laugh.

Then silence descends between us, and it's so heavy, oppressive, and palpable. I feel like I could reach out and touch it, skim it away from the surface so that I could look up and beyond to the galaxies overhead. I'm not sure I'll be able to sleep so close to him. I can smell the clean scent of his detergent but also new scents because he's used my soap. I imagine leaning forward and pressing my nose against his shoulder, pressing my body against his, wrapping my arm around his waist, and seeing if we fit together like spoons in the drawer.

"Fuck," he whispers with barely a sound, but the silence makes it sound like he's yelled it.

"What?" I ask him.

"Huh?"

"You say something?"

"I don't think so," he says.

I know he's lying, which makes me curious, but I don't press.

That's the last time any words are said. Somehow sleep finds me in spite of the way my body is coiled like a spring. I don't sleep soundly, cognizant of movement. At some point, I turn. Griffin turns. His arms find me and pull me against him. It's then I relax, settle in against him and revel in the fact that somehow, we do fit perfectly, and Griffin's warmth is what I need to find peaceful sleep.

It's the cold that wakes me up.

"Griffin?" I move, looking for him.

"I'm here." His voice is gruff.

"It's cold."

He slides from the bed and tucks the covers around me. "I'm going to go."

"What time is it?"

"Early.

I roll to look at him. "I don't want you to go."

He hits something in the dark. The chair, because it knocks against my desk. "Shit. Sorry. I have to get back." I hear the whisper of his clothes. "I have a class in a few hours."

I move to join him. "I'll get up and walk you down."

"No." I feel his weight on the bed. Maybe a hand or a knee, and he leans over me, a hand on my shoulder. "I can find my way. You sleep."

I grasp his hand, pull him toward me, and wrap him in a hug. His weight releases against me, a beautiful pressure. I nestle my face into the space between his neck and shoulder. "I miss you."

He presses his lips against my temple. "I'll text you when I get there, okay."

I nod because there aren't words to say about him leaving.

Still in my arms, he takes a deep breath, and I wonder what he wants. This, even if I'd like to lie to myself, feels like more than friendship just like it felt more than temporary months ago. I release him from my embrace, and he gets up, stands there a moment, then disappears through the dark of my room. The door shuts, and he's gone, but the essence of him lingers long after he's left.

I slip back into sleep with Griffin on my mind and in my heart.

17

I'm nervous when I walk into the coffee shop and scan for the woman who gave birth to me. Indigo is already there, sitting at a corner table, her hands wrapped around a paper coffee cup. I notice the rings on her fingers, one on her ring finger. She stands when she sees me, and I'm struck again how put-together she looks, a rose-colored sweater that looks like cashmere, dark jeans with brown boots that climb over her calves to her knees.

I stop at the table.

"Do you want to order something?" she asks.

"No." I don't think I could ingest a thing. I sit.

She sits.

We sit.

Eventually, she breaks the silence. "Thank you for meeting me."

I offer a quick nod, but now that I'm here, I don't really want to talk. This woman left me. Maybe there are extenuating circumstances, maybe she was too young, just a few years older than I am now, and maybe she was suffering with her own internal demons that I can't fathom, but she left collateral damage. I want her to know that I am strong, that I don't need her, that Dad—beyond his reasons for moving—made me who I am. I want her to know she wasn't necessary, even if I know there's a lie in there.

"How's school?" she asks, starting with small talk.

"I'm not here to do that with you," I say. "Why are you here? After all this time?"

She nods as if she was expecting this. "I needed to face this choice. My therapist suggested closing all the circles."

I feel like I've got rocks in my stomach. "So, finding me is an exercise."

Her eyebrows jump up. "I didn't mean it like that. Yes, in a way, but no." She stops, seeming to realize she isn't making sense and takes a deep breath. "I'll start from the beginning?"

I sit back in my chair and wait.

"I wasn't well then, and I was self-medicating with drugs after you were born."

"That's why you left? To do drugs?"

She sighs and looks out the window at the people walking past.

"When I met your dad, I felt whole. He was so steady and sure of things, and I was out of my mind." She looks down at her cup and rubs a thumb over the cup's sleeve. "When I was with him, I felt like a better version of myself, and thought that together we would be enough. We were—it did—for a while. When I found out I was pregnant, we got married, and I was sure it was the right thing. You were born, and a dark spot hung out in my head."

"Because of me?"

She shakes her head. "No. No. It was me. My struggle. I've always had it, that dark spot. It just kept growing and getting bigger. So, I went back to doing what I'd been doing before, using drugs to alleviate it, but it grew and grew. And as much as Cal—your dad—tried to help, he couldn't fix it, couldn't fix me or us, until all of it just made him angry and distant." She leans forward as if to correct what she's said, but her eyes never meet mine, remaining on my hands. "I don't blame him. Don't think that. I made my choices. That day I left, I didn't leave thinking I wouldn't come back. I'd planned to find a way to get rid of that dark spot, but I got stuck there."

I don't know what to say. I don't understand, but then there is nothing to be said for it, so silence seems best.

"Your dad found me, and my parents stepped in to take the reins like usual. I started rehab and therapy to face my mental struggles. During that time, I decided that I couldn't stay married to your dad because I'd married him for the wrong reasons—though he is a good man—I wasn't in any frame of mind to be a wife and mother. So, I divorced him and signed over my parental rights."

"Then why did you say he stole me. He didn't."

She swallows. "I shouldn't have said that."

"Yeah. No. You shouldn't have. It was messed up."

She has the good sense to look apologetic. "I'm sorry."

"Did you look for me?"

Her eyes flash to mine. "Yes."

But there's something in the way that she says it that has me asking, "When?"

She hesitates, and in that hesitation, I know that it wasn't the whole time. "This last year."

So, she was okay with not being in my life all of these years and hated being my mom for the first five. I take a deep breath and sit back in my chair. "Got it."

Indigo sighs and leans back, mirroring me. "This is more difficult than I thought it would be."

I narrow my eyes. "You thought it would be easy?"

She shrugs. "I thought you might be happy to see me."

"Happy to see you," I repeat. I chuckle with shock, and the flippant assumption makes me nauseous. "Let me get this straight: you left me when I was five, signed away your right to be my mother, never reached out until now, and then when you find me, you tell me my father stole me and think I'll be happy to see you?"

She bites her bottom lip.

"So within the last year, you and your therapist think now is a good time?" I ask. "Why now?"

She doesn't answer.

I look at her hand again, now draped over her folded arms. "Are you married?"

She nods.

"Do you have kids?"

"No."

"Why now?" I repeat the question

"I'm trying to save my marriage," she says. "And I'm trying to find closure."

"I am an exercise, then." And I'm so glad I didn't order anything. I grab my bag and stand.

Indigo stands too and grasps my arm. "Please don't go. There's more to say."

I stall and look at her hand. "You didn't choose to stay. You didn't choose me," I tell her and see all the ways her walking away has impacted my beliefs about myself, my hopes in her return, my thoughts about how if she couldn't see me, then no one could. The idea that I need to look to the horizon and keep walking in order to find myself. But it's been a lie. She couldn't choose me because she couldn't choose herself. And now, she is choosing herself, but I am nothing more than a therapeutic tool to achieve that end.

I look at her, and I realize I don't need her to choose me. It's the unequal equation. Dad has lived choosing me over and over again. We are the balanced equation. I suddenly understand the truth—I must choose me first, only then will I be able to choose someone else. Dad has already taught me this. I never needed Michael to choose me, or the people at every school I attended who didn't. I don't have to feel hurt by Griffin not choosing me or obligated because Ben wants to. My life is defined by the way I see myself as worthy and loveable. I can feel emboldened and joy because Cassie was my friend and Renna is now. The wisdom always existed in Cal's lessons.

I pull out of her grasp. "But I do. I choose me. And I don't know you." I turn and leave the coffee shop.

It isn't until I'm a block away and can duck into an alcove of a building that I start crying, sucking breaths like I might be dying. The emotions of the confrontation rush over me like I've been doused by a bucket of cold water. The freedom of understanding I am nothing like her despite my fears that perhaps my looking to the horizon made me so hits me with a force I don't quite understand. The absolute pain in the realization that she didn't want me. It hurts. While the clarity of the moment is that Dad—in all the difficulty of moving from place to place—has taught me what it means to stay, she reinforced the struggle to see my own worth.

I'm nothing like her.

I realize, I don't want the adventure of leaving to find myself because I already know who I am, who I come from, rather than where.

I just want my dad.

I use my phone to dial him. When he answers, all the emotion spills out all over again. "Mom's here," I cry.

A whine of a saw drowns out his words, but I catch some of them as it unwinds. "Hold on," he yells. The high-pitched careening of the saw dims. "Hey Max-in-a-million. What a surprise."

"Dad."

"Whoa. What is it, honey? Are you crying?"

"Mom's here."

"What? Shit. Oh." I can hear the panic in his voice. "Honey?"

"I'm not okay."

I can hear the rustle of movement. "I'm getting stuff together." He sounds distressed, his thought process random. "I have to move things around, make some calls. I'll be there in a few hours. Max? Deep breath. Max?"

"Yeah?"

"I'm on my way."

I take a deep breath. "Okay."

"I'll call you when I get there."

"Okay." I sniff.

"I love you."

"I love you, too," I tell him, feeling like I'm seven, and he's picked me up off of the ground.

After he hangs up, I text Griffin.

> She only showed up because I'm a therapy exercise.

> What?!?

> Yeah. She's married. No kids. And her therapist thought she should "close the circle."

> What the fuck!?!?

212

> Are you okay?

No.

> Need me to come back?

As much as I would love to see him, I text him:

Thanks. No. Dad's on his way.

> That's where he went in such a rush.
> He just gave me the next 2 days off.

Lucky you

> Not really. Means I have to sit in my
> head and think.

This makes me smile. I reply:

Brood, you mean. You're like a
professional brooder.

> Shut up.

Don't brood too hard, or you'll
screw up that gorgeous face.

> Hard.

Shut up.

I take another deep breath, feeling more balanced. My father on his way. Griffin offering comfort.

Thanks, Griffin.

213

Later, I'm sitting across from my dad at a diner. He's on edge and worried, his eyes crinkled at the edges with concern rather than humor over the top of his menu; he isn't looking at the options but keeps glancing at me.

"Know what you're getting?" I ask, hoping to defuse the tension. I know it's because he's waiting for an explanation. I still haven't told him what happened. There hasn't been an opportunity yet.

He closes the menu and sets it aside. "I can't focus on the menu. What happened? Is she here?" He looks about the restaurant as if Indigo will materialize.

"In town until tomorrow, unless she left already. I sort of walked out on her."

Dad takes a deep breath and wipes his hand over his face.

The waitress appears, and we order food. She looks at my dad with an appreciative gleam, and I realize that during my life that has happened a lot. Women see him. He either ignores it or doesn't notice. He's a handsome man, not that I thought much about it before. Tall. Dark hair. Kind, light eyes. Handsome face. Ready smile. Funny. Responsible. Respectful. He's like the perfect package; no wonder no one ever measures up if he's my pattern.

"Wells, I'm dying here," he says.

"She caught me after a class, yesterday. Asked to meet. So, I met her for coffee earlier today, before I called."

"You didn't call me yesterday?"

214

I knew this would hurt him. "I didn't know what to think. I was trying to process it."

He wraps a hand around his water glass, and takes a drink. When he sets it down, it's a little too hard and makes a loud sound. He's obviously freaking out. If my dad is anything, it's calm, cool, and collected, and those wouldn't describe him at this moment

"I was shocked and freaking out. Especially after—" But I stop. I don't want to tell him what she said. Rationally, I know it's a lie, but there's that emotional misplacing of information in my brain about all the moving making waves of my thoughts. A *what if* that I'm afraid to hear that might impact the way I see my dad.

"After what?" His brow scrunches up with the question.

"She said—" I pause, knowing there isn't a gentle way to say this— "you stole me."

He speaks with a tight jaw. "That's ridiculous. She signed over her rights."

"I know. She admitted that."

He looks out the window we're sitting next to and travels somewhere else for a moment.

I've seen my dad a myriad of ways. He's been kind and generous, determined and focused. I've seen him as a perfectionist with his work and persevere in the direst of conditions. There's his resilience in the face of raising me all by himself. I've seen him angry at me when I did something wrong that deserved discipline, but I never questioned his love. I'm watching my dad, now, distressed and distraught, emotions I can't remember growing up except once when his mother passed away.

"Dad?"

His eyes return to mine, and though he isn't crying, I can see the emotions outlining them. He shakes his head. "Please, just tell me," he says.

"She told me that she was looking for me this last year. That she needed to therapeutically close the loop."

"What the fuck does that mean?" he snaps loudly. "I'm sorry," he says, lowering his voice. "I'm not angry at you, Wells."

"Other than the fact that somehow speaking with me was supposed to be a part of her therapy in order to save her marriage, I don't know what it means."

He shifts in the booth, runs a hand over his head with sharp movement, and swears under his breath. He looks so angry, and this level of anger hasn't been something I've witnessed. Sure, he's been angry with me before—case in point: the night he discovered I snuck out—but not this agitated.

"Dad?"

His eyes fly to mine, and the edges soften. "I'm–" He stops, weighs what he's feeling but bites it, so it doesn't escape his insides. He flips what's on his mind and shines the light back at me. "How are you feeling?"

"Angry. Confused. You?"

"Angry."

"I see that."

"I put this away."

"What does that mean? Because you loved her?"

"I dealt with it, and I didn't expect her to just crop up again, but dammit, I guess I should have." He takes a deep breath and looks out the window again. "I don't love her anymore, if that's what you think. It isn't that. I haven't for a long time. But I do love you, Maxwell, and this side-swipe to use you has me livid."

Her showing up did feel like an ambush. "Was she kind of right? I know you had sole custody of me, but is that why we moved so much?"

He swallows and looks down at the table, moves his silverware from one side of the table to the other. He sighs and returns to looking out the window, and I'm not sure he's going to answer my question.

The waitress returns with our drinks and a ready smile.

Then she's gone.

"When I found your mom—"

"What do you mean, found her?"

"I looked for her. After she left. Knew her haunts and finally found her holed up in drug den, out of her mind. Called her parents, got her to the hospital, and they weren't going to hold her, but her parents got her to agree to sign herself in. They got her to agree to go to a treatment facility."

This is the most I have ever heard of this story; he's never been willing to tell me this side of things. Maybe he didn't want to paint her in a bad light because in his mind maybe abandonment was better than the realities of drug addiction. "Had she been using a long time?"

"I think she did a little before we met, like a party thing. I ignored it, even though my instincts warned me. I was willing to overlook it because I was crazy about her. When she got pregnant, and all the way until you were born, she didn't. But, after you were born, she sank into depression. It didn't matter what I did or suggested, she couldn't seem to climb out of it. She started using. I tried to help with you until I was doing it all. I tried getting her to go to therapy. I tried whatever I could think of while still trying to hold us together financially and emotionally, and I just couldn't do it all." He runs a hand through his hair. "I was only twenty-two, when you were born. Still lots to learn." He looks at me, and I can see that he feels responsible.

The unequal equation.

"It just got worse, and up to her disappearing, I was frustrated, and angry because I couldn't fix it. I kept telling myself we could figure it out, get her better. I was willing; I loved her then."

The waitress returns with our plates.

"So, she'd disappeared before?"

He nods. "Yes. Not like that last time. Hours, sometimes a day, but she'd come back, or I'd go find her. I just wanted to keep us together. But after that last time, I knew that we couldn't continue that way. I thought rehab and therapy would finally put us back together, but then the divorce papers arrived with her agreement to give you up."

Give you up. I don't think he's meant it like that, but I hear it. She gave up on him. On me. I know it isn't that simple, but it feels that simple. "And?"

"We stayed there for another year. I had hope that she might

218

change her mind. I gave her the opportunity to be your mom, reaching out after she was out. She didn't respond, and I eventually spoke with her mom—your grandmother—who said Indigo was back in treatment because she'd started using again. She hadn't been out a month. That's when I decided we—you and me—couldn't stay on the yo-yo.

"I didn't initially start out thinking we'd jump around from house to house, place to place. I thought we just needed a fresh start, somewhere new. But financially, it wasn't great. So, we moved, and moved, and moved again, until it just became our normal. I was able to work, be home with you, and make money to save. And–" He stops.

"And what?"

His gaze meets mine. "I didn't feel bad about it."

He leans back as the waitress returns with our food.

After she leaves, I ask, "Bad about what?"

"Making it more difficult to find us." He looks at his cup, twists it in front of him, and then up at me. "I would have done—will do—anything to protect you, Wells."

I get what he's saying. I do. I understand it, but a part of me begrudges it. Not him. Not his choices. I begrudge the horrible way moving felt. I hate the feeling that Indigo didn't want me, and he's here, so I take it out on him. "Well. That settles that then."

"What–"

"Just so you know, I hated moving. I hated it." I can't sit anymore. I feel itchy. I feel like my chest might be splitting open. I toss the napkin on my barely touched plate and scoot from the booth. "I hated that I never had friends. I hated that everyone teased me. I hated that we lived in dumps. I hated it. I hated it." I stand as tears streaming from my eyes.

"Wells," Dad calls after me, but I don't wait.

I escape out into the night to Rust Bucket, which I'm guessing might be on its last leg after that rushed drive.

After a few minutes clearing my emotional pipes, leaning against the truck, and moving pebbles around with my feet, my dad stops and leans against Rust Bucket next to me.

"I didn't know you hated it," he says.

I turn into him, burying my face against his arm. "I don't hate you, Dad." I mutter against his shirt.

He adjusts me so I'm under the crook of his shoulder and pulls me close. "I'm sorry."

"I'm sorry, too," I say.

He turns to face me, turning me into his embrace, and holds me. I cling to my dad, grateful he's here and strangely glad this happened. I feel clearer. Clearer about Indigo. Clearer about Dad's motives and reasons. Clearer about where I fit in all of the moving parts.

"I'm glad you're here," I tell him.

"I wouldn't want to be anywhere else," he says.

I know that's the truth.

18

"I'm so glad you're coming with us," Renna says, twisting back and forth in front of the mirror. She's dressed for the party she's insisted I come to with her and Carlos. "Ben will be glad to see you."

I slip an elastic hair tie over my wrist. "I've been avoiding him."

"Why?"

"You know why."

"Griffin?"

I don't answer, figuring the non-answer is enough of one. "I guess I want to know if there's a chance."

I'm counting down the days to going home (and I acknowledge that thinking of it this way is dangerous). October has come and gone, thankfully, and we're diving deeper into November. The Thanksgiving holiday will be the first time I've returned to the farmhouse since leaving in August, and the first time I'll see Griffin in person since he visited. I find the focus on a return perplexing given before I left, I was counting down the days to leaving, and now I'm counting down the time, excited to return. A little over a week to go.

"I get it." She grabs a jacket and her purse. "Ready?"

I follow her from the dorm room. "Do you think I'm being foolish?" I ask her.

We walk side by side down the hallway.

"No. I think if your heart is leading you that direction, then you should allow it every opportunity to know for sure."

"I hear a *but* in there."

She looks sideways at me. "What if you aren't giving someone else the chance to sweep you off your feet because you're hanging out at a dead-end?"

I don't like this question, though I also see she has a valid point. "I think I would always wonder. About Griffin." And that is why I'm so excited to return home. I will have the answer to my question about whether I'm making more of what's between us. All the texting that feels flirtatious, the FaceTime videos, the incongruous looks and tension when he visited. I'm not sure if Griffin is just avoiding it, or if he doesn't recognize his own feelings, but I have every intention of making him face it so I can know for sure how to move forward.

The house party is raging by the time we arrive, people spilling from the doorway with drunken laughter. It's dark, the inside packed, and the atmosphere electric. We pay at the door, get a stamp, and inch our way through bodies, finding the bar set up in the kitchen. I get a beer from the keg with every intention of it being the only one, then tag along with the group around the perimeter of the makeshift dance floor in the living room out to an enclosed deck. It's cold but refreshing after the interior of the house. That's where we find Carlos's friends, Ben among them.

I glance at him.

His dark eyes pause on me, then shift away, connecting to Carlos. They offer one another a bro handshake.

The bass booms, rattling the windows, and our collective group lumps up together, drinking, talking, laughing. Carlos and Renna rib each other for our amusement, intermixed with other commentary by various members of the clump. I do my best to remain present, but truthfully, I keep returning to Renna's question: *what if Griffin is a dead end?*

I glance at Ben talking with someone else, so I can actually look at him. There is a quality about Ben I like. He's steady, I suppose, and I'd be lying if I said I didn't like that he sees me, but every time I consider Ben, my feelings for Griffin get in the way. What if I am passing up a possibility?

My phone vibrates in my pocket, and when I see SK in the notification, it almost feels as if the universe has spoken to my internal meanderings.

Hey. I need help.

I smile and text him back:

> You do, SK. You good?

> All good. Eating French fries. How's Ben?

That makes me frown. I glance up. Ben's watching me. He smiles.
I offer him a polite smile back and return to my phone. I look around
imagining Griffin here, but I know he's not. He's eating French fries
somewhere.

> Ben who?

> Maybe you didn't go to that party
> since your dad showed up?

> Oh, THAT Ben.

This makes me smile wider, and my heart skitters about like a
happy dog excited I've come from being away.

> Why? Is there more than one Ben?

I can't keep the grin off of my face.

> Tons of them! I'm at a party right now.
> Ben's a few feet away staring at me
> probably thinking I'm weird because I'm
> grinning as I text you at said party. There's
> also Derek. Hank. BillyBob. The Hulk.

> Only I get to say you're weird.

> Says who?

> Me.

This is a possessive response that pushes my pulse a little faster. Though I don't want to make more of it than I should, I totally am. I look up again. Ben is still watching me. Several weeks ago, he'd acted a kind of possessive at the pizza parlor, and I hated it. Ben sips his drink, then glances at my phone. I return to texting with Griffin, hopeful that his possessive comment is one to offer me hope that perhaps his feelings for me are shifting, rather than something else.

> Can I ask you something? I need your female expertise.

This statement confuses me, since it seems uncharacteristic of Griffin. My nose scrunches, and a frown tugs at my mouth.

> My eyes just narrowed. Are you being sarcastic?

> LOL! No! I just had this girl from class text me. I'm not sure how to interpret it.

My pulse freezes. Fuck. My stomach bottoms out, and I look up again. Ben looks at me and mouths: *You okay?*

I nod, but my belly crash lands, skidding across my internal landscape, carving up my hope.

> Are you trying to make me jealous?

No. Are you?

I turn away from Ben and the group. With a finger pressed to my uncovered ear, I call Griffin. I don't have it in me to rely on my emotional text interpreter.

He answers. "I didn't call you because I thought you might be busy."

"Hold on," I tell him and leave the confines of the screened porch, pushing through a screen door into the open air of the night. "Okay. What's this about some girl calling?"

"Texting. Are you at a party?"

I walk down the steps out into a grassy yard. "Yeah. With Renna."

"How is it?"

"A party, which for the record, I don't like all that much. You're changing the subject."

The screen door creaks, and I turn to look. Ben is standing in the doorway at the top of the steps. "Everything okay?"

"Yeah." I tell him. "This is private. Thanks." I wait for Ben to disappear into the house. "Sorry about that."

"We can talk later. If you need to go."

"No! No. I want to talk to you. It's just loud and someone–" I take a deep breath, feeling like I might be unravelling. "So, a girl texted you."

"Yeah. From class. She asked me if I wanted to get together to work on class stuff, but I told her I couldn't because I work. I offered to meet her for coffee or something. She just texted me."

My heart hurts. "Why do you need me for that?" While I've been content to be his friend in other ways, I don't want to be this kind of friend.

"I don't know what it means."

I swallow, unable to speak, my heart compresses into its smallest form as everything inside me pinches closed.

"Max. You still there?"

"I'm here. Just thinking."

"Thinking what?"

I close my eyes. "She's interested in more than coffee." I stall a moment, then add, "The question is, are you?" My stomach hurts, but I take a deep gulp of my drink.

"I'm not sure."

"What aren't you sure about? It fits with all of your rules." I hate that I've said that. It sounds petty in my own ears, and I know he'll hear it. He's observant enough.

"My rules? This isn't partying. I've never gone out with a girl except... for you."

"Your rules still apply. Willing partner and all that." I look down at the ground. The grass is frosted with cold.

"I haven't been partying. I don't think that—never mind. Maybe I shouldn't have bothered you with this."

I pinch the underside of my arm to remind myself I'm living and breathing even if I suddenly feel like I'm not. It isn't my place to keep him all to myself. I can't make Griffin see me or want me, so I force myself to say, "Coffee won't hurt, I suppose, but if you aren't interested, you shouldn't string her along."

Suddenly I don't know if I'm talking about coffee-girl or me. I don't want him to choose her. I want him to choose me. This isn't about needing him to choose me, just wanting it. I want to choose him, but I can't without him being the balanced equation.

"Wait. What? I haven't answered her, yet. I'm not stringing her along."

"You suggested coffee. She might have hope."

"Are you mad?" he asks.

"Why would I be mad, SK?"

"I don't know. You seem irritated. And I don't understand what you're talking about."

I turn back to the party and sigh. I've been pining for him. Wanting Griffin to see me, and I knew. I knew and still I hoped. I sigh. *What if he's a dead-end?* "I have to go, Griffin."

"Wait! Are you coming home for Thanksgiving?" He says it in a rush.

"Yes. I'll be home."

"That's good. Your dad's been kind of a mess."

"I'm coming home." I don't add how just a few minutes ago the thought was keeping me afloat, but now, realizing that there are other girls, and that he's asking me for advice, has popped my balloon. I'm deep in the friendzone, and I'm not sure there will be a way out. The image of him with another girl crushes me.

"My mom invited you guys over for Thanksgiving dinner. If you're interested. Your kitchen is being torn out this week, so you might have to take me up on it."

I look up at the sky. It's overcast, the clouds backlit by the moon. I wish I could see it more clearly, see everything more clearly. "Great."

The silence stretches a few seconds too long. "Are you sure you're not mad?"

"Not mad. Thanks for the invitation. I'll be sure to tell my dad."

"I'll see you in a couple of weeks, then."

We hang up, and I stand there in the cold, numb to it, looking at the frozen grass. The hope and excitement I felt about going home has slowed and frozen inside me as well. While I'm still looking forward to returning to a place and seeing my dad, I'm afraid to see Griffin. Afraid that maybe I've put hope in signals I've misread that would have him choose me. That he would see me—Maxwell Wallace—and he might reciprocate my feelings.

The screen door opens again. "Max?"

I look up. It's Ben. Ben likes me. Feisty me. He sees me and is interested.

What if you aren't giving someone else a chance to sweep you off your feet because you're hanging out at a dead-end?

I walk up the steps, and cute Ben hands me a drink.

"I thought you might be ready for another," he says and smiles.

"Thanks," I tell him and take a sip, willing my brain to have a talk with my heart so I can forget Griffin. I'm confused, jealous, angry and unsure, and these are unfamiliar feelings that make navigation unwieldy.

"Is everything okay." His head tilts, inviting me to share.

"Yeah. Just trying to figure some stuff out for myself," I say.

"You want to talk?" he asks. "I'm a good listener."

I shake my head. "Not really." I take another sip and follow him back into the screened porch, where I settle next to him against a wall. People move about the room, the vibe lively. I will my heart to engage here, to be here, instead of hundreds of miles away with Griffin who's been invited to coffee with a girl from his class that he hasn't said 'yes' to. Maybe I've overreacting, but I can't seem to climb out of the spiral.

What if he's a dead-end?

Ben's shoulder bumps mine as someone moves past, bumping him. "Sorry," he says.

What if you aren't giving someone else a chance?

I allow my gaze to meet Ben's. "I'd love to dance," I tell him. It's out of my mouth before I can take it back, and I know it's motivated by hurt and bitterness.

He grins, takes our cups, sets them down on the windowsill. With my hand in his, he leads me back into the house, into the crowd of moving bodies. We dance, bodies pressed together, laughing, and all the while I imagine Griffin doing this with coffee girl, and my heart aches. So, when Ben kisses me later, I kiss him back. His kiss is enjoyable, but I can't help wishing that he was Griffin, and I hate myself for it.

19

My dad waiting at the bus stop fills my body with relief. For the last week, I've been leaking emotions of dread. Feeling undone by the arrival of my mother and the tender exposure of my insecurities about Griffin have stripped me down to my naked truth. I am not as put together as I'd like to think. While my dad sees me as I am—or so I'd like to believe—he is like a lighthouse in the storm of this increased self-awareness.

He takes my bag, wraps an arm around me, and presses a kiss

against my head. "It's so good to see you," he says.

"It's nice to be back."

He drops the bag into the back of Rust Bucket.

"RB is still kickin," I say.

"Ole Reliable here is stubborn enough to outlast me," Dad says, climbing in behind the steering wheel. He starts the truck, and it rocks itself to life. "But, I may have to cave for a new truck sooner than later, however."

We drive through town toward the farmhouse.

"It's strange being back," I say as the buildings on the main street slide past. A coffee shop, a bookstore, an ice cream parlor and a dozen office spaces. A clothing shop, a bank, and a hardware store. I scan for faces I recognize, though I'm aware I don't really know any.

"Why's that?"

"It's the first time I've returned. To anywhere."

"We returned to visit Grandmee," he says, referencing his mother who passed away two years ago.

"Doesn't count," I say. "That counts as a visit. This is where you live."

He seems to chew on that, going silent, then says, "I've been thinking about what you said."

"About?"

"Hating all the moves."

I want to jump in and tell him I'm sorry about that, but then the truth is I'm not. I'm sorry for hurting him, but not with offering the truth. "Yeah?"

"It just got me thinking, Max. I can't change the past, but I can think about what's next, I suppose."

I look at him, and he glances at me with a tentative smile. "I want you to think about you for once, Dad. What you want. You've chosen me the last almost-nineteen years."

He looks like he wants to say something but clamps his mouth shut and nods.

When the farmhouse comes into view, I sit forward. "Wow. Dad! It looks beautiful!" Rather than the dilapidated haunted house ready to fall down, this looks like a gorgeous home that might be featured in a magazine, with perfect white paint, black trim and matching shutters. The front porch is painted to match the house, with a new black front door without the giant crack. "Wow. Dad!"

"I told you."

I hear the smile in his voice and look to see it on his face. "You did. But eight weeks?"

He chuckles. "Yeah. We've only started making headway inside."

We. He's said *we*. It makes me think of Griffin and how much a part of our lives he is.

"It's all torn up, so we're living with a hot pot and out at restaurants while you're home, but we've been invited to Griffin's for Thanksgiving."

My heart flutters. "Okay."

"You okay with that? I mean, we haven't really ever been invited to a Thanksgiving except when we went to visit Grandmee way back when. I know it's always just been us."

"I'm good with it, Dad," I say. I give him a reassuring smile and realize it's the truth. Regardless of what my feelings are for Griffin, his importance in our lives isn't going away. Thinking about it from an objective space, his feelings aren't in opposition to mine, I know that. His feelings are his and about what he needs, even if it might hurt because they don't match mine; I just have to be prepared to accept whatever they are. "It will be fun."

When the door opens to Griffin's house on Thanksgiving, I'm using my dad as a shield, hiding behind him. My heart races. I'm so nervous to see Griffin. Waking up in his arms, the memory of his body pressed to mine and fantasies of possibilities, has sustained me. Now that there's a coffee-girl, and I've kissed Ben—not that it means I'm *with* Ben—I'm apprehensive. Nervous, because I know my feelings for Griffin will be written on my face and shouldn't be. Anxious, because even though I kissed Ben, I can't get Griffin out of my head and heart. Apprehensive, because I don't know if he's brought coffee-girl to Thanksgiving, and what if he did?

My dad steps into the house I've visited once, leaving me exposed on the step outside the door.

Griffin's gaze moves over me. It's slow enough that I feel it like a touch.

"Hey, SK," I say.

"Happy Thanksgiving." He offers a half-smile and clears his throat.

I step closer, suddenly afraid to touch him. Unsure of myself, which I know is weirder than usual. I'm the girl who sits with strangers at tables, not giving a fuck.

He leans closer, and he smells so good, just like my imagination conjured to sustain me. Clean, like soap and spice.

"Close the door. It's cold," a man across the room says, and I have a feeling it's Griffin's brother. They resemble one another, though Phoenix is obviously older, a touch shorter and has tattoos. It makes me wonder if Griffin has any tattoos. I don't remember ever seeing any, but I've only seen him without his shirt once in the dark at the Quarry. I hadn't looked for any then.

I step in, and Griffin shuts the door behind me. He introduces me to Phoenix, and I follow Griffin into the kitchen, where Dad is talking with another man and a woman Griffin introduces as his mom and her friend, Bill.

Griffin's eyes meet mine, and we leave the old-people conversation behind to stop at the table already set with place settings, cranberry sauce, a dish of olives. I reach for the olives and place one on the tips of each of my fingers, then wiggle them at Griffin to lighten the mood with my silliness. Mostly to help myself find some balance more than anything else.

"I love olives."

"I don't think I've done that since I was a kid."

"You're missing out then." I bite one from my finger.

Griffin's eyes watch my mouth.

I can feel the look as much as if he stepped closer, my lungs dropping into my belly at his perusal. Then I chastise myself for imagining it.

Coffee-girl, I remind myself.

"How are things with your dad?" he asks.

"Fine." I shrug and eat another olive.

He indicates that I should follow him and leads me down the tight hallway. There are a few hanging pictures I wanted to look at last time I was there. I peruse them as I walk by. Small Griffin is gawky and adorable. Then I walk into a room and pass Griffin, who has stopped to watch me. I sit on the twin bed and look around. Plain faux-wood paneled walls without any decoration, a dresser with stuff strewn on the top, a closet—closed—and the bed with a blue comforter neatly made. It's so sterile, not how I would have pictured Griffin's space.

"You sure you're okay?" His eyes are on his hands in his lap as he messes with his fingers.

"It's good. Dad and I talked." I'm able to admire Griffin in his navy collared shirt and jeans—so handsome. His manners are different from the last time I saw him, but I'm not sure why. He's a little more tentative. Nervous. These are things I can understand since I'm feeling them too, but I know why I am; I don't know why he might be.

"Still upset at him?"

"No. I wasn't really ever upset at him. Just the circumstances, you know. Indigo disappeared like I figured she would, and I realized that's what he was trying to protect me from."

He joins me on the bed, and I turn to face him.

"He misses you. And when he got back, whatever happened shook him up."

"Yeah. I understand. It shook me too. He's all I've got."

Griffin looks up from his hands in his lap. His eyes are grayer and bluer today than green and gold. Darker. His mouth is as kissable as always, slightly frowning, and I pull back on the instinct to kiss him like I did back in August, even if the desire is still there.

"You have me," he says.

My gaze fuses with his, and his words don't assuage the urge to kiss him, so I turn away and press my hands down into my lap. "I'm glad."

I stand and move into the center of the small room to put some distance between us. "So, this is SK's room." I look at him over my shoulder. He leans back onto his hands, and I notice how the shirt stretches across his chest, his shoulders wider and rounded with muscle. "This doesn't look like a serial killer's room." I offer him a smile.

"That's because it isn't. What does a serial killers bedroom look like?"

"Oh. Full of all the news clippings about their nefarious activities."

"Nefarious? Speak English," he teases.

"I am. Sinister. Come, SK. But there isn't much here. It doesn't reflect you. Where are your posters? Trophies? Pictures of friends?"

He glances around and sits back up. "I took down the one poster I had."

I smile. "I bet I can guess what it was."

His eyebrows rise up with challenge.

I put a finger to my cheek, thinking about the boy I met four months ago, then I return to sit on the bed. "A picture of a hot girl in a scandalous bikini."

He smiles. "Close."

"And a car."

He chuckles now. "Closer."

"Why did you take it down?"

"It just didn't feel like it belonged anymore."

I look away from him, unable to squelch the sparkles effervescing in my belly at our proximity.

"Would you like me to take your sweater?"

"Sure." I stand and draw it off of my shoulders.

Griffin stands up behind me to help.

I turn my head, surprised when his fingertips graze my bare skin. Electricity travels my nerves, zapping energy through me. The sizzle. I look up at him and freeze.

He's looking down at me, his face bare of the mask. I can see his feelings, and the way I feel is reflected back at me. Now, I know how his manners are different; he sees me. I shiver, affected, and shrug back into the sweater, afraid I've misread him, that I'm seeing what I want to see.

He doesn't move. "Max."

My name. He's said my name, and I don't know why he's said it. I draw my hair out from the collar and turn toward him. "Griffin?"

He steps closer, and any closer we could feel one another's heartbeats. Mine's racing, my breath shallow, and I think perhaps his might be too. The tension between us is stretched like the truth just on the edge of a lie. I curb the impulse to close the gap, step into what

I think might be the truth, just to end the torture. But my risk didn't work so well last time. I can't risk it again.

"I'm afraid," he says, so quietly I almost can't hear him.

I take another step closer. "Me too." His heat radiates across the distance that separates us. I squeeze my fingers into a fist to keep from placing my hand on his chest.

He reaches out and takes a strand of my hair in his fingers. Watches it slide against his fingers, then looks at me as he places his palm against my cheek.

I lean into his touch.

He leans closer to me, and I think he's going to kiss me! Not coffee-girl. Me!

"I want to kiss you," he whispers.

"Hey!" A voice pops the tension as if it were a balloon.

I whirl toward the voice.

Griffin's brother, Phoenix, stands in the doorway, grinning at us like he knows what's up. "Dinner."

"Okay," Griffin says from behind me.

Antsy and unsure, I move toward the door, afraid to hope that what I think happened really did happen. Had Griffin admitted he wanted to kiss me? I'm afraid I imagined it, afraid to look at him. He'll see my soul laid bare.

"Ready," he asks and touches my shoulder.

I nod, steal a glance, and I'm overheating. "Starving," I say, but it isn't for the food, and I'm not sure how to fake it.

Thanksgiving dinner is a cozy affair. Griffin's mom, Kat, has set up the food on the bar between the dining room and the kitchen. Six of us scoot in around the oval table. I have my dad on one side of me and Griffin on the other. It's a tight squeeze between them, and in all honesty, after what just happened in Griffin's bedroom, my awareness is zeroed in on him.

I attempt to follow the track of the conversation, answer questions that come my way, smile, laugh, do all the things appropriate while a dinner guest. Mostly, I'm thinking about Griffin on my right, and his left forearm resting on the table near my right hand. If I just stretched out my fingers, I could graze him, but I don't. Obviously.

When I lift my eyes from my plate and take a peek at him, he's looking at me.

He gives me a smile and looks back at his plate.

My heart is no longer listening to my rational brain wondering if I'm setting myself up for disaster. What if I've misread things? I'm intelligent, however. I don't think I have. Griffin said, "I want to kiss you," so it can't be plainer than that. Of course, he could change his mind, but the electricity arcing between us would indicate that he hasn't.

After dinner, I help Griffin with the dishes. We stand side by side, saying very little other than small talk or directives about our shared cleaning endeavor. Our arms graze because we're standing close to one another. With each touch, the energy zips with the speed of light through my nerves straight to my heart, which heats the rest of me.

Griffin clears his throat as though he wants to say something, but he doesn't. Instead, he hands me another bowl to dry.

"Where should I put this?" I ask when I'm done drying it. I turn my head to look at him.

He moves to show me. "In here." It seems he's trying not to touch me as he reaches around my body to open the cabinet door.

I turn, and my hip and back come in contact with him.

He stalls. Stays. One of his hands finds my hip, and his touch lingers. He leans closer.

Heat pools through me, around me, rushing across my skin. I rise up onto my tiptoes and reach to place the dish where I find matching dishes nested inside the cupboard. Griffin doesn't move, keeping his hand where it is.

When I'm done, I glance at him. He's watching me, that look from his room still etched on his features.

I turn toward him. "Griffin?" I ask. I want to figure this out.

He clears his throat again and steps away, flustered, submerging his hands into the soapy water. "Sorry."

I swallow and return to face the same direction as him, drying dishes he's washed. I want to have this talk, to rush through it so I know what's happening, afraid of being wrong. But instead of allowing my impatience to lead me, I focus on the moment and say quietly, "Are you? Sorry?"

I note his hands stop washing the dish in the sink water. I follow the contours of his arms up to his shoulders, up over his neck and jaw, to his eyes, which are studying me.

Griffin gives his head a shake. *Not Sorry*, his eyes tell me. Then he offers a smile though it's subdued and more reflective of early Griffin only without all of the walls. That one was angry; this one is just unsure.

My insides inflate and float, and I am content, for the moment, to just be next to him, washing dishes and knowing he wants to kiss me, be near me. But I miss the banter. The quiet between us, the uncertainty and this tension are new and make me want to find that easy interaction to melt it away.

Before we can have a conversation, however, my dad is ready to leave, and though I'm sure Griffin would be willing to take me home so we could talk (and maybe other stuff, like kissing), I'm not confident with my own processing to actually share what's on my heart. Truthfully, I'm scared, which maybe shouldn't be a surprise given my lack of experience in this area of my life. I realize that my bravery and boldness are readily available when there's nothing on the line. Even with Michael, who I cared for, but see now the superficiality of my feelings, I wasn't really risking much. Now, however, my heart is exposed, and Griffin has the power to eviscerate it. I'm not only risking the heart of me, but a friendship that means so much.

Our goodnight is rushed and stilted.

"That was nice," Dad says as we're driving home. He flips on the windshield wipers as snowflakes begin to pepper the glass.

"Yes," I say to respond rather than to what he's said.

"Everything okay?" he asks.

"Hmm? Oh. Yes. Sorry."

"You seem a million miles away."

I smile. "I wasn't." I was actually just a few miles back. "Just thinking."

"Feel like talking?"

Do I? Maybe, but I don't want to talk to him about Griffin, not when I don't understand things for myself yet. I don't want to unnecessarily complicate their relationship. So, I give him a partial truth. "I have some school stuff to do for next week. I was thinking about that."

Dad reaches over the seat and takes my hand. "I'm glad you came home."

"Home." I repeat and look up from our hands to his face. "I like the sound of that."

20

After my run—which was cold—breakfast at a diner with Dad, and a stop at the grocery store, I text Griffin:

> When are you coming to get me?

He doesn't answer right away, and I wait. The longer the time stretches, the more I wonder if I imagined the night before, but I know I didn't. I know the chill of awareness that raced across my skin wasn't my imagination. That his gaze, his pulse, his words—*I want to kiss you*— weren't in my imagination. The weight of his hand on my hip. Admitting he wasn't sorry. No. I know what happened as clearly as my breath puffed steam as I ran.

When my phone finally pings, I nearly launch off my bed for it.

Now.

Dress warm. We're going out.

I do a little dance in my room, get redressed into something more conducive to both looking good and being warm, then go downstairs where my dad tinkers with some side project. Everything is a mess, especially the kitchen, which is just a shell, but we have nice new clean walls that need paint, which I've volunteered to help cover this weekend.

Dad looks up from his project. "You look nice."

I twirl in my favorite green sweater for him.

"Where are you going?"

"Griffin's coming to get me."

He sets down the tool and looks over the frame of his glasses at me. "Griffin." He hums a noise and shifts his glasses back on so he can study the project again.

"Why? You like Griffin."

"I do. I do."

"Dad. We're friends." Which isn't a lie. We are one hundred percent friends, and nothing has actually occurred between us other than my ill-advised, one-sided kiss.

He harrumphs like he's not buying it and looks up at me. "I remember when you told me that you and that Michael kid were just friends."

"Dad. Michael again? Griffin isn't like Michael, and we are just friends."

"I like Griffin more than that other kid. What are you going to do?"

"Play tourist." I pick through a cooler that holds our groceries to make some sandwiches for lunch. Our make-shift kitchen makes this a challenge. "We're going to a park."

Dad watches me rather than resuming his work on the radio or clock, whatever it is he's fiddling with. "Which park?"

"Grossman's Bend."

"That's quite a ways away."

I give him a sound of vague agreement.

"And it's supposed to snow. Maybe you shouldn't go so far away."

"Griffin's car has four-wheel drive. And he's a very good driver."

"What if there's a blizzard. You might get stuck."

"Not in the forecast. I checked. Besides, if that happens, we'll have each other for body heat."

He gives me a vexed look. "Hilarious, Max. I'm laughing uncontrollably on the inside."

I smile at him. "Dad. I'm smart."

"I know."

"Then don't worry."

He swallows, watches me a bit longer, then nods. "Okay."

I don't wait for Griffin to park the car when he pulls into the driveway. I grab my backpack, the small cooler, kiss Dad's cheek, and hightail it from the house out into the cold.

Griffin has opened the car door and stands just inside of it. "What's all that?"

"A surprise. Just open the back." I slide the cooler and backpack under the hatchback and turn to look at Griffin. He's wearing a dark green hoodie. We match. Again. Blue the night before. Now green. "That doesn't look very warm."

"I brought a jacket," he says and closes the back hatch.

"Where am I driving," he asks when he climbs in behind the wheel and starts the car.

"The Bend."

He turns in the seat. "What? It's freezing. And it's supposed to snow."

"Scared?" I know he can't handle the challenge, appealing to his competitive nature.

He turns back to the wheel. "You know you can't dare me like that. I'll bite every time."

"Let's go then."

The visitor center is deserted because it's winter. Wrapped in our jackets and carting my stuff, we step around the gate and make the hike. The sounds of our conversation and our footfalls on the frozen earth are muted under the overcast sky. It isn't windy and strangely feels warmer. The ghost town looks even emptier, which is weird, but November, almost December, presses in against its edges with stark winter versus warm summer.

"What made you think of this?" Griffin asks as we traipse through the town.

Snow has begun to fall, intermittent flakes, and I remember last time it rained.

The truth is that I'd dreamt about it, which compelled me to return. "I woke up thinking about it."

"What about it?"

I'm leading him to the building where we waited out the rain. I shrug. I don't have a reason, other than I just wanted to create a new memory with him. The last time we were here, he'd been emerging from his shadow self. Now, he's so much more fleshed out. But I don't say those things.

"Let's see if anything has moved," I tell him and lead him to the house, then the saloon.

Everything is the same.

"It's like it's frozen in time."

"Like us? Right now?" I turn my face to look at him.

He meets my gaze, waits a moment, and nods.

"Did you expect it to be different?"

"Yeah. No. I mean, I knew it wouldn't be, but it feels like it should look different."

Snowflakes fall, big ones, and the sound has dimmed around us so that it feels like only Griffin and me in the world. I watch as the flakes fall in his hair and melt away, collect in his lashes and melt. I nod. "I get it."

When we get into the building, the space is cool, but it's insulated from the frigidity of winter. Lit by the openings at each end, the building feels hushed, isolated, and safe with us inside. "Here," I say and set the backpack down. I unzip it and withdraw a gray blanket, fluffing it out near the place we sat the last time we were here.

"What is happening?" Griffin asks.

"A picnic." I glance at him.

"In November?"

"What did you think?"

His eyes shift away. "You probably don't want to know."

The words touch my body with warm edges, and I suppress a shiver. "Put the cooler here," I tell him to distract myself.

He does and sits after I do.

I set out the food I've made: sandwiches (turkey and cheese), sliced veggies, fruit that's easy to eat on the go, and some sparkling cider. "Ta da," I say.

"Wow. You put my sandwiches to shame."

I offer him a grin. "But those were some incredible PB&J sandwiches. Best I ever had."

"Liar."

"Never," I tell him, then say, "I think I woke up thinking about this place because I woke up thinking about your name. This is where you told me about it."

He looks at me with a question mark on his face.

"I mean, to answer why here." I take off my jacket, now warm, and set it aside. "Last time we were here, you told me your name meant 'monster.'"

He removes his jacket and adjusts the strings of his hoodie. "Yeah.

249

That's a weird thing to think about and not particularly confidence building for me."

I can't help but laugh. "I looked it up."

"You did?"

I'm afraid I've revealed too much but keep going. "You know it doesn't just mean monster, right?" I hand him a sandwich. He takes it and shakes his head. I continue. "Did you know that a griffin was considered a majestic creature in mythology? That really, in most articles, the griffin wasn't really a monster at all, but a powerful guardian of priceless treasures?"

"Really? A guardian of treasures, you say?"

I pour him some cider. "Yep." I hold out the cup, and he takes it.

"That's definitely better than a monster." I watch him set down the cup, then flip the wax-paper covered sandwich in his hands. He's thinking. I've learned this about him. Movement equals processing. His gaze jumps from the sandwich to mine. Thought loaded. "And that's what made you think about coming out here?"

I stall. There is an unsaid question in what he's actually asked. I hear it, and I sit back onto my legs. I wonder if I should tell him what I'm really thinking? If I should take the risk again, but in a more mature way, less about impulse and more about the nature of feelings running under my skin. I would want that of him, so I say, "I thought about how I wished I'd told you about what I'd been really thinking last time. A do over."

"And what's that?"

I start to tell him, but my throat closes. I look at all of the food and deflect instead. "Let's eat."

"Scared?" he asks with a grin.

I grab a carrot stick and munch on it, smiling around the food.

While we eat, we talk. I replay what happened with Indigo and my dad in more detail than what happens over text and FaceTime. He tells me about school and work.

"And the girl? Did you go to coffee with her?" I hate that my insecurity is on display.

He fiddles with the now empty cup. "Nah."

"How come?"

"I didn't want to. I realized I have feelings for someone else. Wouldn't want to string her along."

I make a noise and busy myself with cleaning up to hide how happy that makes me. So, so happy. Griffin helps me pick up the remnants of our picnic, returning items and trash into the cooler.

We talk about what's left to do this semester before finals and all the homework that I have to accomplish over the weekend, moving back and forth between the blanket and the cooler. Until we both reach into the confines of the space, and our hands crash together.

My breathing changes, moving like a springtime creek, fast and shallow.

I don't move, but I look up at him.

He doesn't retreat and instead runs a thumb over my skin, but he's staring at our hands.

I grab his hand and pull it out with mine. Pushing the cooler aside, I move closer to him so we're facing one another. "The last time we were here—"

"What were you thinking?" Griffin asks, returning to the earlier question.

I turn my hand in his so our palms touch and thread our fingers together. "That if I'd been braver—" I look from our joined hands to his face. I'm afraid, but I can't hold it in anymore. "If I'd been braver, I would have told you that I couldn't stop thinking about you. I would have told you I like you. I would have admitted that every time I called you a silly name, it was because I was afraid."

He catalogues my face with his eyes, lingering, memorizing. "Afraid?"

"Because every time I say your name, it's a tattoo that I feel." I reach over with my free hand and press it over his heart. I can feel its strong, racing beat under my hand. "Here."

He draws me closer.

I shiver.

"Are you cold?" He brings a palm to my cheek.

I shake my head and lean into his touch, our hands still joined, my other one over his heart. "Are you still scared?" I whisper back.

He moves his hand over my cheek, caresses my jaw with his thumb, his eyes tracking his movement. He nods.

"How come?"

"I don't want to fuck this up," he says.

"Then don't."

We meet in the middle, his gorgeous mouth and mine. This time it's mutual, both of us wanting this kiss. He moves his hands to frame my face, and I wrap my arms around him, holding him against me. I think there has never been a more perfect moment. How beautiful it feels to be chosen back.

21

"I get to meet him this time," Renna insists as she finishes packing a bag.

Griffin is coming to stay the weekend with me. He's done with finals. I still have a week and a half, and that just feels too long to go without being in the same space. Kissing. My stomach trembles and the rest of me grows hot and melts. We haven't really crossed many other physical boundaries mostly because of space and time, but I want to. Bad.

Renna has agreed to give me the dorm room. She's going to Carlos's place, but she's adamant about getting some FaceTime with who she's calling "the character."

"Look. You're one of my best friends, Max. I need to meet this character and determine if he is good enough for you."

I smile at her. "Best friends?" She doesn't know what those words mean to me.

"Yes. Sisters from other misters. Goodness. Does this surprise you?"

"No. And I would love for you to meet him."

She flips her hand at me. "Good. There's a party tonight. You should both come with."

I grimace. "Will Ben be there?"

She shrugs. "Does it matter?"

While I know it doesn't (though I do feel a little bad about kissing him when my heart was elsewhere), I don't want anything to interfere with my time with Griffin. "They've kind of met, and it wasn't great."

"Ben will be fine. Even if he's jealous—or whatever—he'll deal. And he's cute so I'm sure he'll find another honey." She grins. Then she folds her hands together and bats her eyelashes at me. "Please."

"Fine."

My phone pings. It's Griffin:

Here.

I give a little squeal of excitement, twirl a little. "He's here."

"You've got it bad," she says and clicks her tongue while she finishes packing.

I escape through the maze and down the stairwell, move through the door, down the sidewalk, and into his arms. I kiss him, hands in the hair at the nape of his neck because it's been over a week, and his mouth meets mine with equal fervor. His hands frame my face, and our tongues speak of all the ways we missed each other.

"I. Missed. You," I tell him between kisses.

He leans back, still holding me. "I missed you, too."

I wait for him to grab his bag, impatient to touch him, but he takes my hand, so I don't have to wait long. We move through the dormitory together, filling one another in on the minutiae of our daily lives until we make it to my room.

Renna turns to watch us walk inside, and I introduce her. She lifts her chin.

"Hi," Griffin says. "Thanks for letting me crash here."

I heat, thinking about later. "Renna's staying with her boyfriend, Carlos."

Renna looks at me with a knowing smile. "No problem. It's nice to finally meet you. I've heard a lot about you."

Griffin's eyes hit mine, and he looks worried. "Nothing bad, I hope."

"What bad is there?" Renna narrows her eyes.

"Nothing." He draws out the word as if he isn't sure if it's a trick question.

I jump in. "We're going with Renna to a party tonight. Okay?"

He nods. "Whatever you say."

Renna smiles. "I like him. That was the right answer."

The party isn't where I want to be. It's yet another house filled with strangers, music thumping against walls and bodies, drinking, singing, everything loud. I want to be alone with Griffin, but if I get to dance with him, then I suppose the detour will be worth it. We both get a drink, and I notice that Griffin's face is masked.

"You're frowning," I say into his ear.

Ben passes us to get to the drinks. He looks at me, then at Griffin, and after offering a polite 'hello,' keeps moving.

I breathe a sigh of relief.

Griffin glances at Ben's back, and I wonder if he remembers him, but he smiles at me and pulls me closer. "I'm good. I'm here with you." He kisses my cheek.

I lead him to the dance floor.

I want to feel his body against my hands.

I want to move with him.

Though we're surrounded by other people, dancing feels good. It's as if it's only us feeling the beat, moving to the rhythm with one another. The chaos around us fades. All I feel are his hands on my hips, my arms curled around his shoulders, his mouth nipping at my neck.

I watch the clock. Countdown the minutes before we can make an escape.

We dance.

Drink a beer. Chat it up with Renna and Carlos.

Dance some more.

"I'm so glad you're here," I say into his ear, competing with the noise.

He pulls me closer.

"Do you want to get out of here?" I ask him.

Griffin nods, and I lead him from the house.

We burst out into the cold December night, bodies steaming, not only because of the warm house. We slide our way across campus, laughing and touching, stopping to kiss. By the time we get into the dark dorm room and through the door, Griffin pulls me back against him. "Max," he says, and it's weighted with desire.

I shiver both with cold and with unspent energy that's been building all night.

He devours me. "I've thought about this all night."

I revel in his mouth with mine. "Me too."

Every part of us collides.

Every atom leaning toward the positive charge of us. Hands roaming, mouths and tongues meeting, exploring, moving deeper into the room toward the bed, until we're both stretched out on it, together. Two cells combined.

"Griffin." I breathe his name, rolling him to his back. His hands on my hips guide me astride him. I can feel his hardness pressed between my legs. *Hard.* I smile, but it's short lived because the pleasure I feel as I move against him makes me gasp.

We're still dressed, but I draw my shirt from my body and rock my hips.

He moans. "Max." His hands grip my hips to still me, then his calluses leave a perfect trail over my skin. When his hands tease the lace of my bra, I lean into him, and he rolls me over. I spread my legs so he can settle between them. I wish our clothes were off. I tug at his shirt, and he removes it. "I wanted to do this to you last time I was in your bed." He breathes the words through the pleasure of our movement and finds my lips again. Kisses me breathless, moves against me so I'm keep myself afloat by holding onto his shoulders as if he's my life raft.

"You did?" I ask when his mouth strays. His words wind me up.

"Yes," he says against my collar bone.

"You didn't."

"I didn't want to ruin things."

With my hands framing his face, I draw him back up to mine. "You say that a lot."

"What?"

"That you ruin things." I tilt my hips toward him, and Griffin sucks in a breath.

"Max. You're making me crazy. It's been a while."

"Why do you say you'll ruin things?" I wrap my legs around his jean clad hips.

He grasps my hips to stop me moving and freezes. He looks at me. "Max. I want you."

I rise up onto my elbows. "Answer my question, Griffin." With a hand against his chest, I push him until he's on his back. I kiss his jaw, his throat, move my way down his chest. "Tell me."

I continue. Lower. Tongue and mouth creating a song against his skin. I've done this before, poorly, in a basement while Captain Kirk and Spock tried to save Bones. *Bones.* I suppress a laugh. I want to give this to Griffin, to do it better and with power. I stop at his waist and unbuckle his belt.

He looks at me. "Oh fuck, Max."

"I want to know," I tell him. "May I?" I ask. "Kiss you here?"

"Max. Yes." He helps me remove his pants.

I take him in my mouth and offer him pleasure in exchange for intimacy. "Why?" I lick, grip, suck, kiss. I make him combustible.

"I can't. I can't think." His hands are in my hair, and he's panting. "I don't say the right things. I don't do the right things." He's saying my name. "Max. I use people. I ruin things."

I don't stop.

He doesn't either. "They leave me. I push. They leave. They leave me." He tries to pull me back up the closer he gets to his release, but I resist, committed to seeing this through, wanting to give to him my devotion. I will stay. I will stay.

He gasps, curling around me as he spends himself, holding on like I am his life raft. When his body relaxes, I kiss my way back up his skin, replaying the song. Once I'm level with his face, he has his arm shielding his eyes, hiding.

"Griffin," I say and move his arm to make him look at me.

He does, and I can see his eyes shining in the dim light of the room. I don't know if they are tears or just reflections of his emotion, but he grasps me and holds me against him in a fierce hug.

"Can I kiss you," I ask, unsure if maybe doing so would cross a boundary. Michael had been repulsed by the idea.

He adjusts, grabs my face and kisses me senseless—again.

He rolls me onto my back, then follows the trail on my body I made on his, but I hold him steady when he kisses my belly. "Is this okay, Max?" he asks, his head tipped up to look at me.

"I'm a little scared," I confess. "I haven't done this before." The adventures in the basement to the soundtrack of Star Trek were one-sided.

"I won't if you don't want me to."

"What if you don't like me. You know. After?"

He moves, rising up and over me so that our faces are level with one another. "That's an impossibility," he says and kisses me until it's impossible to string coherent thoughts together. "Can I make you feel like you made me feel?" he asks against my skin.

"Yes," I breathe.

He retraces the path, slow and sensual with lips and tongue, making me burn, until his mouth settles between my thighs. His mouth works magic, slow and sensual, savoring, so that all my thoughts and insecurities flee. I float, becoming only me, existing in the moment, with Griffin and nothing else between us.

After we're both satiated, we cuddle on my bed, legs entwined, and my hand moving in a rhythm over Griffin's chest. He feels a million miles away. "What do you think?" I ask, referring to his earlier statement about people leaving. He doesn't answer, and I wonder if he's asleep. "What do you think?" I repeat.

"About what?"

"Have you heard a word I've said?" I ask.

"Sorry. Kind of zoned out."

"Griffin!" I give him a playful smack.

He grasps my wrist and twists me until I'm lying on my back underneath him. He swivels his hips, and I moan.

"Max. You feel so good." He leans down and kisses me again.

I want to have sex with him, but I also can feel the fill-in-the-blanks of things still needing to be settled between us, which pushes my brain and mouth toward talking. "You know, before?" I ask, going backward because this feels very important and needs attention.

He growls and leans down, kissing my neck.

"I'm not going anywhere."

He stops, raises his head and looks at me.

"What you said about everyone leaving. I'm not going anywhere."

He sighs, his head dropping forward so that his hair tickles my nose. Then he sits up, rocking back to sit on his heels. "You can't say something like that. No one can."

"I can. I know myself. At least not without a serious conversation." I smile at him, reaching out to touch him. Maybe this relationship wasn't what I expected. Perhaps I'd set up expectations in my head about college and finding home that were inaccurate, but I'm confident that I am more my dad than my mom. I choose Griffin, and I want us to be the equal equation. "I'll follow the rules."

He turns and sits on the edge of the bed, running a hand through his hair. "It wouldn't be because of you, though." He glances at me. "Remember the night at the Quarry?"

I nod.

"Most of the shit I told you about the douchey guy, everything you heard from those girls in the bathroom. It was true. I have told lies to get what I wanted. I've gotten so drunk I couldn't stand up. I've used drugs. I've used girls. I used my friends. I pushed my best friends away because I didn't want to listen to them." He looks away. "You see? It's me."

I sit up and situate myself next to him. I put one hand on his shoulder blade, and with the other, I take one of his hands. "You act like I didn't know all that beforehand. You told me, remember?"

He shrugs.

"I still choose you."

He doesn't respond.

"I don't remember my mom walking away when I was five. But her return and the truth of it is really clear, now."

He turns and looks at me. "She's missing out on the best thing."

"You think I did something to make her leave?"

"Fuck no. That was all her."

"I think you've forgotten something important."

"What's that?"

"Your dad, your brother—you didn't cause them to leave." I tighten my hand around his. "And you aren't being that other guy anymore."

"You sound so sure."

"I have a really good feeling about you." I set my chin on his shoulder.

He smiles.

I stand, keeping hold of his hand.

Griffin twirls me, then draws me back to stand between his legs.

He presses his head against my body. "I don't deserve you."

"We deserve what we believe we deserve." Cal's wisdom. I pause and press my lips against his hair. "Until we both see it, we should keep things simple."

He looks up at me, and I use my fingertips to brush a lock of hair that's covering his eye.

"Simple? I'm not sure what we just did was simple." He squeezes me with his arms.

"I just mean, we probably shouldn't have the baby-making kind of sex, yet."

"You're the boss."

"But I'm afraid that if I leave you to go take a shower, I'm going to miss you too much."

"Are you suggesting that I follow you into the shower and make sure you're extra clean?"

"Yes." I smile at him and pull him after me.

"Girl. I can't promise that I won't have a raging boner seeing you naked. If you're prepared for that, okay, but I'm not sure that's simple."

I laugh. "It sounds simple enough to me."

The remainder of the weekend moves too quickly. Griffin and I co-exist in a bubble of getting to know one another better, intimacy, laughter, and studying for my finals. We barely leave the dorm room except to eat. What I knew to be attraction when I first met him has sprouted into friendship and then bloomed into feelings with roots that reach toward him like vines. I'm wound up in my feelings for him, and while I once thought that whatever we had was temporary, I know that isn't true anymore. What I feel for Griffin reminds me of the depth of emotion I have for my dad, and I wonder if this is love? The idea is sobering because I wasn't expecting that when we drove up to the farmhouse Dad claimed would be done in eight weeks.

When Griffin leaves, and I remain behind at school, I realize how different I'm thinking about what I perceived would solve all of my struggles with the moving. Though college has provided me with Renna, and a place where I feel like I am finally stepping into skin I understand, I'm not looking ahead to the next thing. I'm looking over my shoulder where Griffin is, behind me in a town where there's a farmhouse he's helped my dad fix up. Five months later, instead of counting down the days to leaving, I am counting down the days to returning. Five days and counting.

22

Griffin wants to tell my dad. I'm putting him off. We agreed it would be an "US" thing, but for some reason I'm avoiding it. If I examine my motivations, there's a bunch of anxiety wrapped up in the idea of my dad knowing. Dread that he won't approve and that I couldn't take. Concern that I'm pretending. How could someone like Griffin choose me? Fear that like what Griffin said, I don't deserve him. Panic that at the moment I share my happiness aloud in the universe, it will get taken away. But the first week home, with Griffin moving through the house with my dad while they work, I'm a guitar string strung too tight, and I know Griffin's right. Stolen kisses aren't enough.

A few days before Christmas, Griffin is somewhere upstairs, working in a bathroom they are redoing, and with my dad off on an emergency job somewhere else, I steal up the stairs. It's time to make a plan. When I reach the landing, I hear his movement, the clank of old tiles, the scraping.

I stop in the doorway.

Griffin is crouched down, using a tool to get up what looks like a pesky strip of tile. His back to me, I admire the way his white shirt stretches to accommodate his movement, accentuating the beauty of his form. He replaces the scraping tool, grabs a hammer and uses it to tap what is probably a nail that's decided to take a peek above the subfloor.

"Hey," I say.

Griffin looks over his shoulder. He smiles and stands. "Hey." He glances at the door, looking for any sign of my dad. That's what we've devolved into: thieves of stolen moments.

"He isn't here."

"He should be back anytime. He said mid-morning."

I step into the room, closer to him.

He steps back. "Max." He shakes his head. "I'm working."

"I know." I step closer. "And it's so sexy."

He chuckles. "Stop." He holds his ground when I take another step toward him.

"You sure? Because I was thinking–" I reach out and touch the sinew of his forearm.

He growls at me. "Please don't tell me what you were thinking.

Please don't."

I wrap my arms around his waist.

He capitulates and leans down to kiss me. Really kisses me. Deep and thorough. And like it always does between us, the kiss explodes. His hands are on my hips, and he's walking me backwards until I'm pressed up against a naked wall that's been stripped to the board. Griffin's hands are mapping me, slipping beneath my shirt and molding my soft places. I'm moaning and biting and wanting more than this stolen moment; I don't know how much longer I'm going to be able to do this "keep it simple" thing. I'd like to be stripped and naked.

As his mouth trails across my jaw to the sensitive space below my ear, I attempt to voice a thought, but Griffin's hands are speaking enough for both of us. "I was thinking you're right."

"About?" he says against my neck.

"We should tell him."

Griffin stops kissing me and leans back so he can meet my eyes with his, but all the rest of him is pressed against me. I'm stuck between a wall and a hard Griffin. Hard. I don't want to be anywhere else.

"Really?"

I nod.

His apparent relief fades to worry.

"Why are you worried."

"I don't want him to hate me."

"My dad doesn't have a hate-bone in his body. A mad one, yeah."

"That's what I'm afraid of."

"You've been nagging to tell him, and I don't want to sneak around anymore, either."

Griffin resumes kissing my neck and speaking against my skin. "I want to take you out. I want to tell the world that I get to kiss Maxwell Wallace." His mouth finds mine again, slow, tender until it isn't.

The door shuts downstairs.

We jump apart, our breathing labored with the exertion of unattended want.

"Max?" Dad calls from somewhere in the deep of the house.

"Upstairs," I yell.

"Shit. Shit. Shit." Griffin whisper-swears and does some quick adjustment in an attempt to hide his arousal.

"Hard," I whisper to him with a smile.

"Shut up," he says, gives me a quick kiss on the mouth, then crouches down again as my dad's footsteps start up the stairs.

I move to lean against the door jam, hands in pockets, casual even if my heart strains toward Griffin, who's now looking busy with his task.

Dad's head appears as he comes up the stairs, and his body follows. "Hey. What are you doing bothering Griffin while he's working?"

"I'm no bother," I tell him. "We were talking about how *hard* pulling up tile is." I glance at Griffin when I say it. His shoulders tense a moment, then he shakes his head. "How was the emergency?"

"Watery, but mostly fixed until the part comes in." He walks past me into the bathroom. "Looking good. I think we're almost ready for flooring."

Griffin, now on his knees, looks at my dad over his shoulder and that's when I see it: Griffin's version of admiration. His face is relaxed, and his mask gone. Focused. I've seen this look too. He's given it to me. My heart expands in my chest, pushing other parts of me away, including the fear, because I realize why telling my dad means so much to him. Griffin may not say it out loud, but that look does; he doesn't want to lose my father any more than I want to lose Griffin. He glances at me, offers a small smile.

"I invited Griffin for dinner," I announce and push off of the door jam.

Dad looks at me. "Sounds like a great time, then." He smiles at me. "I'll be right back. Left my measuring tape in the Bucket," he says and tromps past me and back down the stairs. He stops and stares at me. "You might want to brush off, Max-in-a-million. You've got drywall dust all over your shirt and in your hair." Then he disappears down the stairs.

Griffin, now standing, stifles a smile.

I try looking over my shoulder, pulling at my shirt to do so.

Griffin steps toward me, turns my body, then brushes off the remnants of our foray against the wall. "Tonight then."

"Tonight."

From behind me, Griffin wraps his arms around my waist, clasping his hands in front of me, and presses his face into the space between my neck and shoulder. He takes a deep breath as though he needs me to be alive, then releases me. "Back to work."

Later, after Griffin's left to go home and clean up, Dad and I cook a meal that smells delicious in our renovated kitchen. We're hanging out in the now-beautiful living room with hot cider. The weather outside the windows is still, glowing in a strange blue-white light of snowscape and moonlight, and the Christmas tree twinkles, the light reflecting in the window. There's a fire glowing in the refurbished fireplace, over which we've hung two stockings.

"I love it here," I tell dad. "What you've done so far is amazing."

"Took longer than eight weeks."

"Knew it would." I smile at the fire.

"Is it just the house that makes you love it here?" Dad asks.

I look away from the fire at him. He's more aware, I think, than I give him credit for. "Yeah."

He makes a humming noise, looks away at the fire, and takes a sip of his cider.

The knock at the door announces that Griffin's back.

I jump up and open the door. As I do, I'm struck with the memory of opening this door to him almost half a year ago. How different we both are now. Then, I was so adamant about getting away, leaving, and he was so closed off and wounded. Now, I don't want to leave. I want roots—these particular roots—so bad, and he's standing there with a part smile on his face, and his eyes sparkling.

I step out onto the brand-new porch and grasp his face, pulling him into a kiss.

He's holding something in his hands, and it keeps me from getting closer. Plus, Dad is on the other side of the door.

"What was that for?" he asks.

"I just couldn't contain myself."

"A lot different greeting than the first time I showed up on your doorstep."

This makes me smile because he's been remembering too. "Come on. It's cold out here."

He sighs, which I think is probably because he's nervous. "Right."

We stomp into the entry, and I lead Griffin into the living room.

"Cold out there?" My dad asks from his spot in a chair near the fire.

"Freezing," Griffin says. He lifts the pan he's carrying. "From my mom. She started baking. Made you some brownies."

"Does she have a 1950's mixer?" I ask him with a smile, thinking about our trip to Triple B's.

He smiles, recalling it too. "No. I guess you can bake without one."

"I'll get you some cider," I tell him and take the pan.

I glance at my dad who's observing, and I want to throw something at him because I'm pretty sure he's already guessed what's what and hasn't said anything. So all the nerves are probably for nothing. When I return to the room, Griffin is still standing, Dad is still sitting, and it looks like nothing has been said; they're just awkwardly in the same space.

Griffin takes the cider, and I take his hand.

His eyes widen.

"We're dating," I blurt, glancing from Griffin to my dad.

Dad takes a sip of his cider, cool as a freaking cucumber, but it's December, so maybe a cucumber isn't the right description. Whatever. He just looks at us over the cup.

"I mean, I decided... we decided–" But my voice trails away because he just looks so unfazed by it. Had we made more of it than we should? No. I know my dad. He's always grown and bolstered my own mind, but he always has an opinion. It's just his face is devoid of anything, and that's a bit more disconcerting.

Griffin sighs, then adds to my impulsive rant, "I asked Max if she would let me take her out, and she agreed."

Yeah. That sounds better.

Dad hums like he did earlier. I hate that sound. It tells me nothing, and even though I've lived my whole life with this man, I don't know what he's thinking. In all fairness, though, I'm sure he'll make it clear. He did when it came to Michael.

"I'm sorry I didn't tell you sooner."

I squeeze Griffin's hand with a warning and look at him. He just gave us away.

Dad sits up straighter and sets his cup on the table near him. "How long has this been going on?"

"After Thanksgiving," I say. "A couple of weeks." It isn't a lie exactly. That's when we officially took our friendship elsewhere.

He nods and makes that sound again. Looks at both of us, sees our joined hands, nods again, and says nothing.

Griffin tenses next to me, and I glance at him.

He's looking at me unsure what to do next. I don't know, so I shrug.

Dad stands up, grabs his cup, and walks from the room.

I'm panicking a little bit. This isn't what I was expecting. I mean, besides Michael—who my dad wasn't too crazy about, and after the fact, I learned Dad thought he was a selfish jerk—this is the first person I've brought home. Dad had made his opinion clear about Michael: "That boy isn't mature enough for a relationship, Wells," he'd said back then. He also expressed that he knew I knew my own mind, and he wasn't about to go to war with it. Maybe he's just biding his time to talk to me alone.

"Dad?" I release Griffin's hand and follow dad into the kitchen where he's bent over peering into the oven at our roast.

"This is ready," he says and straightens looking for potholders, patting the pockets on the back of his pants like they're there.

"Are you upset?" I ask him.

"Should I be?" he asks, and draws the meat and vegetables from the oven, setting it on top of the stove. "You're both adults. Why does my opinion matter?"

Griffin looks stricken. I realize he's never done this. I make assumptions he's so much more worldly than me, and maybe in some ways he is, but not in this. No more than me. I take his hand so he knows everything will be fine because we're doing this together.

"It matters because I love you." I tell Dad. "And—"

"—and I was worried about betraying your trust, sir," Griffin adds.

Dad looks at us over his shoulder, and for a moment he looks like a wise old man rather than my dad. I imagine him as a wizard, then the image is gone. He turns and steps back to lean against the counter, away from the hot stove. "I was young once."

"You're still young," I say, even though I'd just imagined him as an old wizard.

"I respect your choices, Wells. And if Griffin is your choice, my opinion is of little import." He looks at Griffin. "My opinion, Griffin, with respect to this situation is of little consequence to you. I feel that the line between boss and father of the girl you're dating shouldn't be blurred. My opinion isn't the opinion of a boss, but of a father. You understand what I'm saying?"

"I think so," Griffin replies.

"That said, I trust Max. Maxwell trusts you, then I support that trust."

"Yes sir."

My father looks like he might say more, but instead he just offers a nod and turns back to the roast. "I'm hungry," he announces. "Let's eat."

As we sit down to dinner, offer a prayer of thanksgiving, and begin eating, we rediscover our rhythm together, and I know it's going to be fine. We talk and laugh. We joke and share. I'm happy. I refuse to consider that because I've claimed this joy, that it will fade. I figure, I'm entitled to a little happiness, right?

Sometime later, after I've walked Griffin out to his car, I return to the kitchen to help dad finish cleaning. I watch him for a few beats, moving between the sink and the dishwasher, hit with the sudden realization that he's right. I'm an adult now, and my dad—though only in his forties—is getting older too.

"You don't approve?" I ask and lean on the new island facing him.

He turns, pulls the dishtowel from his shoulder, and leans against the counter. "Would it matter?"

I consider that a moment and realize that he's right. Even if Dad was dead set against my seeing Griffin, it wouldn't matter. So much of my chemistry is mixed up in following that mixture through to its ultimate reaction. "You're right. Probably not. But is it so bad that I want you to approve?"

Dad moves across to the island and leans toward me on the opposite side. "Wells, I told you months ago that boy liked you."

"Nothing happened," I say. "He didn't say anything until after Thanksgiving."

"And that's maybe why I'm hesitant. Griffin's still getting his bearings as a man. I keep thinking about that kid standing on our porch, and while he's made a ton of progress, he's got a long way to go. I'm afraid you'll get caught in that."

"I still have a long way to go."

Dad smiles, looking down at the counter, but it isn't a joyous smile. It's one of those feeble kind like he's reminiscing about something painful. "We all do. Life propels us this way and that, twists us up in all kinds of ways to force us to find our way."

"Like you and mom?"

He looks up, his gray eyes connecting with mine. "Sure."

"Do you regret that even as painful as it was."

Dad reaches out and lays a hand over mine. "Absolutely not. I have you."

"So even in the chaos of life, we find blessings."

"Absolutely." He gives my hand a squeeze, then lets go.

"I'm looking for the blessing, Dad."

Dad's eyes search my face, then he nods and straightens. "Unneeded approval granted." He hangs the dishtowel to dry, gives me a kiss, and disappears into the living room.

I follow him with my eyes but stay in the kitchen a few more breaths, thinking about what he's said, positive that there will be blessings between Griffin and me. It's not like we're getting married; we just started seeing one another! It isn't like there's an agreement between my family and Griffin's in which my dowry has been negotiated and agreed upon. I scoff aloud at the thought.

Dad calls at me from the living room and asks me to bring him a cup of tea.

I skirt the island and set the pot to make him one, considering my dad's wisdom, and hopeful that whatever has blossomed between Griffin and me will multiply with blessings. I shiver, wanting more shared kisses like those a few moments ago outside in his car, refusing to imagine anything different.

23

Two official dates (one to dinner and one to the movies which I will never again do with Griffin because he can't sit still or stop asking questions while the movie plays), one dinner with Griffin's mom and brother (who I think are awesome even if Griffin gets a little embarrassed), and time spent every other night together at my house, I'm not sure I could be any happier. All we've been building filled with blessings. The impending deadline of my return to school in three days is creeping up much too quickly.

It's New Year's Eve. Griffin says he's taking me to dinner, then we'll come and ring in the New Year with my dad while we watch the ball drop on TV. Dad has complained that he probably won't even be able to stay awake until midnight (of which I'm hopeful because maybe tonight is the night we can stop "keeping it simple").

I take care to get ready. A pretty black dress that Renna helped me pick out over FaceTime. I've done my hair and even applied make-up. So I know I look good. I know Griffin will appreciate it. When I'm ready—and he should be arriving any moment—I go downstairs and join my dad where he's sitting at the table, playing solitaire.

Griffin's late.

I glance at my phone. No call. No message.

"A hand of cards while you wait?" my dad asks.

I smile at Dad. "Sure." *He's just running a little late,* I tell myself.

Dad deals a hand of Rummy. "You look pretty."

I organize my cards in my hand. "Thank you."

"Where's Griffin taking you?" he asks as he draws and discards.

"He won't tell me. Said it's a surprise."

Dad smiles and takes what I discarded from the pile. "It will probably be great then. That boy is crazy about you." He lays out a hearts' run and then discards.

"How do you know?" I draw from the pile and glance at the time.

"Well besides the obvious..."

I blush, hold onto my smile, and discard.

Dad picks up the card I set down. "Rummy." He plays it on his hearts run. "Where are you? You wouldn't usually miss that."

"Sorry. Distracted." I temper the doubts beginning to beat wings inside my belly and glance at the time again.

"He looks at you like the sun is shining," Dad says.

"Really?" I stop to look at my dad.

"Be careful with his heart, Wells."

"What about my heart?"

He discards. "You're stronger than he is."

"How do you know that?" I ask and draw a card from the pile.

While I organize my cards, Dad takes a beat to answer, drawing from the pile. "You've had more opportunity to face struggle and overcome it."

"How do you know Griffin hasn't? His dad and everything."

Dad hums a note and makes a play on the run I've laid down. "That isn't to say he hasn't faced heartache, only that you've had more opportunity to build the skill to be resilient."

"Like with Mom?"

Dad nods. "And with all of the moving. With Michael."

"Did you think I was going to hump him and dump him?" I crack up at my joke.

Dad looks incredulous, dropping his cards, and huffing out a puff of air. "I am so disturbed by that, Max."

I continue laughing. "I'm just kidding, Dad! You know I am. I really like Griffin."

He picks up his cards and reorganizes them in his hand with a shake of his head. "I sure hope so," he says, then smiles and chuckles.

I set the cards down and text Griffin:

I'm ready and waiting. Where are you?

He doesn't answer.

Nearly thirty minutes later after sending the text and an hour late,

Griffin texts:

> Sorry. On my way.

Though it should make me feel better, it doesn't. The doubt beasties kick up dust inside me a little stronger now. Something's wrong. I can feel it in my bones, and it bothers me. Now I'm thinking about all that Dad has said the last few weeks, and if something really is wrong, I don't know that my heart is strong at all.

When the headlights of his car flash in the window, I take a deep breath, relieved. I watch him get out of the car and walk to the door. I stand on the inside of the door, waiting for his knock, but he doesn't. He stands on the outside of the door, staring at his keys in his hands. He looks up at the door. I can't see the details of his face, but I can see his body language, which looks more like the Griffin during the summer. He's weighted, his shoulders curled with it. I watch him take out his phone and type a text.

My phone chimes.

Griffin:

> Something's come up. Can't make it.

Now the doubt monsters gnaw my insides raw.

He turns and walks away.

There's no way I'm letting him get away with that, so I move through the doorway. Once I'm outside, Griffin halfway across the yard back to his car, I call out. "What's come up?"

He turns and looks at me.

"Griffin? What is it? You've been standing out here for almost five minutes."

He takes a step toward me but then stops. He looks nice, like he took care to get dressed in slacks and a long-sleeved, buttoned shirt. Like he dressed up for a date. His hair is styled. He isn't wearing a tie, or a jacket, which makes him look a little unfinished. He shoves his hands into his pockets and looks down at his feet. This is the kid I first saw sitting outside the convenience store; he looks broken.

"Where's your coat?"

He runs his hand through his hair, messing it up, but it never really looks a mess; it just flops back into place. "I forgot it."

I walk down the steps and take his hand. His skin is cold, so I lead him to the car. "Get in. Heat on," I say.

He complies and doesn't say anything about me being bossy. My stomach clenches with dread. Something terrible is happening with him, and my dad's warnings suddenly feel prophetic.

I get into the car and turn to look at him. "What's going on?"

He stares at the house. Then with a resigned sigh, closes his eyes, slumps down in the seat, and leans his head against the headrest. He swallows his emotions. While he isn't wearing his mask, he just looks... lost.

I'm starting to freak out, wracking my brain for what could have caused this turn. "Griffin?" Maybe his dad? Something bad happened with him? Or his mom? His brother? "What is it? Are you okay? Is it your family?" I reach out and touch his arm. It's light and he flinches away from me.

He shakes his head. "No. No. I'm not okay. I didn't want to do this now." He sits up, agitated.

I try not to feel hurt by the tone of his voice. It's harsh and different, more like the guy from the Quarry, but he doesn't seem to have been drinking.

"You can talk to me," I say.

"Not about this."

I sigh, then try humor since that can usually draw him from his funk. "What is it? Did you get some girl pregnant?" I snicker at the joke.

He doesn't laugh. His eyes fly open, and his head turns sharply to look at me.

My laughter stops, and my smile shrinks.

My stomach drops through me, and I feel like I'm in a freefall.

I guessed it.

"That was a joke," I say, willing it not to be true.

No. No. No. My mind spins with the word. *I'm happy. I'm happy. I'm happy.*

"Except that it fucking isn't," he says and shoves his hands into his hair, folding forward, his head against the steering wheel. "I slept with Bella, on my birthday, and I didn't fucking follow my own rules. We were both drunk as fuck. I didn't use protection because she said she was on the pill. She showed up tonight to tell me she's pregnant, and she's keeping it. That I'm going to have a kid. I'm fucking nineteen." He slams the steering wheel with his hand. "Is that a joke to you?"

I start at his anger, but I don't feel frightened. I can tell it isn't at me, and I'm caught on *the who* he's talking about. "The Bella who was a bitch to you?"

He lifts his head, but he doesn't look at me; he just stares straight ahead, mask firmly in place now. "One and the same." He sounds so calm, detached.

"No, Griffin. I don't think this is a fucking joke. You can keep your self-righteous, asshole routine to yourself." I'm grasping to understand. I'm not angry he had sex with someone. Jealous for damned sure, but that was before any agreement between us. I'm just trying to grasp onto something concrete. "You slept with the girl who said those awful things about you?"

He shrugs, his mask ruling everything about him. "She was willing."

It feels like a dig at me. But then again, it could be because I'm fucking reeling. "Right. Your rules." I face forward in the seat and stare at the Christmas tree blinking in the window. I don't know what I feel. I'm shocked.

Insecurity sparks to life in the cracks of my confidence, widening the crevices. "Do you love her?" I turn and look at him.

He gives me a look that stops my heart. "No. I don't love her. I just fucked her."

It's such a cold thing to say, and I recognize this Griffin as the one he told me about. This is the one who hurts people because he's hurting; the one that makes them leave. This is the one who will hurt me before I can hurt him.

Don't make decisions when you're emotional—another dad-ism.

I take a deep breath. We can figure this out, I think, but before I can say it, Griffin implodes.

"I fucking told you. I told you," he says, shaking his head, and there's a slight crack in the mask; I can hear the tears, but there aren't any.

"Told me what?"

His hands come up to his hair, and he runs his hands back and forth over his head. "I ruin shit. See? You should just go."

While I can rationally see what he's doing—trying to save me—insides of my body tighten into sharp points. There's anger, but it's not anger so much as it is disappointment. And maybe, if I was better at this whole relationship thing, I could see his words for what they are: his fear and hurt, but I'm not. I'm hurt by him, hurt by the situation, and feel like the moment I accepted something good, something that might have been mine, it gets ripped away.

I swipe at the tears falling from my eyes and look at Griffin. "I told you that you couldn't ruin this." I pause because he is. He's pushing me to leave just like he said he would, and I'm falling right into the trap, ignoring my rules. "I was wrong. Know this Griffin, it isn't because you got some girl pregnant. It's because you didn't trust me to be on your side."

I get out of the car, slam the door, and walk back into the house. Once inside, I lean against the door and glance around. A week ago, this felt like home. Now, though, I feel like maybe I was deluding myself into thinking I'd ever have one.

"You're back already?" My dad appears in the cased opening between the entry and the living room, and when he sees my tearful face, he opens his mouth to say something.

I shake my head. "Please don't–" I start but my voice breaks on the tears that have started to fall.

He closes his mouth and watches me as I walk past him, through the hall to the stairwell.

I walk up the stairs, my surroundings a blur through the tears. When I get into my room, I strip out of the pretending clothes, put on comfortable things I always wear, climb into my bed, and cry my eyes out, wishing I'd never met Griffin Nichols.

24

I get Griffin's first text in my first class of the new semester. It's a few days removed from our—I'm not sure what to call it since *fight* doesn't seem like the right description. I'm in an art history class, with a professor droning on at the bottom of an auditorium about the slides on the gigantic screen. The teacher's words move faster than my brain, and I'm struggling to keep up; I want to be engaged, but I don't feel like myself. I feel like a water-logged, drowned version of me.

My phone vibrates in my bag, and I figure it's probably Renna but hope it's Griffin. When I see SK in my notifications, my heart speeds up, darts about, looking for a bush to hide behind and wait it out. I feel my throat close and tears sting my eyes because all I want is to open it and see that there's a chance. Even hoping that is fruitless because… because…

I open it.

Griffin: Max. I'm lost.

I get up, leave the class, and career into the first bathroom I find, where hide away in a stall and ugly cry. I promised to never leave. I said I wouldn't, but then, he didn't give me much of a choice either. It's just my heart is a bundle of contradictions.

I have all of these rationalizations bouncing around in my mind. There are the justified angry ones that paint me as the victim: *Griffin slept with another girl. Griffin is having a kid because he didn't follow his rules. Griffin didn't trust me.* Then there are the rational ones: *Griffin is in as much shock as me. It's okay that I'm freaking out because who wouldn't. Griffin is having a kid.* The guilty ones are the worst: *I told him I wouldn't walk away, and I did. I left him.*

I have never felt more like my mother.

So, I don't answer him. I can't. I don't know who I am anymore. I think Maxwell Wallace has perhaps slipped out from underneath my skin and left this ghost in her wake. I return to my dorm room and look about as if I'm in a stranger's room. What girl used to like 80's rock bands? And why are there twinkle lights, so soft and feminine in the same place as edgy hair bands? Why is that comforter so bright?

Going to classes feels like the only thing that keeps me upright, and Renna notices it.

She invites me to a party a few days later; I decline. It makes me think of the last one I went to and how Griffin became the skin holding me together.

He texts me a few days later. I'm standing in the dining hall waiting for my dinner. The crowd of students moves around me as if I'm a boulder in the middle of a swift moving river. I stare at the menu above the station, but I don't really see it. I miss Griffin. I miss the sound of his voice. I miss his hand in mine. I miss his laugh, which was difficult to get so it meant that much more when he did. There have been a million times I've tried to compose a message, but then I delete it and move forward without him. *He's going to have a baby*, I think, with another girl who he was attracted to enough to have sex with. Who is beautiful even if she's a bitch. I don't have a place there.

I let myself fall too hard.

Hard.

I smile, but the movement exhausts me.

My phone vibrates in the kangaroo pouch of Griffin's black hoodie I'm wearing. The sweatshirt makes me feel close to him even if it's just a piece of clothing. I imagine him with me. I imagine his arms around me, hands clasped at the small of my back. I think the text is from Renna, telling me she is going to be late, or my dad with a check in, though I wish it to be Griffin's name. It is. I swallow and swipe to open it, afraid it will be his earlier three words, but he's written a book.

Griffin:
> I've gone round and round about what happened when I went to see you.

I'd like to tell you, but I don't know if any of it makes sense.

I told my mom about the pregnancy. I expected her to flip out. She didn't.

She was really helpful, actually, and it made me wonder how many other times I iced her out when she could have been there for me.

The thought made me circle back to you and what you said...

that I hadn't trusted you to be on my side...

My mom was on my side, and I told her the truth. She asked me a question no one else did: What do I want?

I know what I don't want. I don't want to be like my dad.

I want to be like Cal.

I don't want to always push people away. I don't want to be THAT version of Griffin anymore.

I've decided to tell Bella what I want.

I read it again. And reread it. Over and over. So much said with so little. My heart beats with heartrending angst and reinforces the emotional evisceration. He must want Bella. My dad asked my mom to marry him when they found out about me. I don't consider how that turned out. I need to step back and bury my emotions. I slide the phone back into the pocket and try to tell my heart to let go.

It isn't like me not to respond, but I also can't find it in me to text him back, so I don't. I do compose responses in my mind though. *I wish you'd trusted me. I love that you told your mom. I love that you're seeing that there are people on your side. I was always on your side because I love you.*

Yes. Of that I'm sure.

I love Griffin Nichols.

Otherwise, why would this hurt so much? Why would I think that my departure from his life is the right thing when it feels so wrong? He's having a baby with another woman.

I'm not sure who I am. I don't feel like myself. I didn't stay, and even if he didn't give me a choice, I feel upended about that. Who am I if I can't hold to my word? My mom promised. She left. I promised. I left.

Over the next day, a million variations of the same message come to mind. I type it and erase it. Type it again, then erase each one of them. I can't seem to find air to breath for myself, so how does one put that into words?

He's going to be a dad.

With another girl.

While I can accept he had a life before me, I'm unable to rationalize away the insecure jealousy I feel about it. I freaking fell in love with him, and he will share this link forever with another girl.

Who am I to get in the way of that?

Renna comes into our room like a whirlwind after her last class and flops on the bed. She rolls to look at me. I swivel in the desk chair to face her.

"You okay?" I ask.

"That's my question. Are you ready to talk to me?"

We've been back almost two weeks, and I know I'm treading emotional water and barely keeping my nose above the waterline. It isn't natural for me to reach out to someone else—someone who isn't my dad—because I've always relied on myself. So Renna looking at me with her gigantic, brown eyes—waiting and hopeful—makes me think about Griffin's text about his mom: *She was really helpful, actually, and it made me wonder how many other times I iced her out when she could have been there for me.* The thought cracks me open inside and releases a little of my hurt.

"Griffin and I got into a fight." Even if fight doesn't seem right, it seems the best way to describe it to her.

"It must have been a doozy," she says. She sits up on her bed and tucks her feet under her.

So I tell her what happened.

"Holy shit," she says. "Don't tell Granny I said that. She says shit isn't holy. Oh, my goodness." She moves and has me in a hug, and I can't contain the tears even though I try. Her tiny ass gets my giant ass up out of my desk chair and walks me over to my bed so she can sit next to me. When I'm done crying, and she's emptied a box of tissues to help me wipe up my snot and blow my nose, she says, "This deserves a girls' night Rom-com film fest."

"I don't think I can," I tell her.

"How many times have you watched Rom-coms with the girls after a fight with your bf?"

"Never," I say.

"Me either." She giggles. "Let's see if it works."

We buy candy from the vending machine in the lobby and set up her laptop and stream Rom-coms until we're belly laughing about how ridiculous some of them are. We fall asleep in the same bed until she kicks me in the shin, and I move to my own. Somehow, I wake up feeling clearer though undecided about what to do about Griffin. I don't know what we are. Ended? But I feel foolish texting him to clarify since I can't seem to text him when he's opening up.

His next text comes through that day. I'm walking across campus to go to the library for a research project that's coming up, and my phone vibrates in my pocket (yeah, the same black hoodie; it smells like him). Once I'm inside the building, because it's too cold to stand outside reading text messages, I weave my way through the stacks until I find an empty carrel. I slop my backpack onto the desktop, sit down on the chair with miniscule cushions designed to ensure we won't fall asleep, and open Griffin's text:

> When Bella showed up at my door, I'd been getting ready to come and get you for our New Year's Eve date.

> There she was and I freaked out because I didn't want her there. I wanted our date.

I tried to get rid of her and then she dropped the news about the baby. I didn't do a very good job of hearing it. When am I ever very good at the emotional stuff?

She told me I didn't have to be involved just that I should know. The first place I went was to Tanner's.

Yeah. Weird huh?

From a fight and we don't talk for six months to me showing up on his doorstep.

You know, he wasn't mad. I said I was sorry, of course, but he apologized too. I told him about the baby and about you. And you know what he said,

that I needed to tell you and trust you to know what you needed.

I thought he made sense, and I planned to do that.

I stood outside your door, trying to find words to tell you. Then I freaked out because none of them worked in my head.

And when you followed me, you looked so amazing—you always do—and I wasn't prepared to face you. I was prepared for the worst-case scenario in my head—you not being a part of my life—because there wasn't a best case.

There usually isn't a best-case scenario in my head, ever, so I've always made the worst case happen.

That's how I ruin things.

I don't blame you or anything for leaving. I blame myself for pushing you out the door. I don't hold you to what you said, you know, about not leaving. I made it so you didn't have a choice.

My heart feels compressed after I've read it three or four or fifteen times through. I set down my phone like it might bite me. My body feels like it's been pumped with helium, floating, and I've risen too quickly into the atmosphere so I will slip away into the non-gravity of space. Nothing to grasp ahold of. I'm not sure what to do. I don't know what to say. I'd felt upended about walking away. Guilty, even. I wonder if this is what my mom felt. Griffin's acknowledgement that he made the choice for both of us feels like he's offered me an exemption, but it's a club dipped in broken glass and weaponized. Only it isn't Griffin swinging it. It's me swinging it at myself.

With a sigh, I grab my phone and put it back in my pocket. I wander the stacks, wondering why he hasn't called, but then this is Griffin who struggles to string words together when they involve emotions. Texting seems to be easier for him.

I bump into someone. "Sorry," I whisper and turn to find I've walked into Ben.

He smiles and whispers back, "Hey. Happy bumping into you here. Literally."

I tuck a strand of hair behind my ear. "Research." I think about our kiss, cringe, and wish myself far away.

"Me too. I have this sociology thing to do."

"History."

Silence dances around us like an awkward parental attempt at something hip.

"I should get back to it," I say and point with my thumbs.

"Yeah. Good seeing you, Max."

"You too, Ben. I'm sure we'll bump into each other again." I turn away and roll my eyes at how stupid and suggestive that sounded.

"I hope so," he says after me.

I keep walking and do my best to avoid him in the stacks. Eventually, with a couple books discovered about my topic, I return to the carrell and reread Griffin's text. It doesn't feel like he's expecting a response when I reread it. Almost as if he's just trying to process what he's going through, and I think about the rules. How I told him he needed to talk and share. He's sharing. But I don't respond or share back. It's me breaking the rules, not him. But what do I say when everything I'm thinking is the exact opposite of what I want? I don't want him to be with Bella. I don't want to not be a part of Griffin's life, but isn't it the right thing to let go?

Instead, I open a word document on my computer to type him my own letter. I get the *Dear Griffin* written, then the cursor blinks at me with harsh judgement because I don't know what to write. This is a man I love, I love, I love, and I can't figure out what to say. He's having a baby with someone else! I close the computer, pack up my bag and leave the library.

The next day he sends a series of texts:

> I fixed my phone screen. It's good as new. No more cracks.

> I should have started with 'I'm sorry.' I'm sorry, Max.

> I talked to two people I need to talk to, and it wasn't easy.

> The first one was Bella.

> I told her I wanted to be involved in my kid's life, you know.

> Like co-parents or whatever they call it. I told her I didn't want to be like my dad and not be involved. She's agreed and invited me to the ultrasound next month.

> This DOESN'T mean there's a Bella and me, like a couple.

> Nope.

> We both agreed on that.

The second person—and the more terrifying of the two—was Cal.

I haven't gone to work, and I knew I needed to face him about stuff.

I told him about the baby. He was really helpful.

And he called me out on some of my shit, which is definitely something I needed. He always knows exactly what to say.

I still have one more person I need to talk to:

You, Max.

I need to talk to you.

I don't respond. But I read through his texts over and over, and my heart fills with tender hope. Read and reread it, again and again, until the ache isn't as harsh.

Later, I'm walking with Renna to a party at Carlos's house. She's finally gotten me to agree to come for a little while. Ben hands me a drink and smiles at me. I can see he still likes me, and I'm going to have to figure out how to navigate that. My feelings for Griffin are so big, but maybe not the safest place for my heart.

I reread his last texts. My heart hurts. I put my phone back in my pocket and take a sip of my drink, my eyes scanning and unfocused, my insides trembling with... it isn't hurt anymore. Sure, I'm still aching at what happened between us, at what felt like a betrayal of what I'd thought we were building, but it isn't as acute. Now, it feels like I've split into two Maxes again. The one who wants Griffin and the one who's afraid to want someone that much. The latter one is the louder one.

Ben, who's standing a few feet away leans over, "Would you like to dance with me, Max?"

I swallow and shake my head. "No thank you. I'm–" But I can't finish it, all wrapped up in the emotion of my own making. Truth is, Ben is a distraction from all the feelings I have for Griffin, a way to numb them into something easy and bland. It isn't Ben (because he's nice), it's my feelings toward him. And yet when I look at him, I know he's safe. He likes me, and maybe he wouldn't tear my heart to shreds. Then again, I will never feel like I'm glowing from the inside out like Griffin makes me feel. Perhaps that's what happened to my parents. They burned so hot, so quickly, they couldn't find a way to reignite it when the fire went out. I look at Ben. "Another time, maybe?" Is a low burn the better option?

When I get back to the dorm room, my phone alerts me that there's a voice mail. I open it and listen, nearly dropping the phone at the sound of Griffin's voice. I feel the reverberation in my belly, vibrating through my insides because I miss him.

"Hi. Um. I'm not sure this is the best way to talk. No. It isn't. Shit." He pauses and sighs, and I can picture him running a hand through his hair. "I feel like I need to talk to you rather than to myself. Um...

I know I hurt you. I'm sorry. And I'd just like to be able to tell that to you, but I respect that you need to decide what is right for you—even if it's hard for me to accept it. I do accept it. For you. Because I care about you. So, maybe if you're willing to talk to me. Um. Or not. Let me know. Yeah. Okay."

Or not. Not.

The idea of not talking to him is just as bad as opening my heart to talking.

He's right. I'm not talking. I'm not following my own rules. I've travelled away from the person I was a few months ago, the one who made up those rules; the one willing to sit down with a stranger at a table outside of a convenience store and outrageously call him a serial killer. Where did she go?

It's late, after midnight, but I sit down at my desk and open my computer anyway. I pull up the document I started in the library. Dear Griffin, and the nagging cursor. Then I just write:

> I'm so hurt. Hurt doesn't feel like the right description. Hurt feels like something that can be mended. Oops. I tore a hole in my favorite pair of jeans. Patch it up with an I'm sorry iron on and move on. Put those big girl pants back on, all patched up and keep wearing them. This feels like more than that to me. Truthfully, I don't know if it's about you. You've been so open and honest about what you're going through. You've been transparent. You've followed the rules, and I've been stuck, quiet, and reflective, which as you know, isn't my usual plan of attack toward anything. I feel so strongly for you, Griffin... that's a lie. I love you. I love you. I loved you. Loved. It isn't past tense. I do, still.
>
> That night... I did make the joke about you making a girl

pregnant. I'm sorry for that. I was trying to cajole you into talking to me like usual. I didn't know. And when you just shut me down, shut down any possibility of us talking about it together, working through it together, I felt blown apart.

I feel crushed, like I'm trying to find all the pieces to put myself back together, but they are spread out and I'm picking through what's left to find them. Then as I find them, they don't seem to fit back together right. I've made a liar of myself. I claimed I would do anything to work through a problem, nagged you to do the same and here I am. I've run. Like my mother. Shit. I don't know where I'm going with this.

I've spent my whole life never measuring up to anyone outside of my father. Ever. All the fair-weather friends I had at any stopover on my dad's and my odyssey, I shifted to fit. I made myself the version they wanted me to be so they would keep liking me. Then we'd move on. Chameleon Max would adjust to the next place. Even with my first and only boyfriend, I found a version that he liked, hoping that he'd stay even knowing that I wouldn't. And when he didn't, while I was hurt by his denial of me as someone important to him, I sloughed off that skin.

Then I met you, and for the first time in my life, I felt seen and understood. You didn't tell me I needed to lose weight or do my makeup a certain way to be prettier. You didn't tell me to tone-down my humor or my impulsivity. You didn't treat me like I was a card-board cutout or that my mind and what I had to say wasn't worthy. You made me feel like my dad has, important, relevant, and worthy just as I am. Oh. Shit. Griffin. I didn't know until I wrote that, what was happening in my mind. I should probably do this more often. I don't even know if I will send this because fuck, I just laid myself bare.

Here's the thing, when you sat in the car that night and didn't trust me with the pain you were in, it was like I was asked to go back into hiding. You didn't do that. I did. I went back to all those places… houses 1-9 where people and relationships were as fragile as glass, and no one ever chose me for me. I never let them though. I let you in. I trusted you and thought you felt the same. I shut the door, cut you off because all of these real feelings hurt so much. I couldn't stay and fight. I don't know whether I'm coming or going. I know I love you, but I don't know if that's enough. My dad loved my mom, and it wasn't enough. I feel stretched out on a rack and about ready to break because I don't know how to find the breath I need. Is it to find a way back to you? Is it to let you go and move forward?

Ultimately, I'm trying to find out what Maxwell Wallace needs. What makes me the best version of myself? Notice I didn't say who, because I know it can't be a who. Dad taught me that a long time ago, but I also think that a who can contribute to that version. I have to figure this out standing on my own two feet in order to be part of an equal equation. It's time to stop being a chameleon. Whatever happens, I love you. I love you. I love you.

When I'm done, I close the computer, crawl in my bed with a tear-streaked face and a sore throat from crying, and find solace in sleep.

25

It has been nearly two months since I've been back at school, and while spring arrives with the rain and blossoms, the silence I've created between Griffin and me keeps me stuck in winter. I've reread the letter I wrote every day. I've considered sending it but haven't. I figure my silence has probably ended things officially, even if I can say that isn't what I want. Truthfully, I don't know what I want. I haven't crossed over the threshold to try to put things back together, but I also haven't stopped rereading Griffin's texts and wishing for more. There's a lot of emotions in play. Guilt for walking away and allowing it to go on this long. Insecurity about the fact that Griffin is having a baby with someone else. Shame for feeling so weak. Loss for allowing my understanding of who I am and what I want to slip away when a few months ago it felt so clear.

I'm walking through the dorm hallway back to my dorm room after my evening class when my phone chimes. I pull it from my jacket pocket to look at who's texting me. I haven't gotten one from Griffin after his voice mail, and the silence has been loud. When I see SK in my notifications, my heart wakes up, jumps up and down and twerks a little bit.

As soon as I get into the empty dorm room, I lean against the door and open the message.

Griffin:

> I know you aren't talking to me. I hope it's okay to still text you to share, because the only one I wanted to share this with was you.

> I got to hear the baby's heartbeat today.

> I didn't know. Max.

> I didn't know what it would do to me. How I would feel.

> After the appointment, I got into my car and cried.

> Maybe that's weird, and maybe that makes me seem weak, but hearing her heartbeat for the first time filled me with so much feeling; it was all I could do to hold it in until I could find a place it felt safe to let it go.

Oh Yeah! The baby is a girl.

I'm going to have a daughter.

I never thought I would be excited to say that I'm going to be a dad, but Max, my feelings have changed since I first learned I was going to be a father.

I've been wondering if that's how my dad felt?

I wish I had my friend Max back to talk to. I miss her.

I reread his message, and I find that I'm smiling. My heartbeat is in my ears, crashing against the bottom of my throat, and this time, I don't hesitate. I text him back.

Me

I think it's beautiful, SK. I'm sure your dad was just as excited about you.

I push send so I don't agonize over it. I miss him, too. So much.

My smile fades, the heaviness of knowing he's going to be a dad with someone else pulling the floating feeling that made me smile back to the earth. I push away from the door. The three dots pop up, disappear, reappear, disappear, reappear. Then he presses send.

Maybe I should go see my dad.

I don't reply. I've put a safety clamp on my heart and while sending the first text has relieved a bit of the pressure, I've closed it back up in the name of self-preservation even if I'm not clear yet on what I'm preserving myself from.

I think of my mother, then, wondering.

I rummage through my desk drawers until I find the crumpled-up paper with her number on it. Allowing my impulsivity to drive me, I dial it. The phone rings.

"Hello? Max?"

"How did you know it was me?" I ask.

"I programmed your number into my phone. Last time."

Time stretches between words like taffy, thinning out, getting ready to break, then it folds back up and thickens when my mother says, "I didn't expect you to call. Hoped, but…"

"I wasn't going to."

"Are you okay?"

"I don't know." I close my eyes and imagine her the last time I saw her, standing in the coffee shop, so put together, trying to close the loop. And maybe that's what I'm doing, right now. "Was it easy to leave?"

She takes a deep breath. "No."

"Then why–"

"Wait, Maxwell. Wait. Let me–" She interrupts my question and continues. "Leaving, or I should say not returning, wasn't easy, but it was the right thing to do. I was in no position to be a good mother. I regret that every day, but I don't regret deferring my rights to your dad. That last time—when I saw you, I shouldn't have blamed him."

I look at the stack of books on my desk and think I should end this call, but then she says, "Me leaving wasn't your fault, or his." I look up from the desk and out through the window at the trees speckled with new growth and new blossoms. Tears press against the back of my eyes and fill in the spaces like a flood until they fall, blurring the view.

"It wasn't because I didn't want you. It wasn't because I didn't love you and your dad. I think in some twisted way I did, but I was an addict. I needed that more."

I clear my throat. "Thanks for the truth," I say through my tears, and mean it.

"I'm glad you called."

I'm not sure if I am. Then, I suddenly know why I did call, considering the thoughts Griffin shared about his own father. I've been feeling like her, having walked away, and gone silent and maybe, in my own way, I can empathize. Last time she was here, she was looking for a way to close a choice she made, and while I don't agree with how she did it, I don't hold it against her anymore. "I called because I wanted to tell you that I forgive you."

That taffy silence stretches again, and she sniffs. "Thank you for that."

"I have to go," I say.

She sniffs again. "Okay. Goodbye, Max."

I wipe my eyes and stare out at the greenery beyond my window. I think a piece of me thaws.

A few nights later, I'm at dinner with Renna and crew at the pizza place where I took Griffin. We sit at a table near the giant fireplace. Renna sits on one side of me, Ben on the other. I let myself just exist in the moment of hanging out with friends without worrying about it. I'm just myself and feel that spark of who I once was effervesce in my belly.

Ben, reaching for pizza, grazes my arm with his chest. He offers me a smile that reach his eyes.

My phone vibrates. I glance at it and see it's a text from Griffin:

> I went and saw my father, told him about the baby.

> I'm not sure how I expected it to go.

> It's always tense between us, not because of him, but because of me.

> This time, I felt like I wanted it to be different, so I didn't run away, which is what I have done since he got out.

> My dad told me that he wants to be better, and I decided that if I want people to trust in me, I should probably do the same, right?

> I keep circling back around to that night when I didn't trust you to be on my side.

I wish I'd made a different choice, but like Cal said, that sometimes life kicks you in the balls, and you have to figure out if you're going to lay there or get back up.

Okay. He didn't say it exactly like that. ☺

I spend nights wishing I'd made a different choice.

Replay it over and over, wondering how it would be different.

I know it was my fault, Max.

I didn't trust you because I was just a coward.

Afraid you wouldn't choose me because I wouldn't choose me.

I know you've moved on, and I'm happy for you.

I just miss my friend.

His words—afraid you wouldn't choose me—hit me square in the chest, my own fear coming alive in his fears. I've always chosen Griffin, except... I haven't. The other sentiment—trust—swirls around in my mind too mixing up with what happened with Michael all those months ago. He couldn't trust us—how confused I was about it.

I reread the message: *I didn't trust you because I was just a coward.*

The realization hits me like the pull chain of a naked lightbulb in a dark basement. Michael's ending of us hadn't been about me at all. Just like what my mother said: *it wasn't your fault.* Michael's decision to end it had been whatever he'd been going through, like my mother. The safety clamp on my heart eases a bit, and I release a little more pressure sending a text back to Griffin immediately.

> I miss you too, SK.

That's the truth.

"Everything okay?"

I look up at Ben, who's watching me, and offer him a nod.

"We should all go to the beach for spring break," Carlos suggests. He looks at Renna and wiggles his eyebrows.

"And how do you think we'll pay for that," Renna asks. She pulls a hot slice onto her plate.

"My grandparents have a rental in the Keys," Ben says and leans for another slice of pizza, making sure to touch me as he does. "I could ask them. They probably wouldn't charge their favorite grandson."

"Oh, I love this idea! You'd come too, right, Max?" Renna asks.

"That would be fun," I say. The idea has a certain appeal, but it also makes me feel like I've swallowed stones. The rocks make it heavy to keep swimming on the surface, and instead of lingering in the space to reflect on why that is, I just allow it to happen, a passive recipient to the current, and its pull.

Ben smiles.

Renna takes a photo of us all, then posts it to Instagram.

Spring break plans make a race for the finish line, and I remain caught up in a current. Floating in it feels safe because I don't have to think about Griffin and how much I miss him. I don't have to sit in my insecurity and disassociation with myself. I don't have to ponder Ben's looks and Renna's excitement, I just exist there, resting and healing.

I call my dad a couple of days later to tell him.

"Max-in-a-million! Oh, I miss you, sweet pea," he says.

"Hey, Dad. How's the house?" I really want to ask how Griffin is, but I don't.

"It's coming along. Griffin has been a big help. The kid's a hard worker. Not sure how he's fitting school and work and all the other stuff in. And the house, we're renovating the upstairs now, new flooring is going in, bathrooms are almost done, and we should be getting to your room soon. I'm hoping it's done before you come home for spring break."

Thanks Dad, I think, grateful to hear about Griffin. "About spring break—"

"You're not coming home?" His disappointment is in his voice, and it draws me back to all those months ago when I knew me moving on would leave him behind. The pressure valve cracks, and I realize I'm not sure if leaving is what I want anymore, yet I continue to float away in the current without the strength to fight it yet.

"My roommate and a bunch of friends are talking about going to the Keys. One of them has a vacation rental out there."

"Oh." There's a pause. "Well, that's nice. I think you should have adventures," he says. recovering like a champ.

"Yeah. Um– I thought I should call and let you know."

"I'm glad you did."

We talk about school and other mundane stuff until I have to go to work on a research paper.

"I love you," he says.

"I love you too, Dad."

I'm finally feeling less like a water-logged rat, and back to my old, sexy mermaid self. Running again, even in the cold. Clearer about who I am and what I believe about myself. When I look in the mirror, I'm beginning to recognize my reflection again. I see the girl who is a series of wild contradictions, who used to be wildly impulsive though that impulsivity has tempered. I see the girl who truly fell in love for the first time, who can't compromise on what she wants in a relationship: trust, mutual respect, open communication. Non-negotiables. They were always there. I described them on that day we went to the Bend. What I don't know is what I want moving forward. The thing is, I know I haven't followed my own non-negotiable rules. I haven't talked or shared what's going on with me. I haven't allowed Griffin in to trust him with my own pain and fears and that's why I walked away wasn't it? What a hypocrite.

Then there's Ben. I don't love Ben. I like him. He's sweet and thoughtful. He's attentive, and I know that if I gave him the green light, he'd try to be everything I wanted him to be. I just don't know what it is I believe about what I want for myself. I agree to meet him for coffee, just us. This is me opening myself to other possibilities to know how I feel, and if crossing that spring break threshold is what I want.

Ben seems nervous when we sit down at a table. He swipes his hands over his pants as he sits. I notice he likes his coffee with chocolate and cinnamon, and it makes me think of Griffin, who likes it with a touch of cream.

I set my hazelnut latte on the table and sit.

"You packed? For the trip?" Ben asks.

"Started packing. I haven't decided what to bring."

"Swimsuits." He smiles.

"Those. Yes. Check." I take a sip of my coffee.

The silence between us stretches, becoming awkward. Besides some alcohol fueled kisses and dancing many months ago, there isn't a lot between Ben and me. I'm not sure what to say, so I don't say anything. I think about Griffin and how I never felt like I didn't know what to say, how talking with him just felt easy. Maybe that's because we were real friends, and I haven't given Ben a shot at even that.

"It was nice of your grandparents to let you use the house," I finally say.

"I told you. I'm their favorite grandson. Truthfully, I'm their only one." He smiles.

I laugh. "By default, then."

He nods and fiddles with the handle of the coffee mug. "May I ask a personal question?"

I swallow my sip. "Sure."

"What happened with that other guy? The one from the party?"

"What do you mean?"

"Well, you guys seemed into each other. When you came back after the break…" He stops and then blurts, "Renna said that you'd broken up."

Freaking Renna. I wonder what else she's said.

"She did, huh?"

"Don't get mad at her," he says, leaning forward. "I coerced that information out of her. And she might have been under the influence when she mentioned it. That's all she'd say."

I look down at my cup, then out the window at the trees lining the street, focusing on the warmth of the coffee cup seeping into my hands. "It feels weird to talk about it."

"At all or with me?"

I pause, considering the question. Is it because I don't want to talk about Griffin? Or because I don't want to open up to Ben? I feel like I'm leaning back and away from him. "I'm not there yet. So, both, I guess." I haven't even talked to Griffin. I need to talk about it with Griffin.

My heart picks up speed thinking about that. Yes, I need to talk to Griffin.

Ben nods. "I don't want to, like, dance around things. I think you know, already, Max. I like you."

I meet his gaze. His dark eyes hold mine. I wait for the butterflies, the thudding heart, the physical response to his declaration, but it isn't there. I offer him a slight nod of acknowledgement, so he knows I've heard him.

"And I just–" He sighs and sits back. "I'm not doing this right."

"What?"

"Just telling you that I've liked you for a while. And I've been hoping that maybe during spring break you might give me a chance? With you."

He sees me. He's choosing me, and yet the declaration doesn't offer fireworks. That's what I'd always wanted right? To be seen? To be chosen?

I swallow. This is opening up. For sure. I don't like the way I feel like I might crawl from my skin at the idea of kissing someone who isn't Griffin. It isn't Ben I want to see me. It's Griffin, and he does. Every single one of his texts proves it. It isn't the words, it's the actions.

I look at Ben and understand that whatever I say is important not only for him but more importantly for me. I'm not the girl who rides the current, and that's exactly what I've been doing. I'm the girl who sits down at tables and laughs with—Griffin. "I've been in a tough place," I tell him.

Ben nods. "I'd like to be someone you can lean on."

I offer him a smile. "You're my friend, Ben, but that's all I can offer." The words come out like heartbeats because my heart constricts with the idea that I might be hurting a very nice person.

He looks at his coffee cup, and I can see that he's disappointed by the shape his mouth takes. I understand, but I also don't feel the need to apologize for my honesty. That feels good, more like the version of me I recognize. My insides breath a deep sigh of relief as if I've broken away from the current and have started swimming again.

"You love him?" he asks.

I look up from my half-empty cup, meet Ben's gaze, and nod.

"You should tell him how you feel."

That night, while I'm in my dorm room packing for spring break, I get a text from Griffin and smile because it's like he conspires with God for the perfect timing. My heart rate picks up its skirts and runs toward him. Renna is chattering about all the plans for the week, and I'm half listening to her, but mostly I need to read what he's sent me. It feels so long since I've heard from him, and the compulsion to connect drives me forward.

Griffin:

> You know you told me one time—

> that time we went to the Bend—

> that my name meant a "guardian of treasures," and you believed it.

> I loved that you did.

> It made me feel like it could be true.

> All my life I thought my name meant monster and that's kind of how I've acted.

> Like one of those self-fulfilling prophecies or something.

The truth is, though, Max,

that I didn't guard my treasure, I pushed her away.

I wish there was something I could say to fix it,

But I messed it up.

I'm sorry for that.

I heard you aren't coming home for spring break which made me sad.

I had hoped to tell you 'I'm sorry' in person, but I get it too.

You're moving on.

Maybe with the many number of Bens in your life ☺

I hope you have fun and enjoy your break.

I'm trying to follow your relationship rules, so, I wanted you to know that no matter what, I want to be a better treasure guardian.

I will always treasure our friendship—

I miss that, most.

I will always treasure the lessons you taught me,

and the way you made it clear you believed in me.

I will always treasure the way you made me feel like I was the best version of myself,

and now that I know what that feels like, I can work for that on my own.

I treasure that you made me face my shit

(well, you and Cal). ☺

So. for all of that, thank you, Maxwell Wallace.

Your friend forever, Griffin.

I sink, phone in hand, to my bed.

"What is it?" Renna asks.

I look up. "A text from Griffin." I hold out the phone to her.

She pads across the room in her thick, colorful socks and sits next to me, takes the phone, and reads it.

As she does, I stand, unable to sit and pace instead.

"Wow," she says.

My skin breaks out with goosebumps, and my breathing hikes up. "What am I doing, Renna?"

"What are you doing?"

I look at her. She's sitting on the edge of my bed still holding my phone but watching me. "I don't know. I feel all jumbled up. I mean, I feel better than before, but I'm confused."

"Do you love him?" she asks.

"It isn't that simple. He hurt me."

"It is that simple, Max. Just because you love someone doesn't mean they won't mess up and that you won't ever hurt one another. That's a part of building a relationship, you know?"

Balancing the equation.

My mom didn't stay to balance the equation. But I didn't either.

"I think you need to answer the question: do you love him?" Renna asks and holds my phone out to me. "Do you love him enough to work at it?"

And then it hits me. My rules. Forgiveness. I'd forgiven Griffin a long time ago even if I hadn't told him. Every text made that possible. I haven't forgiven myself for walking away. "I can't go—" I look at her— "with you."

She smiles and nods. "Ben will be heartbroken. But he's a handsome guy. He'll find another honey."

I hug her.

Then I open my computer and book a bus ticket home for the next day. I need to tell Griffin how I feel, and that means going home to do it, face-to-face. It is time to stop running.

26

When I'm standing outside of the farmhouse, bag in hand, I stare at the front door. I know Griffin is inside because his car is in the drive. I don't see Rust Bucket. I'm nervous, my insides jittery with anxiety and all of the what if questions streaming through my consciousness. What if I waited too long? What if I misread his texts? What if I feel more than him? But more than those questions is the overarching need to know for myself where I stand with Griffin. It's defining my next steps one way or the other.

I set my bag down on the porch and take out my phone to text him.

Hey.

Hey

Is my dad home?

No. Out on a job. Why?

I open the door and walk in, shutting it behind me, then put the bag down and glance around. Months ago, I walked into the dump of a house and thought it was probably the worst one my dad had ever bought. Now, it's breathtaking. Like a home. My home. It hurts to think he's going to turn it over. This place has become so much more to me than house numbers 1-9. House 10 is where I found something wonderful. Myself.

I hear footsteps upstairs.

And Griffin.

"Cal?" Griffin's voice calls from the landing. That's where I imagine him. My heartbeat doubles, and I feel tears press against my insides, threatening. His steps reverberate through the floor as he moves down the stairwell. "Cal? Need some help–"

He freezes when he sees me. "What the–"

I swallow and grasp my hands twisting them up to put the anxiety somewhere tangible. I can't find my voice. He looks perfect. The Griffin of my dreams and fantasies. The same. Steady and strong. But different too. No mask. His face is gentler, his hair a little shorter. His mouth is still perfect and kissable. I want to kiss him. I want to tell him everything in my heart. I want to tell him about my journey and how I'm different even if I'm the same, but I restrain my impulse.

He takes the final stair and stops. "Are you okay? What happened? You're supposed to be—not here."

I nod and think about saying something, but I can't. I feel like the moment I do, the tears behind my eyes are going to flow out like a raging river. And it will be ugly. Seeing him here, now, makes me understand how much I shut myself away from the feelings. These weren't going anywhere, and I was a fool to think that I could find that elsewhere.

I don't want to be without him.

I want to be a part of this balancing equation process, if he wants to do that with me.

He shoves his hands in his pockets, then removes them and crosses his arms and waits.

I squeeze my eyes shut because looking at him is painful. He might not want to balance the equation with me. So I say, "You're painting." Inane and completely not what I want to say.

"Finishing upstairs. Working the punch list to finish it out." His eyes don't stray from me. "What are you doing here?"

"I didn't go."

"I see that."

I smile but look at the floor, trying to wrangle my thoughts. "Right. Let me fix that." I look up at him and hope what I'm about to say is the right thing. "I didn't *want* to go." I take a step toward him. "I thought I did, but the closer it got, the more I thought about home."

About the people who make me feel at home in my own skin.

I see his throat work as he swallows. He puts his hands back in his pockets. The gray t-shirt, spattered with paint, stretches around his shoulders which seem even wider. "Your dad will be happy."

I take another step toward him. "Yeah. Um, he will be. But he isn't the reason I came home." I take another step closer, a couple of steps more to go. "I wanted to see you, Griffin. I miss you, and–"

But he doesn't let me finish. He closes the distance, takes my face between his hands and kisses me. Wraps me up in his arms and kisses me like I'm oxygen. I kiss him back, grasping onto his shirt, holding on as if he's the life raft in the middle of the storm, and the tears finally fall. "I'm sorry," he repeats between kisses. "I'm sorry." He draws back, looking sheepish. "I should have asked."

I smile through the tears. "I was hoping it wasn't too late."

He crushes me against him in a tight hug. "I'm sorry, Max. So sorry. You were right."

I hold onto him like he might slip through my grasp. "I should have stayed and fought with you. For you. I shouldn't have walked away. I'm sorry, too."

He kisses my forehead. My temple. "You're here now. Do we still need to fight about it? I could muster some fighting words if you give me a moment, I'm sure."

I laugh against his chest and shake my head, leaning back to look at him. Then I kiss him, wanting him to feel my emotions, my love. Griffin kisses me back, and like it always is, the fire ignites and spreads, moving through us until we're both panting and needy.

"Max. Max." He withdraws and puts his forehead against mine. "I'm at work. And I have to not get fired because your dad will have my head if I mess up again."

"Again."

"Yeah. I can't let him down."

"I'll help. Help me with my bag?"

He follows me up the stairs, our hands linked.

"It's beautiful," I say. "The house."

He nods. "It is, but not as beautiful as you."

"The sweet talk will get you anything you want." I smile at him, feeling buoyant, but I also know there's more to say. More to address. "Show me my room?"

He takes the lead, and I follow him across the landing and into the room I chose. It looks different. The walls aren't bleeding wallpaper anymore. They are painted the soft gray I picked out for downstairs, the baseboards, the crown molding, the doors are all white. There's a window seat now, and I know those bones had been there but nonexistent months ago. The tree outside the window is trimmed back. My bed sits in the same space with the same comforter, but it's up on a frame. There are actual nightstands, one on each side instead of crates. Even lamps. "Your dad didn't change the paint color you picked for downstairs."

I sigh, turning to take it in, light at the beauty of it, but it crashes down because it can't be mine. "No. Neutral color is better for resale."

Griffin sets down my bag at the end of the bed and looks about everywhere but me, as if he's nervous and shy. "Well. I should get back to work." He swipes his hands over his back pockets, then walks back toward the door.

I stop him with a hand on his arm before he passes me.

His eyes meet mine, and my heart both expands, then takes a breath. "Can we talk? While you work?"

He nods, then disappears through the doorway.

I change into something work ready and find him in the new bathroom with a putty knife and a small container of putty. He's bent over the windowsill. He turns when he hears my footsteps, watches me walk into the small room. I remember the last time we were in this room. We made out against the wall, almost right where I'm standing. Griffin must remember too, because he ducks his head, looking away.

"Was Renna upset that you didn't go?" he asks and scrapes putty against a nail head.

"Maybe," I say. "But she understood."

He glances at me. "And Ben?"

I smile. "Worried about all those Bens in my life?"

He turns and takes a deep breath. "Just one."

My face heats, and I step back until I'm leaning against the new bathroom counter. "Ben and I went out for coffee," I say.

He becomes very interested in the putty and the putty knife he's holding, his face somber, but unmasked. "Yeah?"

"Yeah."

He lifts his head to look at me. "You're here."

"I am." I offer him a smile. "He isn't you."

Griffin smiles, the kind that turns up the corners of his eyes. He sets the putty on the counter next to me. I track his movement, then return to watching his handsome face.

"I've read and reread your texts," I tell him. "I loved them."

He crosses his arms. "I just–" he pauses. "I needed to talk to you. I missed you and I didn't know how else to figure out what was happening. You didn't text back." It isn't an accusation. Just a statement of fact.

"I wanted to, I just didn't know what to say. I wrote you a letter. I just never sent it."

"What did it say?" He leans against the counter next to me and studies his hands, rubbing at the paint on his fingers.

"About how I was feeling and how much you mean to me and about how for the first time in my life, you made me feel like I was just right."

He turns, one of his hips leaning against the counter, facing me. "You are."

"I was—am—insecure about Bella. I don't want to be, but I am."

"Bella and I aren't like that. Even with one night, we weren't really ever anything, you know? We're just partners for the baby." He stops and takes a deep breath. "That's really important to me, Max."

I nod and look down at my hands. "I thought maybe because you were having a baby together, I shouldn't get in the way of that."

Griffin lifts my chin, so I meet his gaze. "There's a big problem with Bella."

"What's that?"

"She isn't you."

I can't help but smile.

He presses his lips just to the right of my mouth. "I mean it."

I turn to face him and draw him into a real kiss, one I hope expresses everything on my heart. My hands are in his hair at the nape of his neck, holding him to me. He groans, lifts me until I'm sitting on the counter, and steps between my legs, hands kneading my hips. I moan, pulling him closer. He leans away from the kiss but doesn't move his body, keeping his hands on my hips.

"Are you okay with the idea of me being a dad? I understand, Max, if you aren't. It's big. I'm having a kid."

I pull his face back and kiss him again. "I'm not scared of that," I tell him.

"I can't promise it won't be complicated," he says, "But Max, if you'll have me, I'm all in."

I smile against his mouth. "All in, huh?"

He grins. "Are you being naughty?"

I grasp his belt loops and wiggle his hips against me.

He growls, head on my shoulder. "I'm at work."

"Fine," I say and give him a quick kiss. "Where's the paint brush? I'll follow you with the paint."

Together, we spend the afternoon working through the punch list talking, kissing, working through the conflict, kissing, smiling, kissing, laughing, kissing. Balancing the equation. I know that whatever comes, we're both willing and able to work through it together.

"Your relationship rules really helped," Griffin says.

"I'm smart like that," I tell him and slap his butt with the paint brush.

Griffin freezes and looks down at his jeans, then his eyes rise up to meet mine. "You're going to get it, Max. SK doesn't take kindly to vandalism."

I laugh and scramble to get out, but he grabs me and draws me against him, trapped, exactly where I want to be. I know that whatever happens next, here in this house or helping dad sell it for the next flip, me at school, Griffin, the baby, whatever is over the horizon, we'll work together. We'll fight and make up. We've got the rules to guide us so we can keep both sides of the equation balanced. As I slip out of Griffin's grasp and lead him through the house on a chase which conveniently ends in my room, near my bed because I need to get him on that thing, I realize home was never about the house, it has always been about the people in it.

So I kiss Griffin when I let him catch me.

I pull him down with me so that we're breathless together in a wonderfully placed bed.

And I show him how he is my home.

EPILOGUE

"Max!" Dad calls from somewhere on the first floor of the house.

I'm standing inside of my bedroom, shrugging into my sweatshirt, feeling the impending weight of what's coming. Looking around the space, the way it's put together with a beautiful bed and end tables, pillows, and fresh gray paint, I feel the fantasy of staying seed itself in my heart. I know better. The house is so different from how it looked nine months ago; the haunted house it once was as opposed to what it has become analogous in some ways to how I feel about myself. But this is the cycle of life with my dad. The impending doom of hearing it's time to sell, it's time to pack up again, it's time to leave, crushes me.

I sigh.

"Max!"

"I'm coming down!" I yell back and my steps thump on the stairs as I descend. The beautiful stairwell has been refinished, shining with fresh stained mahogany. Kissing Griffin here a few days earlier makes it all the sweeter. The hallway is also gleaming with polished wood and new tile. The original stained-glass inserts are refurbished. A quick left, and I enter the dining room. He isn't there. "Where are you?"

"Mud room."

I walk through the gorgeous chef's kitchen that looks night and day from what it was, the gleaming white subway tiles in contrast to the old peeling laminate it was. The new island. The farmhouse sink where I kissed Griffin.

The porch was the last place that they renovated, and now it looks like a beautiful mudroom and laundry room. It's got a bench and a place for hanging coats and stashing muddy boots, as well as a nook for the washer and dryer. Everything is insulated now, so it doesn't feel like a freezer anymore. I think of Griffin standing there, soaked through, and smile.

Dad finishes tying his boots, stands when I stop in the doorway, and smiles one of those award-winning, charm-me-into-submission smiles I instantly mistrust.

"What?"

He presses his fingertips to his chest. "Why are you *what-ing* me?"

"Because that's the look you usually get when you're trying to talk me into your next real estate scheme."

His hands fly up in supplication. "You got me."

I sigh. "Okay. You sold the place."

"I did."

I hate how disappointed I feel. No. It's actually terror because trying to figure out how to maintain a relationship with Griffin is going to get even more complicated without Dad here.

"Put your shoes on. I have something to show you, first. Then I'll tell you the plan. Okay?"

I nod, retrieve my jacket from a hook, and follow him into the workshop, remembering Griffin's revelation about his father. When we get inside, he goes to the doorway between the shop, and the space where he's been parking Rust Bucket to protect it from the cold.

He flips on the light and when I walk in, I stop short.

Parked in Rust Bucket's place is a different truck. Newer, but with all the Rust Bucket necessities that made it a good handyman's truck.

"Ta da."

"Where's Rust Bucket?"

"I sold him."

The sale of the house covered the new one. Shit. I look at my dad. "That's good. I won't worry about you on the road now."

Dad takes my hand. "Come look at this though." He draws me around one side of the truck to the driver's side door, where there's a sign: Callum Wallace Carpentry & Handyman Services. And just underneath it, the address where we're standing.

My eyes fly to my dad. "What?"

He grins and sort of rocks back on his heels. "What do you think?"

I open my mouth to respond, but nothing comes out.

His grin widens. "Max speechless?" He chuckles. "Let me show you one more thing, then I think you'll have something to say."

Confused, I follow him to the closed double doors of the garage. He unlatches them and pushes them open. I follow him outside, where an incredibly delectable Griffin stand next to a small, shiny, yellow car. "What's that?"

"That, Max-in-a-million, is your new car, compliments of Rust Bucket and some savings."

My gaze snaps to him.

He's holding out a key ring with two keys attached. "This one is for your car. And this is the house key anytime you feel like coming home." He smiles, but this time, I hear the catch in his voice.

"Home?"

He smiles a teary smile and nods. "Yep. I sold the house to, well, me. It's already mine. Here." He hands me the keyring. "Welcome home." He clears his throat. "Don't worry. I got all the finances figured out and—"

But I don't let him finish. I just throw my arms around him.

Dad wraps his strong arms around me. "Welcome home, Max," he says quietly. "Welcome home."

PLAYLIST

Music is always a source of inspiration when I write. Here are a few of the songs I listened to while working on Max's story. If you're interested in more playlists related to Max and Griffin, look for In the Echo of this Ghost Town and Griffin's Road Trip Playlist.

How to Get By	Electric Sons
Still Dreaming, Backwards	Ella Voss, Mokita
Fireworks	Hazlett
Pick-up Truck	Kings of Leon
Twenty	Laur Elle
Edge of the Dark	Emmit Fenn
Timing is Everything	EXES
Stormy Weather	Kings of Leon
Your Best American Girl	Mitski
More Than Friends	Mokita
Need You	Kidswaste
Love Me	Smeyeul., Galvanic, Haux
Barricade	Elliot Moss
IDC Anymore	Yoe Mase
Chicago	McKenna Breinholt
Bones Break	EXES
Find Myself	Mont Duamel
You & I	Edapollo, Harvey
All I See is You	UTAH, Jacob Steele

ACKNOWLEDGMENTS

In Max's world, she loves old rock bands. So, channeling Max, I'd like to dedicate some old-school rock songs to some amazing people:

AC/DC's *"Who Made Who"* might be a song about machines and humanity, but in this strange pandemic paradigm, it seems to fit how important our humanity in conjunction with machines has become vital. So many people I've met in the internet sphere with respect to writing have been instrumental in my craft. Thanks is owed to a plethora of people: Rayna York, Stephanie Keesy-Phelan, Misty Wagner, Brandann R. Hill-Mann, and Lavinia Ungureanu. Thank you to my Salon Crew for your tireless support. Thank you to Katherine Lamoureaux; You deserve an award for your editing help. Thank you. Thank you. Thank you! I might have written the story, but you all made it better so the circular *who made who* works.

Journey *"Don't Stop Believing"* is dedicated to Sara Oliver, cover artist extraordinaire. She's made magic with my covers, including this one. She's the embodiment if never stop believing that amazing things can happen (like your amazing covers).

"More than Words" by Extreme goes out to all the READERS! Okay, so forget for a moment what the song is really about and just focus on the idea that there aren't enough words to express my appreciation and gratitude about your support. Hugs.

The song *"Sweet Child of Mine"* by Guns-n-Rose goes out to my family. Your support keeps me afloat when life sort of feels more like *"Welcome to the Jungle"*. I love you Vince, Anuhea, La'anui, Mom, and sisters, Connie and Susan. Your encouragement and belief in me is golden. Vince, Sr., Corina, Kalani, Shanz, Kaleo, Sandi and my niece and nephews. Thank you for being my home.

Finally, *"Frail"* by Jars of Clay (which isn't totally an old-school rock song) goes to my Lord and Savior Jesus Christ whose Grace somehow helps me see characters more clearly. All glory, honor, and praise to You.

EXCERPT

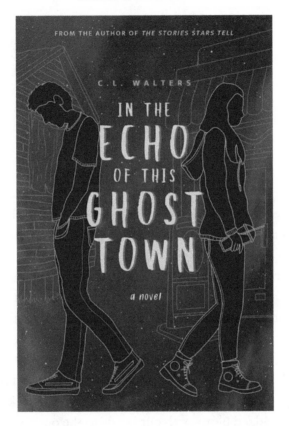

Griffin's story available now.

1.

The cruel asphalt underneath me feels like the truth. Everything about me is a lie. I hurt. Tanner, my best friend, is on the asphalt next to me. We've been in a fight. He says something I don't catch. I'm drunk as fuck. His voice sounds distant as though I'm covering my ears even though he's just an arm's length away. I think I said something about him being pussy-whipped—definitely thought it. He bit back with sharp words, drawing blood, though I'm not exactly sure what kind of weapons they were or where they cut. I'm just bleeding internally. Angry, we sort of collided—two drunks—and rolled across the parking lot outside a convenience store, unable to keep our feet under us. We added blows with our hands to the ones with our words.

I break myself into parts to avoid the feelings—or the hurtful truth of them. There's the Griffin who wants to accept the stark reality of tiny painful pebbles pressing my skin. He wants to find a way to bandage up what's bleeding. That Griffin is the optimist, but he also feels the wounds. So, there's the Griff who adds scar tissue to protect the softer parts. This tougher Griff is filled with so much rage there aren't defenses strong enough to damn the vitriol ready to ooze from my mouth. He's the one who will cauterize the weakness to protect all of me, because gentle Griffin is an infection. Unyielding Griff won't accept heartache; this Griff is all about the lies I tell to keep the tender fragments of myself hidden.

Now, breathing like my lungs might spew from my mouth, I'm trying to remember why this battle was so important. I turn my head to look at Tanner on the ground next to me, disoriented by the movement of the world around me. I wonder why—of all the people in my life—I'm fighting with Tanner. He's my brother—or the closest thing I have to one since my older brother, Phoenix, left me—and right now, I feel like my gut is bruised from the rocks I've been carrying around inside of it. My throat is on fire with the need to cry, or maybe I just need to puke.

Tanner is on his back, like me, drunk, like me, and looking up at a black sky. But I'm looking at him, my best friend since we were fourteen. I'm always looking at Tanner.

"You were my brother, Griff," Tanner mutters up at the sky.

Were.

Were.

Were.

I get stuck in the past tense.

Angry, insulated, scar-tissue Griff tags into the match instead, hops around the ring looking for the next opening to hurt him back. Fury as a default setting.

Everyone leaves.

I recall Phoenix's back as I watched him walk away. He didn't turn around, and I think that's what hurt the most. In my imagination, I've created a version of him stopping at the end of the sidewalk, turning, and looking over his shoulder at me to smile. It's the kind of smile that says: *I see you, baby brother. Don't worry. You've always got me.* He didn't though. He just turned and kept walking toward the bus stop.

I'd looked at my mom, waited for her to change her kicked-out-of-the-house sentencing, unable to register the tears in her eyes for my own anguish. She hadn't. She shored up her defenses, her mouth thinning into a barbed-wire fence, and she waited for me to yell. I just didn't. All that feeling was stuck in my throat. The blame for making Phoenix leave dumped concrete mix down my gullet, filled me up with bitterness, and hardened my insides into stone. I stomped past her, disappeared into my room, and slammed the door but didn't scream. I couldn't. I just went silent. Flopped on my bed and stared at the hot-girls-hot-cars poster Phoenix had given me for my thirteenth birthday. Now, he was gone. First dad. Now him. What did that mean for me?

So, fury is a friend.

I roll away from Tanner. "Fuck you. You're leaving," I say. I know the feeling of being left behind better than anyone, except maybe Tanner whose brother died and whose parents' marriage exploded.

"Where am I going?"

I struggle onto my hands and knees, the loose pebbles of the parking lot biting at my palms. I don't know why I think about the sting of rocks when there's a boulder sitting inside my chest. I need to puke it up, but it's lodged there.

Tanner might be right; he isn't leaving in a physical sense. We both made sure we didn't have options after high school—too much party, not enough school—but that doesn't mean he isn't digging out.

"You left a long time ago." I spit. I do feel like I need to puke. Sick. Somehow, I get to my feet. "Everybody fucking leaves."

Tanner sits up. "I didn't. I tried to talk to you; you wouldn't listen."

I don't want to listen now. Nothing he might say will sway pissed-off Griff. Tanner violated our pact. He broke the Bro Code, and it isn't the part about fucking bitches. Tanner broke what was real between all of us, and that was the promise to always be there for one another. Tanner is choosing to walk away. Phoenix left and never came back; he just sends stupid postcards that don't make any sense. Brother by postcard proxy. Tanner isn't going to come back either.

"We aren't friends anymore," I mutter.

"Guys. This is dumb." Danny's voice punctuates our mutterings with the clarity of his sobriety.

I swing around toward our other friend, swaying as I do. My feet scratch over the scree of the lot as I walk away from Tanner to Danny standing near his tan car. Danny—his arms crossed over his chest and his hands tucked up under his arms—watches us. His brow has collapsed over his dark eyes with irritation which makes me hesitate.

I'm not sure I've ever seen Danny mad. Then again, I can't be sure of anything since I'm wasted.

There's a shuffle in the gravel behind me which I assume means Tanner has gotten to his feet. He says, "You're right. We haven't been friends for a long time." His words add weight to the boulder that's holding down my heart.

I glance around for Josh—the fourth of our gang—but remember he isn't there. He's wherever kids with intact families who love each other go.

Lately, I feel like I've been trying to hold our brotherhood together, trying so hard to keep things the way they've always been.

I thought it would always be Tanner and me. Tanner, me, Danny and Josh.

Tanner says something about walking home.

Danny's arms collapse to his sides, and he takes a step past me. "That's pretty far, Tanner. I can take you."

I shake my head. "No. He isn't our friend."

Danny looks at me, dark eyes narrowed. "He's mine." He calls after Tanner, "I can take you home, bro."

Tanner's voice is farther away. "No."

I hear the slide of his steps across the gravel as he walks away, but I don't turn to look at my former friend. Turning around might tear open the exposed underbelly of weak Griffin. That Griffin wants to reach for when we—Tanner and me—were fourteen and walking down the school hallway, laughing after getting kicked out of homeroom together. Or when we played the prank at the end of freshman year with the fire alarm. All the times we traipsed around town before we could drive, looking for fun and usually making it. The quiet talks when life felt too heavy, so it didn't feel like we had to hold it up alone. That's been a long time ago. After months of trying to bind Bro Code together, I'm not begging Tanner to stay. Instead, I climb into Danny's car and sink down as low as I can in the passenger seat.

Danny gets behind the wheel, but he doesn't start the car. "That was messed up, Griff. What you said about Rory." I hear the disappointment and displeasure in his voice, in the punctuation of his words and the way they run together as if he's speaking Spanish.

"What are you talking about? I didn't say anything about Rory." I shake my head to deny it, but my brain is cement. Why would I say anything about Tanner's dead brother? "Tanner broke the code," I mumble and lean my head against the window, wondering how we'd gone from laughing and drinking a little while ago—Tanner, the prodigal son, returned to the fold after his misguided relationship detour with the Matthews chick—to what had just happened.

"No. He didn't." Danny starts the car; his hands slip from the key because he does it with so much force. "You're the one who broke it."

"How's this my fault?" I stare out at the overflowing dumpster at the edge of the parking lot. I turn to look at him. "Tanner's the one acting like a bitch."

Danny makes a disgusted sound. "He's tried to talk to you for months." He looks over his shoulder as he reverses the car. The staccato of the gear shift moving into first gear adds emphasis to the tension. "And Josh and I tried to tell you. You're so stubborn. That's not how friends treat one another."

"We're going the wrong way. Bella's is the other way."

He swears, and I'm taken aback by it. I've known Danny for three years. Of all of us, he hasn't been the one to let loose with his mouth. That's usually me.

"I'm taking your ass home."

"Whoa, dude. Tanner's the one who broke the code."

Danny goes silent, his hand gripping the steering wheel so tight his knuckles are white. Then he sort of unleashes, slamming the wheel with his hand and yelling, "This isn't about the fucking, stupid-ass code!"

I'm not sure what to say. Of course it's about the code! All of who we have been together has always been about our crew; why else would I be fighting for it? For the last three years, our code has been our navigational system. First Tanner (Josh has always been a ride-along) and now Danny is disabling our operating procedures. That party at

Bella's was my endgame. That's the rules of Bro Code: to help one another freaking get laid. My anger collects, so when he parks in front of my house refusing to go to Bella's, I'm not only shocked by his defiance and disregard of our rules, but I'm also fuming.

"Get out." Danny won't look at me, the last of our gang. The dependable one. The one who is always there. "You're drunk, and I'm going home."

"I'm always drunk."

Danny's face turns toward me then, the shape of his usually kind features sharp and jagged like unfinished granite. "Yeah. Maybe that's the fucking problem." He reaches across me, and the door groans as it opens. "It's time to grow up, Griff. Get out."

The seat belt latch pops and releases, but I can't seem to get my feet under me and roll out of the car instead. When I finally stand, the earth tilts under me, and I sway to correct. "Well, fuck you then." I slam the door and fall with the momentum into the grass outside my house.

Danny drives away, the car huffing and puffing exhaust as if it, too, were angry.

I roll onto my back as the sound of Danny's car disappears in the distance and lay in my front yard gazing at the spinning dark sky. The expanse above me taunts me with my smallness and isolation. I'm alone and shake out my memories to find the last time that was so. They are thin and breakable.

"Fuck!" Angry Griff rages at feeling so small and reinforces his fury by lying about our victimhood.

Softhearted Griffin—who might be able to reinforce the truth if he weren't so small—makes himself smaller to stay safe.

I don't cry even if I feel the sharp points of tears crawling up my throat. Then again, maybe I just need to puke.

 **BOOKS**

Also by CL Walters

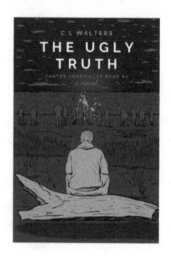

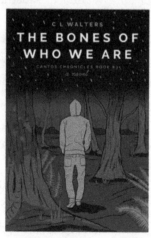

Available Now!

A new Cantos Novel coming Fall 2022

EXCERPT

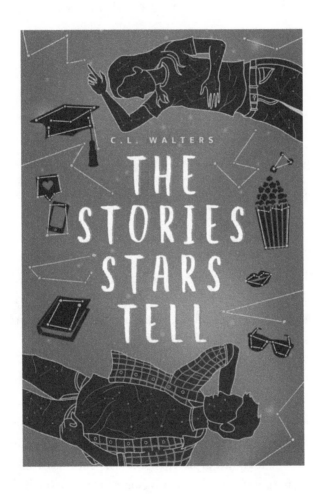

Emma's and Tanner's Story Available Now.

senior year

(14 days to graduation)

emma

I squeeze my eyes shut, terrified I'm about to screw this up. Three deep breaths. Slow. Steady. In. Out. The sound of my breath echoes in my head like the rush of the wind through the tree leaves in my backyard, and the fear of failure, which always sits in the front of my brain, drips down through my body into my stomach.

I could forget my part.

I could ruin everything.

I could be sick.

I picture Cameron, standing in front of his dad's red Ferrari in his khaki pants and suspenders over his dark brown shirt ranting about conquering his fear right before he kicks the shit out of his dad's car. Okay. He's a fictional character from one of my favorite movies of all time, *Ferris Bueller's Day Off*, but still. I'm going to kick the shit out of this, like, speech-Ferrari.

Breathe in. Breathe out.

"Emma?"

The sound of my name, as though it's being called through a

tunnel, draws me back. I open my eyes and look into the familiar bright blue eyes of my best friend, Liam.

"Emma? It's almost time. You're doing your breathing thing?"

He's dressed in a business suit, charcoal gray and red tie with those chic pants and shoes that make him seem like he's stepped out of a male fashion magazine. Far more fashionable than most males in these competitions who look like they're wearing their father's Sunday suits. He is beautiful. Dark haired, thin and fit, handsome and not into me at all (I'm not into him either). We've been best friends since third grade in Mrs. Hale's class.

My insides shimmy, but I nod. "Cameron. Remember Cameron."

"What?" He adjusts his black-framed, hipster glasses which he pulls off to perfection.

"Just channeling Cameron." I tug on the bottom of my matching charcoal gray jacket.

Liam reaches out, fixes my collar, and then takes both of my hands in his. Leaning forward, he presses his forehead to mine. He smells like wintergreen mint, familiar and comforting. "We've got this. We've practiced this. We know it. We. Know. It."

I close my eyes. "We do," I repeat, and my heartbeat slows to the rhythm of his words. Liam. My best friend. "Our last time in duo," I whisper. Tears threaten to fall. "What am I going to do without you?"

He pulls back but keeps hold of my hands. "Do. Not. Cry." Hand squeeze. "You have to keep your make-up looking good. Game faces. Let's kick the shit out of this speech, like Cameron did the car."

I smile, because he knows me, and I nod. "Let's do it."

Our names are called. We walk from the wings out onto the stage and take our marks.

We slay it. Of course we do, because that's who we are.

Later, Liam and I are at my house for our usual Saturday night John Hughes movie of the week. It's what we always do on a Saturday night, except for that one Saturday junior year when I went off the rails. The popcorn is made, drinks are chilling, and *Pretty in Pink* is cued up. While we wait for Ginny — our other bestie — to arrive, we both scroll through Instagram.

"Look at this one," Liam says. He's on the floor with his back against the couch. His legs — fit in cotton twill — are stretched out in front of him, crossed at the ankles. He holds up his phone.

"What is that?" I ask.

"It's Baker's house."

"Baker? As in Atticus Baker?"

He nods. "Party there tonight." He continues to examine his phone, and I watch him.

Instead of scrolling through the feed, he stops and scrutinizes Atticus Baker's page. Picture after picture, even reading the comments. It strikes me, because Liam hasn't ever expressed an interest in anyone specific (he's kind of private like that). As he looks through Atticus Baker's feed, it dawns on me how much of a risk Liam took to tell his truth. How lonely it might be in our small, conservative town. Lately, with graduation impending, I've thought about what kind of risks I've taken in my life (that one time junior year notwithstanding), and the answer has been none.

"I see you, Liam. You think Atticus is hot," I say with a giggle.

"Who doesn't? He's gorgeous."

He continues to study every single picture Atticus has posted, and I recognize familiarity in his actions. I've done it. My own phone, at the moment, is open to Tanner James's IG feed, as per usual. I press on his story and watch a video of him walking into Baker's party, but I don't show Liam. He doesn't approve of my infatuation with one of the biggest f-boys at school. I don't blame him; it's suspect.

Instead, I reach out and ruffle Liam's hair, which I know he hates. "But you like him like him."

"Stop!" He lurches forward to get out from under the destructive force of my hand and adjusts his hair back into place, not that I could have done much to those product-laced locks. "And shut up. I don't." His ears turn red.

"You are so lying." I grin and search for Atticus's IG feed on my phone. "He is really handsome," I say when I find it.

I select a gorgeous picture of Atticus and turn my phone to show him. Liam glances at it but looks away, aloof and noncommittal. Even I can't detach from the beauty. Atticus is gorgeous: tall, black, stylish, fit. He's a basketball player at our high school and got a full ride to St. Mary's in California. All of his pictures have this low-key, I'm-so-casual vibe in a matching filter, so there's no way it's casual. But, damn. "Liam. He's so hot, you have my approval," I tell him, even though I know how horrible and objectifying it sounds. Not that Liam needs my approval.

He groans. "Stop, Emma. For real. Atticus is like—" He pauses and turns his shoulders so he's facing me. "Look—"

"Mr. Liam, sir, I don't much feel like one of your lectures," I interrupt in my best patronizing student voice, because Liam is always lecturing me. Mansplaining. The jerk.

"Atticus is like — out of my league. And that's *if* he's gay." He looks down at his phone again. "I mean, I think I got some vibes, but my vibes are inexperienced. I have no idea what I'm doing. Besides, how many openly gay men do you think there are in this backwater, hick-horrible town?" He offers an old man grunt of disgust and readjusts himself with his back against the couch's seat again. "I can't wait to get out of here."

I understand his sentiment, though my prison is of a different kind: Christian family, striving for perfection where nothing real ever happens. Okay, maybe that's not fair, but it's how I feel sometimes. I can't wait to leave and distance myself from stifling expectations to experience my own version of freedom.

I try to give Liam a pep talk anyway. "None of us know what we're doing. We're all faking it. Ferris is the only one who seems to have it all figured out, and he's a fictional character. No one is like that."

"Has what figured out?" Ginny asks from behind us. Liam and I turn and watch her walk into the finished basement from the stairs. "Your dad said to come down, and he'll bring us some fresh cookies when they're out of the oven."

The third of our Bueller troop flops onto the couch next to me with her fresh-coated vanilla scent. She's been on a new kick to live as a 1970's hippie in order to explore the ideology of antidisestablishmentarianism, mostly to annoy her dad and stepmom. The outfit today: tie-dye cotton maxi-skirt she made herself and a black shirt without a bra (which is very noticeable because of her gorgeous boobs and high beams she's been very proud of since she got them). The whole no bra thing has really pushed the buttons of her stepmom which Ginny loves to do more than anything. She lays her head on my shoulder and threads her arm through mine.

"Life," I say, in answer to her original question.

"Our parents don't even have life figured out. Obviously," Ginny replies. "Case in point: my dad and step-monster. How could we — mere eighteen-year-olds? I take that back. We might have it more together."

"Something new?" I ask. The last installment of *The Life and Times of Ginny Donnelly* had her stepmother forcing her to paint her bedroom since she's leaving for college soon. Her stepmom is determined to convert Ginny's room into a fitness haven and has been taking measurements for her equipment.

"Besides Operation Kick Ginny Out of Her Room? Nothing new. I don't want to talk about them, or the fact that she made me go through my closet to consolidate everything into boxes for storage."

"Sorry, Gin." I squeeze her arm with mine. "On a happier note, we were discussing something intriguing. Specifically, Liam's crush on Atticus Baker."

He turns his back to us and resumes his stylish leaning against the couch, looking like a modern James Dean. He's got it all: the hair, the glasses, the pout.

Ginny sits up. "Atticus Baker? Man, he's hot."

"That's what I said."

"Is he gay?"

"We could run a new operation: Find out if Atticus Baker is Gay," I offer. "We could all slide into his DM, and see?"

"Emma." Liam's voice is threaded with a warning, like a brother who has reached the threshold of annoyance.

I smile. "I'm sorry, Liam. Am I hurting your feelings?" I lean toward him and nuzzle his ear.

He moves to get away from me again. "No." He swats at me. "And no offense, but we know how the last operation you planned went."

I glance at Ginny, who raises her eyebrows and tilts her head. "He has a point."

I know they're referring to the junior year debacle. To be fair, if I was going to sneak out and go to a party, I was going to go all in. Especially if getting caught by my parents was a risk. I hadn't gotten caught, but I had gotten what I'd been after: a kiss — a gorgeously memorable hot kiss that I hadn't been able to forget. From Tanner James. "Everything turned out okay. We didn't get into trouble. Really, when you list out the successes against the failures, that was a win-win."

Liam looks at me like I'm delusional, and perhaps I am. "Emma, if you think you won in that situation, you're wrong. You haven't stopped infatuating about the school's biggest douchebag since. And for someone who claims to be a feminist, that's some contradictory bullshit."

I look to Ginny for backup, which I don't get. "He's right." She shrugs and flops against the couch. "It's been over a year, and you're still struggling with it."

They're both right. I sigh because I *am* infatuated with Tanner James, and I know better. "It doesn't matter. Graduation is two weeks away. We're going to kick ass, say our smarty-pants speeches, and leave for college. Which I will cry about later. Tanner James will be old news. My infatuation with him will be spent as I walk onto a college campus as a co-ed surrounded by beautiful men and women and a playground of sexual awakening."

Ginny and Liam glance at one another with saucer-shaped eyes and then collapse with laughter.

"Emma! I can't believe you just said that." Liam laughs even harder.

"Sexual Awakening. Emma." Ginny shrieks, falling away from me at her waist.

"Wow. You're giving me a complex."

When their laughter subsides, Liam climbs up onto the couch.

With me in between them, sulking, my arms crossed over my chest, I say, "You make me sound like a prude."

"That's not what we mean." Liam pats my leg. "I'm sorry if I hurt your feelings. I just—" He pauses and looks at me over the top of his glasses, reminding me of his dad. "Emma, you're pretty conservative when it comes to stuff like that. And scared about, like everything."

"What? Sex?" I say, still pouting but knowing he's right. I haven't done much in my eighteen years besides masturbate. I'm not ignorant about sex. I may have been raised with Christian parents, but they have been open and frank about sex. While the discussions have moved around the naturalness of the act, the underlying message has been an expectation to wait until marriage. Besides the junior year operation, I'd kissed a couple of other guys. Add to that my date for junior prom, Chris Keller, who tried to pressure me into sex and went so far as to grope me in the limo. I'd slapped him (so much for uncomplicated). Without a doubt, I'm curious and interested in sex, but it's clear my wiring leads to the red wire, not meaningless romps in the back of limos.

"Yeah, sex," Ginny says. "You overthink everything. Sex, like, isn't a thinking endeavor. It's all feeling."

I stand up to get away from them and their words, which I recognize as true but don't want to. "I'm not scared of sex."

Liam stands and mirrors me. "Emma — you're Claire." He points at the TV screen where *Pretty in Pink* waits for us.

I narrow my eyes at him. "I'm not Claire, who's in *The Breakfast Club,* by the way. I'm not a stuck-up, snobby, princess, tease."

"No. Not like that part. Like the sexually repressed part," Ginny says. "The one who secretly likes the bad boy but won't act on it."

"Except—" I hold up a finger for emphasis— "I went into the closet with bad boy John Bender just like she did, only it was junior year with

Tanner James." I want to lash out at Liam who's checking out a guy but is too scared to find out if he's gay. And Ginny, who slept with her last boyfriend because she wanted to "get over" her virginity. With my hands on my hips, ready to deflect, I pause and bite my tongue. It's petty and mean, and I love them too much.

"Emma." Ginny's chin falls against her chest, and she stares at me under her lashes. "You had to be drunk to do it."

She's right. *Operation Kiss Tanner James* required me to be drunk, because I couldn't muster up the courage to be bold. But then when had I ever? If it wasn't about church, or school, or duo with Liam — things that I could control — when had I ever been brave?

"Fresh cookies, hot from the oven." My dad with plate in hand maneuvers down the steps into the basement. He looks up with a smile when he reaches the bottom and pauses a moment, assessing the tension in the room. "Everything alright?"

"Perfect." I cross my arms over my chest.

"Those cookies smell delicious, Mr. Matthews," Liam says, turning on the couch to face my father.

Kiss ass.

"How many times have I said it's okay to call me Mo?"

Liam snags a cookie from the plate as my dad sets it on the table between the couch and the TV. "Thanks, Mo."

Dad straightens, walks over to me, and gives me a side hug. "Thanks, Dad."

"*Pretty in Pink* night?" His eyes bounce from me to Liam to Ginny. He lingers and clears his throat. "Not many of these left, huh?"

We all mumble affirmations at him. I'm sure none of us are truly ready to come to terms with that fact yet, even if we say we're ready to leave.

"I'll leave you to it, then." He squeezes me against his side once more and then disappears back up the stairs.

After he's gone, I look at my friends feeling hurt and vulnerable. They might as well have just said I was the most boring person on the planet — and they'd probably be right.

Ginny pats the couch cushion next to her and holds her arms out to me.

I walk into them, flop forward, and lay against her awkwardly.

"Your Emma-think isn't a bad thing. It's an Emma thing. You're awesome. When you're ready — you'll know," she says. "In fact, because you're you, you'll probably have the best first experience of us all. All that thinking and analysis to make sure."

I move off of her to sit.

"And," Ginny says, "believe me. You don't want a Dean on your hands." Each of us snorts in reference to her first, the aftermath of just trying to "get over it." She shudders and takes my hand in hers. "Maybe it will be like a sexual awakening in college next year, or maybe it will be a hot someone this summer. Perhaps it will be in four years, or maybe it will be on your wedding night. It doesn't matter. What matters is YOU get to decide that for yourself, and that will make it perfect."

Liam sits down on the other side of me and takes my hand. "And I'll be there cheering you on for your first encounter with the D, or the V — whichever you prefer."

"I don't know why this suddenly became about me."

"Here. We can make it about me," Liam says. "I'm still a virgin."

"A status you'd like to change with Atticus Baker." I wiggle my eyebrows at him.

He smacks my shoulder. "Shut it, bitch." Then he chuckles.

"Let's get this John Hughes night moving already. Turn on the movie. Wait, Pretty in Pink? Maybe we should switch it to The Breakfast Club." Ginny lets me go and leans forward for popcorn. "We've got some analysis to do on that dialogue between Allison and Claire tonight, I think."

After an argument about sticking with our planned movie schedule, we watch *Pretty in Pink*. Ginny relents because Andie needs analysis of her attitudes about men: douchebags versus the best-friend. I point out one of my best friends is gay and the other one isn't; it's not an option in all circumstances. We're all in agreement that Andie should have ended up with Duckie (cue giant eye rolls), but as the movie plays, I'm distracted. I attempt to stay in it with my friends since our John Hughes movie nights are dwindling down to a handful. My mind keeps turning back to junior year. I think about how I'd played that night and the aftermath and wish I'd been braver.

ABOUT THE AUTHOR

CL Walters writes in Hawai'i where she lives with her husband, two children, and acts as a pet butler to two pampered fur-babies. She's the author of the YA Contemporary series, *The Cantos Chronicles* (*Swimming Sideways*, *The Ugly Truth* and *The Bones of Who We Are*), the YA/NA Contemporary romance *The Stories Stars Tell* and the adult romance, *The Letters She Left Behind*. *In the Echo of this Ghost Town* and *When the Echo Answers* are her sixth and seventh YA Contemporary novels. For up-to-date news, sign up for her monthly newsletter on her website at www.clwalters.net as well as follow her writer's journey on Instagram @cl.walters.